Jean-Baptiste Molière

The Works of Molière

Vol. V

Jean-Baptiste Molière

The Works of Molière
Vol. V

ISBN/EAN: 9783743390607

Manufactured in Europe, USA, Canada, Australia, Japa

Cover: Foto ©Andreas Hilbeck / pixelio.de

Manufactured and distributed by brebook publishing software (www.brebook.com)

Jean-Baptiste Molière

The Works of Molière

THE WORKS OF MOLIERE.

IN SIX VOLUMES.

VOL. V.

A NEW TRANSLATION.

BERWICK:

PRINTED FOR R. TAYLOR.

MDCCLXXXI.

PSYCHE.

A

TRAGI-COMEDY.

VOL. V.						A

Psyche, *a Tragi-Comedy of Five Acts, performed at
Paris at the Palace of the Tuilleries during the Car-
nival, 1670; and at the Theatre of the Palace-
Royal, July 24th, 1671.*

IN the following play, Moliere thought proper to facrifice the regularity of the conduct to the acceffo-
ry ornaments. As the king was very impatient to
have it foon finifhed, Moliere had recourfe to the ce-
lebrated Corneille, who readily complied with his plan;
for men truly great are void of jealoufy. Quinault
furnifhed the French words, which were fet to mufic
by Lully. The royal magnificence with which it was
attended in the reprefentation, and the concourfe of
famous authors whofe talents were all united, the
more readily to execute the orders of Lewis XIV. add
a new luftre to this piece, which will always be efteem-
ed for feveral beautiful paffages in it, and efpecially
for the new and delicate turn in Cupid's declaration to
Pfyche.

ACTORS.

JUPITER.
VENUS.
CUPID.
ZEPHYR.
ÆGIALE, } Graces.
PHAENE, }
THE KING, Father to Psyche.
PSYCHE.
AGLAURA, } Sisters to Psyche.
CYDIPPE, }
CLEOMENES, } Two princes in love with Psyche.
AGENOR, }
LYCAS, captain of the guards.
TWO CUPIDS.
A RIVER-GOD.
Attendants to the King.

PSYCHE.

PROLOGUE.

The fore part of the stage represents a champaign country, and the back part the sea.

SCENE I.

FLORA, VERTUMNUS, PALEMON, NYMPHS
attending on FLORA, DRYADES, SYLVANS,
RIVER-GODS, NAIADES.

Clouds are seen hanging in the air, which in descend-
ing, move and open, and, spreading themselves o-
ver the whole stage, discover Venus and Cupid attended by six Loves, with Aegiale and Phaene near
them.

FLORA.

WAR is no more, the first of kings doth cease
From his exploits to give the world a peace.
Parent of love, whom all the world obeys,
Descend from heaven, and give us happy
days.

A 3

CHORUS of Sylvans and River-Gods.

A peace profound and fweet we know,
The fofteft joys are here below;
This charming leifure owes its birth
To the moft glorious king on earth.
Parent of love, whom all the world obeys,
Defcend from heaven, and give us happy days.

FIRST ENTRY.

The Dryades, Sylvans, River-Gods, and Naiades, join
and form a dance in honour of Venus.

VERTUMNUS.

YIELD, yield yourfelves, ye cruel fair,
And figh for figh return.

PALEMON.

The queen of beauties haftens here,
To make you gently burn.

VERTUMNUS.

A charming object ftill fevere,
Can ne'er true love infpire..

PALEMON.

Beauty indeed begins t'endear,
But fweetnefs fans the fire.

BOTH TOGETHER.

Beauty indeed begins t'endear,
But fweetnefs fans the fire.

VERTUMNUS.

Let all fubmit to Cupid's dart;
Let's languifh, fince we muft.

PALEMON.

To have no foftnefs in the heart,
Is of all crimes the worft.

VERTUMNUS.

A charming object ftill fevere,
Can ne'er true love infpire.

PALEMON.

Beauty indeed begins t'endear,
But fweetnefs fans the fire.

BOTH TOGETHER.

Beauty indeed begins t'endear,
But fweetnefs fans the fire.

FLORA.

Is one fage,
In blooming age,
Is one fage
To banifh love?
Without ceafing,
Let's be preffing,
All the joys below to prove.
Youth's chief wifdom lies in this,
The knowing to enjoy its blifs.

SECOND ENTRY.

The Sylvans and River-Gods intermix their dances
with Flora's finging.

FLORA.

LOVE charms
Whom he difarms;
Love charms,
Receive his yoke.
All our pain
Will be in vain,
Striving to refift his ftroke;
Whatever chain we lovers wear,
Has fofter charms than liberty by far.

CHORUS of Sylvans and River-Gods.

A peace profound and sweet we know,
The softest joys are here below;
This charming leisure owes its birth
To the most glorious king on earth.
Parent of love, whom all the world obeys,
Come down from heaven, and give us happy days.

THIRD ENTRY.

The Dryades, Sylvans, River-Gods and Naiades, seeing
Venus approach, continue to express, by their dancing, the joy her presence inspires them with.

VENUS in her machine.

IT is too ancient a custom to pay court to me, cease
your joyful songs; such great honours do not become me; reserve them for softer charms. Venus is
no longer in vogue. Every thing has its turn. There
are new attractions to which every one offer their incense. The beauteous Psyche now fills my place; already all the world croud to adore her, and it is too
much for me in my disgrace to find one submit to do
me so much honour. The world is no longer uncertain about our merits, every one quits my party, and of
the surprising croud of favourite Graces whose friendship and cares attended me every where, I have only
two of the meanest left me, who attend me out of
compassion. These dark abodes must lend their solitudes
to my distressed mind, and leave me to hide my grief
and shame among their shades.

Flora and the other deities retire, and Venus with her
retinue descends from the machine.

SCENE II.

VENUS, CUPID; ÆGIALE, PHAENE, THE
LOVES.

ÆGIALE.

GODDESS, we are at a lofs what to do, in the
affliction we fee you in. Our refpect would
keep filence, our zeal would have us fpeak.

Venus. Speak: but if you are defirous of pleafing
me, defer all your counfels till another time, and fpeak
not of my anger, but to allow that I have reafon for it;
this, this was the moft fenfible affront that my divini-
ty could ever receive; but I will be revenged of it, if
the gods have any power.

Phaene. You have greater lights, and wifdom to
judge what is worthy of you, than we have; but, for
my part, I fhould have imagined that a great goddefs
fhould not have put herfelf in fuch a rage.

Venus. That is the very occafion of the extreme
rage I am in. The more refplendent my rank is, the
greater the affront is; and if I was not placed in this
fupreme degree, the indignation of my heart would not
be fo great. I, the daughter of the god who hurls the
thunder; I, mother of the god who infpires love; I,
the deareft wifh of heaven and earth, whofe very coming into light was on purpofe to charm; I who have,
from all that breathe, feen fo many vows perfume my
altars, and who by immortal right have always held
the fovereign empire of beauty; I, whofe eyes reduced
two high goddeffes to the extremity of yielding me the
prize of beauty, fhall I fee victory and my rights dif-
puted by a pitiful mortal? fhall the ridiculous excefs
of a foolifh infatuation oppofe a trifling girl to me?

A 5

shall I, with patience, endure the rash judgment passed
on her charms-and mine; and shall I, from the high
heavens where I shine, hear prejudiced mortals say,
" Venus herself is not so beautiful?"

Ægiale. Mankind are impertinent with their com-
parisons, and it is their way.

Phaene. In the present age they know not how to
praise, without offering outrage to the highest names.

Venus. How well, alas! does the insolent rigour of
those words revenge Juno and Pallas, and comfort their
hearts for the bright glory which the famous apple added to my charms! I see them applaud themselves on
account of my uneasiness, constantly affect a malicious
laugh, and with fixed regard, studiously search for my
confusion in my eyes. Their triumphant joy, at the
force of this outrage, seems to say, insulting my wrath:
" Boast, Venus, boast the charms of your face; by the
" judgment of one only you prevailed over us, but by
" the judgment of all a simple mortal has the advantage
" over you." Alas! this stroke puts an end to me, it
pierces my very heart, and I can no longer bear these
unequalled rigours; and the pleasure of my rivals is
too great a surplus to my lively grief. O son! if ever
I had any credit with thee, and if ever I was dear to
thee, if thou wearest a heart sensible to the indignation
which afflicts the heart of a mother who so tenderly
loves thee, employ, now employ thy utmost power to
support my interest, and make Psyche, by thy darts, feel
my vengeance. To make her heart miserable take
such of thy darts as would please me best, the most
empoisoned of those which thou art used to hurl in
thy anger. Cause her to be inflamed with love, even
to madness, with the lowest, vilest, and most frightful
of mortals; and make her undergo the cruel punish-
ment, to love and not to be loved again.

Cupid. Every one complains of Cupid; people impute a thoufand faults to me; and you cannot conceive the ill, and the foolifh things which they ſay of me continually.   If to affift your anger——

Venus. Begone, no longer refift thy mother's defires; apply thy thoughts to nothing but to endeavour immediately to facrifice a victim to my injured honour. Begone, and let me not fee thy face again till I am revenged according to my defires.   [Cupid flies off.

END of the PROLOGUE.

{*❀{}*❀{}*❀{}*❀{}*❀{}*❀{}*❀{}*❀{}*❀{}*❀{}*❀}

ACT I. SCENE I.

The ſtage reprefents the king's palace.

AGLAURA, CYDIPPE.

AGLAURA.

SILENCE, dear fifter, fharpens fome ills; therefore let us fpeak out our mutual grief; and each breathe out the killing anguifh of our hearts. We fee ourfelves fifters in misfortune; and yours has fo great a fimilitude with mine, that we may blend them both in one, and in our juft tranfport, repine in joint complaints, at the cruelty of our fate. What fecret fatality, fifter, fubjects all the univerfe to the charms of our younger fifter, and, of fo many princes which fortune has brought hither, has not given one of them to our chains? What! to fee hearts haftening from all parts, to furrender themfelves to her, and paſs by our charms without paying any attention to them. What fate have our eyes allotted them, and what have they done to the gods, that they are not to enjoy any homage amidst all these tributes of glorious sighs, which other eyes triumph in? Can there be a greater difgrace to us, fifter, than to fee all hearts overlook our charms, and the happy Pfyche calmly enjoy a troop of lovers attached to her motions?

Cydippe. Indeed, fifter, all the ills in nature are nothing to this; it makes me wretched.

Aglaura. I am often ready to cry with vexation; it has deprived me of all pleafure and repofe; my conftancy is unarmed againft fuch a misfortune; my mind, ftill fixed on this affliction, fets before my eyes the difgrace of our charms, and Pfyche's triumph. At night, an eternal idea of it ftill paffes before me, which prevails above every thing; nothing can rid me of this cruel phantom, and when foft flumber comes to deliver me from it, fome dream immediately recalls it to my mind, which awakens me in furprife.

Cydippe. Sifter, you have juft defcribed what paffes in my breaft; I endure the fame as you do.

Aglaura. Let us confider this affair. How are her charms fo powerful? have her flighteft looks acquired the grand fecret of pleafing? What is there in her perfon to infpire fuch flames? What law of beauty gives her the empire over all hearts? We agree that fhe has fome youthful attractions; but muft one yield fo much to her for being a little older, and be quite deftitute of charms? Do we make a figure to be defpifed? Have not we fome charms, fome graces, fome complexion, fome eyes, fome air and fome fhape capable of captivating fome lovers? Do me the favour, fifter, to fpeak freely to me. Am I, in your opinion, of an air, that my merit should give place to hers? And in what accomplishment do you think that she outshines me?

Cydippe. Who? you, sister? in none. I observed
you yesterday at the chase near her a long while; and,
without flattering you, you appeared to me handsomer
than her. But tell me, sister, without flattering me,
are they visionary notions I take in my head, when I
think myself so formed as to deserve some conquest?

Aglaura. You, sister? In reality you have all that
can create an amorous flame. Your least actions shine
with an agreeableness that affects me to the soul; and
were I a man, I should be your lover.

Cydippe. How happens it then that we see her bear
it from us both; that all hearts surrender when she appears; and that they entirely neglect our charms?

Aglaura. I certainly have discovered the cause of so
many lovers submitting to her laws; and all our sex
join in thinking her charms very trifling.

Cydippe. I guess at it too; there is certainly some
mystery concealed under it. This secret of inflaming
every one is not an ordinary effect of nature; the
Thessalian art is concerned in this affair; and some
skilful hand has without doubt formed a charm for her
to make herself be loved.

Aglaura. I have much stronger grounds for my belief; the charm she attracts with is a free easy air, caressing looks and words, a sweet inviting smile, and
promises of favours. Our glory is now no longer preserved; and the times of those noble spirits are no
more, who, by a worthy trial of illustrious cruelties,
would see the constancy of a lover proved. We are
far fallen, in the age we are in, from that noble pride
which so well became us; and we are now reduced to
lay aside all hopes, unless we make advances to the
men.

Cydippe. This is juſt the ſecret of the affair, and I ſee that you gueſſed it better than I. It is becauſe we are too reſerved, that no lover will come near us. And we endeavour too much, to maintain the honour of our ſex and birth. The men now love what ſmiles upon them; hope, more than love, is what attracts them; and it is by that, that Pſyche raviſhes from us all thoſe lovers we ſee under her dominion. Let us follow the example; let us adjuſt ourſelves to the times; let us condeſcend to make advances, ſiſter; and let us have no more to do with gloomy decorums, which rob us of the fruit of our moſt lovely years.

Aglaura. I approve the thought, and we have an opportunity to make the firſt proof of it upon the two princes who arrived lately. They are charming, ſiſter, and their entire perſons are to me—Have you ſeen them?

Cydippe. Oh! ſiſter, they are both made in ſuch a manner, that my ſoul—They are two accompliſhed princes.

Aglaura. May we not endeavour to gain their tender affections, without any diſhonour to ourſelves?

Cydippe. I think a beauteous princeſs may give them her heart without any diſgrace.

Aglaura. Here they come; how I admire their air and attire!

Cydippe. They do not in the leaſt belye what we ſaid of them juſt now.

SCENE II.

**CLEOMENES, AGENOR, AGLAURA, CY-
DIPPE.**

AGLAURA.

WHY do you fly us thus, princes? does the
fight of us affright you?

Cleomenes. Madam, we were informed that the
princefs Pfyche was here.

Aglaura. Is there nothing agreeable in thefe places
except her prefence adorn them?

Agenor. There may be fufficient charms here, but
we were impatient to find Pfyche.

Cydippe. Undoubtedly fome prefling bufinefs pufh-
es you on to feek her.

Cleomenes. Prefling enough, when our fortune depends entirely upon it.

Aglaura. It would be too great a favour for us to be
informed of the fecret which thofe words mean.

Cleomenes. We do not pretend to make a fecret of
it, fince, in fpite of us, it would come to light; a fecret feldom lafts long, madam, when love is in the
cafe.

Cydippe. That is plainly to fay, princes, that you
are both in love with Pfyche.

Agenor. Both, fubject to her empire, are now going, in concert, to difcover our flames to her.

Aglaura. Two rivals fo well united, is certainly a
great wonder.

Cleomenes. It is true, the thing is uncommon, but
not impoffible to two fincere friends.

Cydippe. It is becaufe in this place there is none

fair but she, and do you find no one here to divide your vows?

Aglaura. Amidst illustrious blood have not you seen one that deserves your flames?

Cleomenes. Do we reason when we are inflamed? Do we chuse whom to love? And do we regard what right they have to charm us?

Agenor. One follows, in such an ardour, any thing that attracts us, without having the power to chuse; and when love affects the heart, reason has no place there.

Aglaura. Indeed, I pity the troublesome perplexity your hearts are entangled in. You love an object whose smiling charms will mingle anguish with the hopes they give you; and her heart will not perform for you all that her eyes promise you.

Cydippe. The hope that numbers you amongst her lovers, will find a mistake in the soft airs she sets out to view; and you will endure very tormenting moments from the sudden turns of her unsettled mind.

Aglaura. A clear discernment of your merit makes us pity the fate this love guides you to; and you may both find if you will, a heart with as many charms, and more steady.

Cydippe. By a much better choice, you may preserve your friendship in love; and we see, in both of you, a merit so uncommon, that we would, out of pity, by a gentle advice, prevent what your heart is preparing for itself.

Cleomenes. This generous advice shews a goodness for us which affects our souls; but, madam, heaven has reduced us to the misfortune of not being able to profit by it.

Agenor. Your illustrious pity would in vain divert us from a passion, the effect of which we both dread;

what our friendſhip has not been able to bring about, madam, there is nothing can do.

Cydippe. The power of Pſyche will—Here ſhe comes.

S C E N E III.

PSYCHE, CYDIPPE, AGLAURA, CLEO-MENES, AGENOR.

CYDIPPE.

SISTER, come and enjoy what here awaits you.

Aglaura. Prepare your charms to receive the new triumphs of an illuſtrious conqueſt.

Cydippe. Both theſe princes have felt your charms ſo ſenſibly, that they are already diſpoſed to diſcover it to you.

Pſyche. I did not imagine that I occaſioned their thoughtfulneſs; upon finding them with you, I ſhould have ſuppoſed quite the contrary.

Aglaura. They only honour us with their confidence, for we have neither youth nor beauty to excite their love.

Cleomenes to Pſyche.] The confeſſion we muſt make to your divine charms is, doubtleſs, madam, a very raſh one; but ſo many hearts ready to expire, are obliged to diſpleaſe you by ſuch confeſſions, that you are reduced not to puniſh them with the thunder of your wrath? In us you behold two friends whom a happy agreement of tempers has united from our infancy; and theſe gentle bonds have been confirmed by numberleſs combats of eſteem and gratitude. The rigorous aſſaults of adverſe deſtiny, the contempt of death and aſpect of tortures, have ſignalized the lovely ties of our friendſhip, by illuſtrious inſtances of mutual offices. But whatever trials it has met with, its greatest triumph is this day, and nothing so manifests its constancy approved, as the preserving of it in love. Yes, in spight of so many charms, its illustrious constancy has subjected all our vows to the law it enjoins us; it comes, with full and gentle deference, to submit to your choice the success of our passions, and to give a weight to our concurrence, that, for reasons of state, the balance may turn to the choice of one of us, this same friendship readily offers to unite our two kingdoms to the lot of him that is successful.

Agenor. Yes, madam, these two kingdoms which we offer to unite, upon your happy choice, we will add as a succour to our love to obtain you. This is what our amorous hearts make no difficulty of, we being ready to make a sacrifice of ourselves in presence of the king your father, to secure this happiness. And it is making a necessary gift to the fortunate person of a power which the unfortunate one, madam, will have no longer occasion for.

Psyche. Princes, the choice you offer me sets before me what is sufficient to suffice the wishes of the most ambitious; and you both embellish it in such a manner, that nothing more valuable can be offered. Your love, your friendship and supreme virtue, all heighten the offer of your passion, and I see in it a merit which opposes itself to what you desire of me. I must not allow my own heart to enter into such alliances; my hand waits a father's commands to bestow itself, and my sisters have rights which go before mine. But were I made absolute mistress of my vows, you might both have too great a share in them at once; and my esteem, suspended between you, could not let my choice fix on either. I would repay the ardour of your addresses with my tenderest vows; but where there is so much merit, two hearts are too much for me, and one heart too little for you. I should have the tenderest wishes of my soul restrained, and behold one of you receive a destiny which would give me too much pain. Yes, princes, I should with ardour prefer you both to all whose love follows yours, but I should never be able to prefer one of you to the other. My tenderness would make too great a sacrifice to him I should chuse; and I should look upon the wrong I should do the other by it as a cruel injustice. Yes, too much greatness of mind is conspicuous in you both, that either of you should be made unhappy; and you should seek the means of being both fortunate in your love. If you have so much regard for me, as to allow me to dispose of you, I have two sisters capable of pleasing, who have it in their power to make your fate happy ; and friendship makes their persons dear enough to me to wish them yours.

Cleomenes. Alas! Can a heart that loves to excess, consent to be given away by what it loves? We give, madam, to your heavenly charms, an absolute power over both our hearts, dispose of them even to death; but pray have this tenderness, not to dispose of them to any other person than yourself.

Agenor. Madam, it would be offering too great an affront to the princesses; the refuse of another passion would be a lot too mean for their attractions. It must be the faithful purity of a first flame that can aspire to the honour your goodness proposes to us; and each deserves a heart that had sighed for none but her alone.

Aglaura. Princes, I think you should have given us leave to explain ourselves concerning you, before you declined the offer. You must think our hearts are very flexible and tender; therefore how do you know whether we would accept of you?

Cydippe. I suppose we would chuse to owe the conquest of our lovers to our own merit; and our spirits are high enough to refuse hearts that want to be solicited.

Psyche. I thought it a glory sufficiently great for you, sisters, if, by being possessed of so much merit——

S C E N E IV.

PSYCHE, AGLAURA, CYDIPPE, CLEOMENES, AGENOR, LYCAS.

LYCAS to PSYCHE.

OH! madam.

Psyche. What is the matter?

Lycas. The king——

Psyche. Well, what about the king?

Lycas. Wants you.

Psyche. What perplexes you so much?

Lycas. You will know but too soon.

Psyche. Alas! You make me afraid for the king.

Lycas. Be afraid for yourself only; it is you that are to be pitied.

Psyche. Thank heaven, my fears are over, since I know I have them only for myself. But tell me, Lycas, what is it that affects thee so much?

Lycas. Suffer me, madam, to obey him that sent me here, and to leave you to learn from his mouth what it is that afflicts me thus.

Psyche. I must go and learn what makes them be so much afraid of my weakness.

SCENE V.

AGLAURA, CYDIPPE, LYCAS.

AGLAURA.

IF your order extends not to us, pray tell us what great misfortune your grief conceals from us.

Lycas. Alas! princess, it is a misfortune which greatly affects the whole court; the oracle has given the following answer to the king, which is too deeply engraven on my heart to forget it. " Immediately lay " aside all thoughts of Psyche's marriage, and lead her " in funeral pomp to the top of a mountain, where you " must leave her; for there a poisonous dragon " waits to take her for a wife." After so terrible a decree, I leave you yourselves to judge if the gods could have discovered their wrath to us in a more terrible manner.

SCENE VI.

AGLAURA, CYDIPPE.

CYDIPPE.

WHAT think you, sister, of this sudden misfortune in which we see Psyche, plunged by the fates?

Aglaura. Why, what think you of it?

Cydippe. Indeed I am not very sorry for it.

Aglaura. To tell you the truth, neither am I. Come, fate has sent us an ill that we may look on as a good.

END of the FIRST ACT.

FIRST INTERLUDE.

The Scene changes to frightful rocks, and discovers, at a distance, a lonesome desart.

In this desart Psyche is to be exposed, in obedience to the oracle. A company of afflicted persons come hither to deplore her misfortune.

Disconsolate Women, and afflicted Men, singing and dancing.

WOMEN.

DEH, piangete al pianto mio,
   Sassi duri, antiche selve,
Lagrimate fonti, e belue,
D'un bel volto il fato rio.

1. MAN.

Ahi dolore!

2. MAN.

Ahi martire!

1. MAN.

Cruda morte,

WOMAN and 2. MAN.

Empia sorte,

BOTH MEN.

Che condanni a morir tanta belta.

ALL THREE TOGETHER.

Cieli, stelle! Ahi crudelta!

WOMAN.

Rispondete a miei lamenti,
Antri cavi, ascose rupi,

Deh ridite, fondi cupi,
Del mio duolo i mesti accenti.

I. MAN.

Ahi dolore!

2. MAN.

Ahi martire!

I. MAN.

Cruda morte,

WOMAN and 2. MAN.

Empia sorte.

BOTH MEN.

Che condanni a morir tanta belta.

ALL THREE TOGETHER.

Cieli, stelle! Ahi crudelta!

2. MAN.

Com'esser puo fra voi, o Numi eterni,
Chi voglia estinta una belta innocente?
Ahi! Che tanto rigor, Cielo inclemente,
Vince di crudelta gli stessi inferni.

I. MAN.

Nume fiero!

2. MAN.

Dio severo!

BOTH MEN.

Perche tanto rigor
Contro innocente cor?
Ahi, sentenza inudita,
Dar morte a la belta, ch'altrui da vita!

E N T R Y.

Six afflicted Men, and six disconsolate Women, exprefs
their sorrow by their geftures in dancing.

W O M A N.

AHI ch'indarno si tarda,
 Non resiste a gli Dei mortale affetto,
 Alto impero ne sforza,
Ove commanda il Ciel, l' Uvom cede a sforza.

1. MAN.

Ahi dolore!

2. MAN.

Ahi martire! -

1. MAN.

Cruda morte,

WOMAN and 2. MAN.

Empia forte,

BOTH MEN.

Che condanni a morir tánta belta.

ALL THREE TOGETHER.

Cieli, ftelle! Ahi crúdelta!

End of the FIRST INTERLUDE.

A C T II. S C E N E I.

THE KING, PSYCHE, AGLAURA, CYDIPPE,
LYCAS, and Attendants.

PSYCHE.

MY lord, the source of your tears is very dear to
me; but it is too much to allow the tendernefs of a father to reign in the eyes of a great prince
on my account. My lord, what you now give to nature is an injury done to the rank you hold, and I
fhould refufe the moving favour. Give your grief lefs
empire over your wifdom, and ceafe to honour my fate
with tears which difcover too much weaknefs in the
heart of a king.

The King. Oh! daughter, my grief is rational,
though it be extreme, therefore leave my eyes open to
thefe tears: Wifdom itfelf might weep, when one lo-
fes forever what I lofe. The diadem's pride would in
vain have one to be infenfible to thefe great reverfes of
fortune; the fuccours of reafon are in vain offered to
make us fee with a tearlefs eye the death of what we
love; the attempt to do it would be a barbarity in the
eyes of the world; and it is more a brutality than a fupreme virtue. I will not, in this adverfity, affect infenfibility, and conceal the anguifh that touches me. I
renounce the vanity of that ferocity, called firmnefs,
and whatever name they give to the lively grief I feel,
I will difplay it, daughter, to all the world, and fhew
the heart of a man in the heart of a king.

Pfyche. I am quite unworthy of fo much concern.
Oppofe a little refiftance to the laws it impofes on a

heart whose prowess a thousand occasions have distinguished. Should you, my lord, for me, renounce that
royal constancy of which you have given a famous ex-
perience under the assaults of misfortune?

The King. On a thousand occasions, constancy is an
easy matter. All the revolutions that hard fortune can
expose us to, the loss of grandeur, persecutions, the
poison of envy, and the insults of hatred, have nothing
in them but what the resolutions of a mind where
reason has the least rule, may easily defy. But that
which brings rigours with it that make the heart sink
under the weight of bitter sorrows, are the rude strokes
of those severe fatalities which rob us for ever of the
persons that are dear to us. Reason offers no arms for
succour against such assaults; this is the most terrible
thunder that the gods in their wrath can lance against
us.

Psyche. You have yet, my lord, wherewith to be
comforted. The gods have crowned your marriage
with more than one blessing; and, by a manifest favour,
in taking me from your sight, take away nothing but
what they have taken care to repair the loss of; there
still remains what may assuage your grief; and this law
of heaven, which you call cruel, leaves in the two
princesses, my sisters, a subject for paternal love to
place all its tenderness on.

The King. Ah! poor consolation for my ills! Nothing, nothing offers itself to me that can comfort me
for thee. My eyes are only open to my anguish; and,
in so dismal a fate, I look upon what I lose, and do
not regard what is left me.

Psyche. You know better than I, my lord, that our
wills are to be regulated by that of the gods; and I
can say nothing to you upon this melancholy occasion,
but what you can much better say to others. The gods

are sovereign masters of the gifts they deign us, and they only leave them in our hands for what time they think proper; when they recall them, we have no right to repine at the loss of those favours which they will no longer continue to us. I, my lord, am a gift which they granted to your wishes; and now that by this decree they are going to resume me, they take nothing from you but what you hold of them, and you should restore me without repining.

The King. Oh! seek a better foundation for the comfort thy heart offers me; and add not a load to that piercing grief whose torment I now suffer, by the falsity of this reasoning. Do you think, by this, to give me a powerful argument not to lament at this decree of heaven? Is not a killing rigour very visible in this procedure of the gods you would have me quietly submit to? - Consider the age in which these gods force me to give thee up, and that wherein my unfortunate heart received thee; you will thus know that they take much more from me, than they gave me. I received of them in you, daughter, a present my heart requested not of them; I then found very few charms in it, and saw, without any pleasure, my family increase by it. My heart, as well as eyes, have acquired an endearing habitude of that present; I have expended fifteen years of cares, watchings, and study, to make it valuable to me; I have adorned it with the amiable riches of a thousand shining virtues; I have, with the utmost care, inclosed in it all the lovely treasures which wisdom can furnish; I have fixed the tenderness of my soul upon it; I have made it the charm and delight of my heart, the comfort of my declining sense, the soothing hope of my old age. All this these gods rob me of, and have I not reason to complain of this melancholy decree, whose cruel stroke I suffer? Alas! their power sports with our fond hearts too severely. Need they have staid to resume their gift, till I had made it my whole happiness? they had better not have given me any thing, than taken it from me again.

Psyche. My lord, how dare you exclaim against these gods, who may avenge themselves?

The King. What more can they do to me? They have reduced me to a condition of being afraid of nothing.

Psyche. Oh! my lord, I tremble at the crimes I make you commit, and should hate myself.

The King. Alas! is it not sufficient that my heart gives thee up to the cruel respect which we must shew them? they may suffer my just complaints, it is hard enough for me to obey them, without restraining the grief which the terrible decree of so hard a lot gives me. I cannot restrain my grief; I will for ever mourn the loss I suffer.

Psyche. My lord, your grief and my fate is too much for my tender heart to bear; spare my weakness in the condition I am in; I have great need of resolution.

The King. Right, I ought to spare thee my inconsolable anguish. Behold the fatal instant that must tear thee from me; but how shall I pronounce that dreadful word? Yet it must be, for so heaven decrees; an inevitable rigour obliges me to leave thee in this fatal place, Farewell, I go——Farewell.

SCENE II.

PSYCHE, AGLAURA, CYDIPPE.

PSYCHE.

LET the king not be alone, sisters, but follow him, and sweeten his afflictions; you will augment his alarms if you expose yourselves longer to my misfortunes. The dragon I wait for may be fatal to you, involve you in my lot, and give me in you a second death. Heaven has condemned me alone to its poisonous breath, nothing can help me; I have no need of an example to die.

Aglaura. Do not envy us the sad advantage of blending our tears with your sorrows, and mingling our sighs with yours; suffer this last pledge of a tender affection.

Psyche. That would be losing you in vain.

Cydippe. It is in hopes of a miracle in your favour, that we accompany you to the grave.

Psyche. What can one promise one's self after such an answer from the oracle?

Aglaura. The oracle frequently gives obscure answers. We understand them the less, the better we think we understand them; and perhaps, after all, you ought only to expect glory and felicity from it; allow us, sister, to see this mortal terror happily deceived by a fortunate issue, or at least to die with you, if heaven does not shew itself more propitious to our wishes.

Psyche. Pay more attention to the voice of nature, sister, which calls you to the king. You love me too much, it is contrary to duty; you know its indispensible law, a father ought to be still dearer to you than I am. Render yourselves a support of his old age; you owe him each a son-in-law and grandsons; a thousand kings, with emulation, keep their affections for you; a thousand kings, with emulation, will offer you their vows. The oracle required none but me; and I alone will die, and without shewing any weakness too, if it be possible; at least I will not have you for witnesses of what nature, in spite of me, leaves of it upon me.

Aglaura. Is it troubling you, to share your sorrows?

Cydippe. Nay, perhaps it difpleafes you?

Pfyche. No, But in fhort, it is putting a conftraint upon me; and perhaps redoubling the wrath of heaven.

Aglaura. You will have it fo, we therefore part. May that fame heaven prove more juft and lefs fevere, and vouchfafe to fend you the fortune which we wifh you, and which our fincere friendfhip hopes for you, in fpite both of the oracle and yourfelf.

Pfyche. The gods, fifter, will never fulfil either your hope or wifh.   Farewell.

S C E N E III.

P S Y C H E alone.

NOW I am alone, and can freely contemplate this frightful change, which from the higheft pitch of glory precipitates me to the grave. That glory was incomparable; the fplendour of it fpread itfelf to the moft remote corners of the earth; all the kings in the world feemed created to love me; their fubjects all imagining me a goddefs, began to accuftom me to the incenfe which they conftantly offered me; their fighs purfued me, without cofting me any; my foul remained free while it captivated fo many others; and amidft fo many flames, I was queen of every heart, and miftrefs of my own.   Oh heaven! have you imputed this infenfibility to me as a crime? Do you difplay fuch feverity towards me for having only returned efteem to their vows? If you impofe this law upon me, that I muft make a choice to avoid your difpleafure, fince I could not do it, why did you not do it for me? Why did you not infpire into my breaft, that which is infpired into fo many others, by merit, love, and— But here come the two princes to difcompofe me again.

SCENE IV.

CLEOMENES, AGENOR, PSYCHE.

CLEOMENES.

WE are come, madam, to expose our lives in defence of yours.

Psyche. How do you think I can listen to you, when I have forced away two sisters? Do you imagine, princes, to be able to defend me against heaven? To give yourselves up to the dragon, which I must here attend, is a despair which ill becomes great hearts; and to die when I die, is to overwhelm a tender heart which has but too many sorrows of its own.

Agenor. We may subdue the dragon; Cadmus, who was not in love, defied that of Mars. We are in love, and love makes every thing possible to a heart that follows its banners, and to a hand whose darts it-self directs.

Psyche. Would you have it serve you in favour of an ungrateful creature, whom all its arrows have not been able to touch, and lay down its vengeance in the very moment it beams forth, and aid you to deliver me from it? Nay, if when even you shall have serv-ed me, when you shall have given me life, what fruit of it do you expect from one who cannot love?

Cleomenes. We are not animated by the hope of so charming a reward; we only seek to discharge the du-ties of a passion which dares not ever presume, do what it can, to be capable of pleasing you, or worthy of inflaming you. Live, fair princess, and live for an-other; we shall behold it with a jealous eye, we shall expire at it, but of a sweeter death than if we were to see yours; and if we lose not our lives in protecting yours, whenever you vifibly prefer an lover to us, we fhall foon die with grief and love.

Pfyche. Live, princes, live; nor think any more of breaking, or fharing my unhappy fate; I thought I had told you heaven requires none but me; heaven has condemned me alone.   Methinks I hear already the deadly hiffings of its approaching minifter; my fear paints him out to me, and conftantly fets him before me; and, miftrefs as it is of all my thoughts, it figures him out to me on the top of this rock.   I fink under it through weaknefs; and a remnant of virtue, with pain, fcarce fupports my vanquifhed heart.   Farewell, princes, pray leave me, for I fear it will prove fatal to you if you ftay.

Agenor. We fee not yet any thing to terrify us; and if your ftrength abandons you when you paint out to yourfelf fo near a death, we have hearts and hands which are not abandoned by hope.   A rival may probably have dictated this oracle, or gold have made it fpeak that which it hath pronounced; it would not be a miracle for a man to have anfwered for a dumb god; and we have but too many examples in all nations, that temples are not lefs free of rogues than other places.

Cleomenes. Suffer us to oppofe to the bafe ravifher to whom facrilege unjuftly gives you up, a paffion which heaven has chofen for the defence of the only beauty for whom we defire to live.   If we dare not pretend to the poffeffion of it, allow us at leaft, in its danger, to follow the ardour and duties of our paffion.

Pfyche. Bear them to my other-felfs, bear, princes, to my fifters, thefe extreme ardors with which your hearts are filled for me; live for them when I am no more; bewail the direful rigours of my fate, without giving them in you new caufe of grief; this is my laft will, and the orders of the dying have always been received as fovereign laws.

Cleomenes. Princefs——

Pfyche. Once more, princes, live for them; you fhould obey me, as much as you love me; do not reduce me to hate you, and to regard you as rebels inftead of faithful fervants to me. Go, leave me to expire here alone, where I have no more voice left than to bid you an eternal farewell; I find myfelf lifted aloft, and the air opens a paffage to me, from whence you will no more hear this dying voice. Farewell, princes, for the laft time farewell. My fate can now be no longer doubted by you.

[Pfyche is carried into the air by two Zephyrs.

Agenor. Alas! fhe is now quite out of fight. Let us both go, prince, and feek on the top of this rock the means to follow her.

Cleomenes. Yes, let us go, and there find the means of not furviving her.

S C E N E V.

C u p i d in the Air.

GO to death, both of you, for having the boldnefs to be rivals of a jealous god; and do you, Vulcan, forge a thoufand brilliant ornaments to embellifh a palace, where Cupid may furrender himfelf to Pfyche, and dry up her tears.

E n d of the S e c o n d A c t.

SECOND INTERLUDE.

The Scene changes to a splendid court, adorned with columns of Lapis Lazuli, enriched with golden figures, which form a magnificent palace designed by Cupid for Psyche.

VULCAN, CYCLOPS, FAIRIES.

VULCAN.

QUICKLY prepare these places to receive
  The gentlest, and most amiable of the gods;
Let each with interested cares obey him.
We ne'er can do enough when love requires.
Cupid will not admit the least delay,
Toil, hasten, strike, redouble still your blows;
And let your ardour to obey and please him
Make all your labours pleasing and agreeable.

ENTRY.

The Cyclops finish, to music, large golden vases,
  which are brought them by the Fairies.

VULCAN.

SERVE such a lovely deity with vigour,
  He takes delight in ardent diligence;
Let each with interested cares obey him.
When love requires, we ne'er can do enough.

Cupid will not admit the least delay,
Toil, hasten strike, redouble still your blows;

And let your ardour to obey and pleafe him
Make all your labours pleafing and agreeable.

SECOND ENTRY.

The Cyclops and Fairies fix in their places to mufic,
the golden vafes intended for new ornaments to Cupid's palace.

END of the SECOND INTERLUDE.

ACT III.   SCENE I.

CUPID, ZEPHYR.

ZEPHYR.

I HAVE faithfully executed your commands, and
carried the beauty from the rock, and brought
her into this delightful palace, where you may difpofe
of her as you think proper; but I am furprized at the
alteration I fee in your perfon. That ftature, mien,
and habit difguife you entirely; it is impoffible for the
craftieft man in the world now to take you for what you
really are.

Cupid. I do not want to be known. I will difcover
nothing to Pfyche but my heart, and the tranfports of
that lively ardour which her beauty has imprinted upon me. And therefore to exprefs the great love which
I bear her, and to conceal what I am from thofe eyes
that impofe laws on me, I have affumed this habit.

Zephyr. I always thought you clever at every thing,
but now I find you more fo than ever. The gods, when
they have been in love, have often transformed themfelves into various forms, to cure their amorous paffi-

on; but truly you far furpafs them. This is the right.
figure to gain you good fuccefs with the amiable fex
you adore. The affiftance of fuch a form is very powerful; and, not to mention either rank or wit, he that
can find means of being fo well made, will fcarce figh
in vain.

Cupid. I have refolved, my dear Zephyr, to continue thus for ever.   The eldeft of the Loves cannot be
blamed for this.   In fhort, I am quite tired with that
long ftate of infancy, and I fhall now fhew myfelf a
man.

Zephyr. Very well. You could not do better; for
you are entering into a myftery that is too deep for a
boy to penetrate.

Cupid. My mother will undoubtedly be vexed at my
affuming this character.

Zephyr. I forefee fome fmall anger upon that fcore.
For though difputes about age ought not to reign among
the immortals, yet Venus, like other beauties, does net
much care to be thought the mother of fo beautiful a
youth.   But the thing that moft offends her, is the
method of your proceeding; it is revenging her caufe
in a ftrange manner, to adore the beauty fhe wants to
punifh.   This hatred, which fhe expects the power of
her fon, whom the gods themfelves fear, fhould anfwer
her wifhes in————

Cupid. Leave off this difcourfe, Zephyr, and tell me
what you think of Pfyche's beauty. Is there any thing
on earth, or any thing in the heavens, which can deprive her of the glorious title of a matchlefs beauty?
But I behold her, my dear Zephyr, admiring the glories
of her new habitation.

Zephyr. You may fhew yourfelf to her, to put an
end to her fufferings, and difcover her glorious deftiny to her; talk together whatever two lovers can fay

with their fighs, mouth, and eyes. I fhall prove to you
a fincere confident, and not difturb you in your amorous
téte-à-téte.

S C E N E II.

P S Y C H E alone.

WHAT a delightful place is this I am tranfported to! How beautiful every corner is adorned with every thing in nature and art the moft pleafing
and magnificent.   Every thing glitters in thefe gardens and apartments, whofe pompous furniture have
nothing in them but what enchants and flatters one;
and where-ever my fears turn, I fee nothing under my
feet but gold or flowers. Has heaven made this charming place for the abode of a dragon? And when, by
this fight, it amufes and fufpends the unequalled rigours of my jealous deftiny, would it fhew that it re-
pents of it? No, no, this is the blackeft, the moft barbarous ftroke of its cruel hatred, which by a new and
unparalleled rigour, difplays this choice it had made of
every thing the moft beautiful in the world, that I may
quit it with more regret. How abfurd is my hope,
if it thinks, by this means, to affwage my forrows! E-
very hour that my death is delayed, has fo many moments of new misfortunes; it lingers the more, and I
die but fo much the oftener. Thou monfter, which
art to devour me, let me languifh no longer, but come
and feize on thy victim. Wouldft thou have me feek
for thee? And muft I animate thy fury to devour me?
If heaven intends my death, if my life is a crime, feize
on the little that remains of it. I am tired of murmuring againft a lawful chaftifement, I am tired of fighing; come quickly, and put a period to my days.

SCENE III.

CUPID, PSYCHE, ZEPHIR.

CUPID.

I AM the dragon, the merciless monster which the astonishing oracle has prepared for you, and which is not frightful to that degree that you had figured it out to yourself.

Psyche. What, are you the monster with which the oracle threatened me; you, who rather seem to be a deity that miraculously comes to my aid?

Cupid. What need have you for aid in an empire, where every thing that breathes attend to take their law from your looks, and where you have no other monster to be afraid of but me?

Psyche. A monster like you gives me not much uneasiness; and if it has any poison, a soul would have very little reason to make the least complaint against a sweet infection, which every heart would dread the cure of; scarce do I see you, but my ceasing fears suffer the image of death to vanish, and I feel an unknown fire run through my frozen veins. I have felt esteem and complaisance, friendship and gratitude, and the innocent feelings of compassion have made me experience the power of it; but I never yet felt what I now feel; I know not what it is, but I know that it charms me, and that it gives me not the least alarm. The more I cast my eyes upon you, the more I am charmed; never was I so moved by any thing I ever before felt; and I would tell you, that I loved you, my lord, if I knew what it was to love. Turn not away those tender eyes that poison me; those piercing but amorous eyes, which seem to share the anguish they give me. Alas! the more dangerous they are, the more I am pleafed to be wedded to them. By what in-comprehenfible decree of heaven do I thus fay to you more than I ought; I, whofe modefty ought at leaft to wait till you explain to me the diforder I perceive you in? You figh, my lord, as I figh; your fenfes, like mine, appear in amazement; it is my part to be filent, and yours to tell me this; and yet it is I who tell it you.

Cupid. Pfyche, you have always been fo hard-heart-ed, that you muft not be amazed if, to repair the inju-ry, love now repays itfelf with ufury of that which ought to have been given it. The moment is come in which you muft breathe thofe fighs you have fo long retained, and in which you muft lay afide your cruelty, and be at once fenfibly affected with numberlefs, fweet, and unknown tranfports, which ought to have touched you during fo many 'lovely days which this infenfible foul has profaned the courfe of.

Pfyche. Have I been guilty of a great crime then, in being infenfible of love?

Cupid. Do you fuffer a cruel chaftifement for it?

Pfyche. The punifhment is very gentle.

Cupid. Love may chufe its lawful punifhment, and, in this glorious day, do itfelf juftice for the failure of love, by an excefs of love.

Pfyche. Wherefore have I not been punifhed fooner! The happinefs of my life is placed in it; I ought to blufh at it, or at leaft to whifper it; but the punifhment has too many charms in it for that. Allow me to fay it, and repeat it aloud; I will fay it a thoufand times, and never blufh at it; it is not I that fpeak; the fur-prizing power, the amiable violence of your prefence, takes poffeffion of my voice, whenever I would fpeak. It is in vain that my modefty is fecretly offended at it, that the decency of my fex would impofe other laws upon me; your eyes themselves determine what I shall answer; and my mouth, subject to their almighty power, no longer consults me about what I ought to say.

Cupid. Believe, fair Psyche, believe what these eyes say to you, which only burn with a desire that yours should inform me of all that passes within you. Believe in this sighing heart, which, as often as yours will answer it, will inform you more by a sigh than a thousand looks can tell you. This is the most sweet, the most powerful, and the most sure of all languages.

Psyche. The intelligence of it was due to our hearts, to make them equally content. I have sighed, and you have heard me; you sigh, and I hear you. But leave me no longer in this uncertainty, my lord, and tell me, if by the same way, Zephyr brought you here after me to tell me what I hear? When I arrived in this place, was you expected? and when you speak to him are you understood?

Cupid. I have a sovereign empire in this sweet climate, as you have an empire over my heart; Cupid is favourable to me: and it is to oblige him that Æolus, at my request, summoned Zephyr. It was Cupid who, to reward my passion, himself dictated the answer of the oracle, by which you are delivered from a multitude of lovers that you were threatned with, and which has freed me from the eternal obstacle of so many ardent sighs which were not worthy of being addressed to you. Ask me not how this kingdom is called, nor the name of its king; you shall know it at a proper time. I would gain you, but it is by faithful services, assiduous cares, and constant vows; by an amorous sacrifice of all I am, and all I can do, without trusting to the splendour of my rank to solicit for me, or without making any merit of my power; although I am sovereign in this happy abode, I would owe Pyſche to no-thing but my love.   Come, princeſs, and admire with me the wonders of this place, and prepare your eyes and ears to feaſt upon its enchantments.   Here you ſhall ſee the groves and meadows conteſt their beau-ties with gold and gems; and ſhall hear nothing but charming concerts; a thouſand beauties ſhall here ſerve you and adore you without envy, and perpetually with rapture and ſubmiſſion ſolicit the honour of your com-mands.

Pſyche. My will attends upon yours, I no longer have any of my own; but the anſwer of your oracle has ſeparated me from the king my father, and two ſi-ſters, who are now lamenting my imagined death. Suffer, therefore, my ſiſters to be witneſſes of my glo-ry and your cares for me, to diſſipate the error which loads their breaſts with mortal anguiſh; lend them as you did me, the wings of Zephyr, which may facilitate their acceſs to your empire as they did mine; ſuffer them to ſee where I now live, and let them admire the ſucceſs of my loſs.

Cupid. Alas! Pſyche, you have not given me up all your ſoul.   This tender remembrance of a father and ſiſters robs me of part of thoſe ſweets the whole of which I would have my paſſion enjoy.   Have no eyes for any but me, as I have not for any but you; think of nothing but to pleaſe me; and when ſuch thoughts dare intrude to divert that———

Pſyche. No one, ſure, can be jealous of the tender-neſſes of natural affection.

Cupid. I am ſo, my dear Pſyche, of all nature.   The rays of the ſun too often ſalute you; too often do your lovely locks ſuffer the careſſes of the wind; while it blows them, I cannot but repine at it; the air itſelf which you breathe, paſſes with too much pleaſure thro'

your lips; your very habit touches you too near; and
as foon as you figh, fomething, I know not what,
ftartles me, fearing left amongft thofe fighs there fhould
be any wandring ones.   But you defire to fee your fifters; go, Zephyr, Pfyche will have it fo, and I cannot but affent to it.   [Zephyr flies off.

S C E N E   IV.

C U P I D,   P S Y C H E.

C U P I D.

WHEN you fhew your fifters this heavenly
mansion, freely beftow on them plenty of
its charming treafures, and lavifh careffes upon careffes on them; and exhanft, if poffible, all the ten-
derneffes of natural affection, that you may give up
yourfelf entirely to Cupid.   I will have nothing to do
with your meeting; but hold not too long a converfation with them; you can have no complaifance for
them that you do not rob me of.

Pfyche. I can never abufe the favours which your
love confers on me.

Cupid. In the mean time, let us go and view thefe
gardens and palaces, where you will find nothing but
what your beauty effaces.   And you, ye little Loves
and youthful Zephyrs, who are animated by tender
fighs alone, difplay with emulation, the pleafure you
felt when you firft beheld the faireft of the fair.

END of the THIRD ACT.

T H I R D   I N T E R L U D E.

C U P I D,   P S Y C H E.

A ZEPHYR, who fings; two CUPIDS, who fing; a
company of CUPIDS and ZEPHYRS, who dance.

E N T R Y.

The Loves and Zephyrs, in obedience to Cupid, fhew, by
their dances, the joy they have in beholding Pfyche.

ZEPHYR.

LET tendernefs, ye youths, your bofoms move;
Join to your happy days the fweets of love,
'Tis only to deceive you, they advife
To fhun love's pleafures, and avoid its fighs;
Then give yourfelves up wholly to its joys.

TWO CUPIDS TOGETHER.

All, all in their turn, love's fweet tranfports muft know;
And the more charms they have, they more to Cupid owe.

1. CUPID.

A heart that's young and tender
Ought always to furrender;
And never have in view
Crofs windings to purfue.

TWO CUPIDS TOGETHER.

All, all in their turn, love's fweet tranfports muft know;
And the more charms they have, they more to Cupid owe.

2. CUPID.

For what reafon ftill refift?
To what purpofe ftill perfift?

Once a day is loſt, 'tis vain
To hope it will return again.

TWO CUPIDS TOGETHER.

All, all in their turn, love's ſweet tranſports muſt know;
And the more charms they have, they more to Cupid owe.

SECOND ENTRY.

The two companies of Cupids and Zephyrs begin
their dances again.

ZEPHYR.

CUPID has always ſtore of charms,
    To him let's render up our arms;
His very cares and tears muſt pleaſe,
And following him your heart's at eaſe.
Indeed to taſte his rapt'rous pleaſure
We muſt languiſh beyond meaſure;
But yet, no mortal truly lives,
Who not to love juſt homage gives.

TWO CUPIDS TOGETHER.

Should cares, pains, and anguiſh a lover invade,
By one happy moment he fully is paid.

1. CUPID.

We've hopes, and fears, and myſteries;
But who a happineſs ere ſees
Obtain'd without ſome miſeries?

TWO CUPIDS TOGETHER.

Should cares, pains, and anguiſh a lover invade,
By one happy moment he fully is paid.

2. CUPID.

What can a mortal better do
Than love and pleaſe his fair one too?
O! how full of charming joy
Is the lover's bleſt employ!

TWO CUPIDS TOGETHER.
Should care, pains, and anguish a lover invade,
By one happy moment he fully is paid.

END of the THIRD INTERLUDE.

&8&*&*&*&*&*&*&*&*&*&*&*&*&*&*&*&8&

ACT THE FOURTH.

The Stage represents a grand and delightful garden,
with verdant arbours adorned with gold, and deco-
rated with vases of orange-trees, and other trees
plentifully laden with fruit. The middle of the Stage
is filled with the most beautiful and uncommon
flowers. At the farther end several grottos are difcovered, adorned with shells, fountains and statues, and the whole view terminated by a magnificent palace.

SCENE I.

AGLAURA, CYDIPPE.

AGLAURA.

I AM quite tired, sister, with beholding so many
wonders; future ages will, with pain, conceive
them; the sun, that sees all things and discovers all
things to us, never beheld the like; it disturbs the
mind. This magnificent palace, this pompous equipage, make an odious shew, which loads me with shame
as well as displeasure. How unworthily does fortune treat us! And how does her indiscreet bounty
blindly waste, lavish, exhaust and unite its efforts, to
make so many treasures the lot of a younger sister!

.Cydippe. I approve of what you fay; I have the fame afflictions; and what difpleafes you in thefe charming places, does the fame to me; whatever you take as a deadly affront, overwhelms me as well, and leaves bitternefs in my foul, and a blufh on my face.

Aglaura. No, fifter, there is not a queen that talks fo much like a fovereign in her own realms, as Pfyche does here, where we fee her obeyed with the utmoft exactnefs; and her will is, by an amorous ftudioufnefs, watched for in her very eyes. A thoufand beauties croud around her, and feem to fay, upon perceiving our jealous looks, how great foever our charms are, fhe is ftill more beautiful, and we who ferve her are more fo than you. She fpeaks, and they willingly execute her commands. Flora herfelf who attends her fteps, throws her moft precious ftores, with liberal hands, around her perfon; Zephyr is in readinefs to fly at her order, and his miftrefs and he quit their own loves to ferve her.

Cydippe. She will prefently have altars raifed to her, as fhe has already gods obedient to her commands; whilft we only have command over wretched mortals, whofe caprice and audacioufnefs hourly, in fecret perfidy, oppofe our pleafure either by murmuring or artifice.

Aglaura. It was a fmall matter, that in our court fo many hearts, with emulation, preferred her to us; it was not enough that day and night, fhe was there adored by crouds of lovers; but, when we comforted ourfelves with the hopes of feeing her in her grave, by the unexpected order of the oracle, fhe muft difplay the miracle of her new fortune in our prefence, and chufe our eyes to be witneffes of what, at the bottom of our heart, we fhould the leaft have defired.

Cydippe. That which gives me the greateft vexation, is this perfect lover, so capable of pleasing, whom she has made a captive of; might we chuse out of all monarchs, is there a king in the universe who bears so noble a stamp? To see one's desires of wealth satisfied is often a success which makes us miserable; there is no pompous equipage or stately palaces but opens some door to incurable ills; but to have a lover of perfect merit, and to find one's self dearly beloved by him, is a happiness so high, so sublime, that the greatness of it is inexpressible.

Aglaura. Let us talk no more of it, sister; we shall die with envy at it; let us rather consider how we may avenge ourselves, and find means of breaking this good intelligence between them.   Here she comes.   I have a net ready for her, that she will not easily avoid.

S C E N E II.

P S Y C H E, A G L A U R A, C Y D I P P E.

P S Y C H E.

DEAR sisters, I am come to bid you farewel, my lover sends you back again; for he cannot bear that you should deprive him of one moment of the joy he takes in being alone contemplating me. A single look, the least word that I part with, even to my sisters, he reckons a tenderness which I rob him of in favour of natural affection.

Aglaura. Jealousy is very nice; and these delicate sentiments give good reason to think that he who has such an ardent love for you is above the rank of common lovers.   I speak thus to you of him without knowing him; you are ignorant of his name, and of his parents, we are therefore alarmed at it.   I take him for a great prince, and of a power supreme, even beyond

that of a diadem; the treasures which he has, with pro-
fusion, sown beneath your feet, might make even Plenty's self ashamed; you love him as much as he loves
you; he delights you, and you delight him; your happiness, sister, would be extreme if you knew but whom
you loved.

Psyche. I care not who he is; I am beloved by
him. The more he sees me, the more I please him.
There are no pleasures which can charm the soul but
what prevent my wishes; and I cannot see what you are
alarmed at, when all in this palace wait to serve me.

Aglaura. What advantage is it that all here wait to
serve you, if this lover will never let you know what
he is? We are only alarmed for your interest. In vain
do all smile here, in vain do all please you; true love
knows no reserve, and he that is obstinate in conceal-
ing himself, is conscious of something in himself that
is obnoxious to reproach. If this lover should become
inconstant now, for change in love has its charms; and,
between us, I will be bold to say, that however great
the lustre of your face may be, there still may be others
perhaps as handsome as you; if, I say, another object
should engage him; if in the condition we now see
you, alone in his hands, and without any defence, he
should commit any violence, on whom shall the king
revenge himself either for the change, or the insolence?

Psyche. Sister, you make me tremble. Heavens!
Can I be so unfortunate as——

Cydippe. Perhaps Hymen's knots are already——

Psyche. O! no more, this would overwhelm me.

Aglaura. But one word more, and then I am done:
This prince who loves you, and who commands the
winds, who gives us Zephyr's wings for a chariot, and
loads you with new delights every moment, when he
thus visibly breaks the order of nature, may perhaps mix

a little impofture with fo much love. Perhaps this palace is but an inchāntment, and thefe golden roofs,
thefe heaps of treafures with which he now purchafes
your affection, may, as foon as he is furfeited with your
careffes, difappear in a moment.   You are fenfible as
well as we of the power of magic.

Pfyche. What cruel alarms do I feel in my turn!

Aglaura. Our friendfhip aims at nothing but your
good.

Pfyche. Farewel, fifters, let us break off our difcourfe; I love, and fear left he fhould grow impatient.
Depart; and to-morrow, if poffible, you fhall fee me
either more content, or in the depth of mortal anguifh.

Aglaura. We will go and let the king know what
new glory, what excefs of happinefs heaven has poured
upon you.

Cydippe. We will give him the furprizing and marvellous hiftory of fo fweet a change.

Pfyche. Trouble him not with your fufpicions, fifters; and when you defcribe this beautiful empire to
him——

Aglaura. We know very well what to tell him; and
need no leffons on that point.

[A cloud defcends and envelopes Pfyche's fifters; and
     Zephyr carries them up into the air.

SCENE III.

CUPID, PSYCHE.

CUPID.

HOW glad am I that you are again alone, and I can again repeat to you, without having your sisters for witnesses, what an empire those lovely eyes have over me, and how excessive the joys are which a sincere ardour inspires when two hearts are once united. I can display to you the amorous ardency of my transported soul; and swear to you that the sole object of those transports is to serve you, to see this ardour attended with an equal ardour, and to conceive no other wish than to be regulated by your desires. But what is the reason, that a gloomy cloud seems to obscure the lustre of those piercing eyes? Have you not every thing here you desire? Or do you disdain the homage of those vows that are here tendered you?

Psyche. Indeed, my lord, I do not.

Cupid. What ails you then? And whence this misfortune to me? I hear more sighs of grief than of love; the fading roses on your cheeks discover some secret anxiety; your sisters are hardly out of your sight before you sigh with regret. Ah! Psyche, when the ardour of two hearts are the same, have they different sighs? And when one truly loves, and has the sight of what one loves, can one think of relations?

Psyche. No, I am not grieved at that.

Cupid. Is it the absence of a rival, and of a beloved rival, which makes you neglect me?

Psyche. Alas! how ill do you penetrate the secrets of a heart that is entirely yours! I love you, my lord, and love is provoked by the unworthy suspicion you have formed. You are ignorant of your own merit, if you are afraid of not being beloved. I love you, though ere now I have ſhewn myſelf haughty enough to deſpiſe the vows of ſeveral kings; and, if I muſt tell you my real thoughts, I never found any one but you who was worthy of me. However, I have a concern which I would in vain conceal from you; a black chagrin is mingled with all my tender paſſion, which I cannot free it from. Aſk me not the cauſe of it, for perhaps if you knew it, you would puniſh me for it; and if I dare yet aſpire at any thing, I am certain I ſhould not obtain it.

Cupid. And are you not afraid that I ſhould be in my turn provoked that you ſhould ſo little know your own merit, or pretend ſo little to know how abſolute a power you have over me? Alas! if you doubt it, be undeceived, ſpeak.

Pſyche. It would be very diſagreeable to me to be repulſed.

Cupid. Pray have not ſuch cruel ſentiments of me, it is eaſy making the experiment; ſpeak, I am quite attentive. If you require oaths to make me be believed, I ſwear by thoſe victorious eyes which are rulers of my heart, thoſe divine authors of my flame; and if that is not enough, I ſwear it, like the gods, by Styx.

Pſyche. After this aſſurance, I am leſs afraid. My lord, I behold in this place all imaginable grandeur; I adore you, and you love me; my heart is delighted at it; but amidſt this ſupreme happineſs I have the misfortune not to know whom I love. I therefore deſire that you would let me know who you are.

Cupid. Pſyche, what is that you ſaid?

Pſyche. That this is the greateſt of my wiſhes, and if you do not grant it me——

Cupid. I have sworn it, and am no longer master of it; but you are insensible what you demand. Leave me my secret. If I discover myself I lose you, and you me. I cannot therefore grant your request.

Pysche. Is this the sway I have over your heart?

Cupid. You can do any thing, and I am entirely yours. But if you think our mutual flames are sweet, lay no obstacle in the way of their charming progress; do not force me to fly; that is the least evil which can happen to us from this desire you are seduced by.

Psyche. My lord, you will try me; but I know what I ought to think of it. Pray inform me of the whole excess of my glory; and no longer conceal from me for what illustrious choice I have rejected the vows of so many kings.

Cupid. And must I submit to your demands?

Pysche. Permit me to conjure it of you.

Cupid. Were you sensible, Psyche, of the cruel accident you draw on yourself by it————

Psyche. My lord, you make me despair.

Cupid. Think well of it; I can yet be silent.

Psyche. Will you not fulfil the vows you have made?

Cupid. Well then, since it must be so, I am a-god, the most powerful of all the gods, absolute both on the earth and in the heavens; my power is supreme in the ocean and the air; in short, I am Cupid himself, who by my own darts was wounded for you; and were it not, alas! for the violence you offer me, which has changed my love into anger, you would have had me for a husband. Your desires are satisfied, you know who it is that loves you, you know the lover that charms you: and now see, Psyche, to what a condition you have reduced yourself. You yourself force me to leave you; you yourself force me to deprive you of all the fruits of your victory. Perhaps thofe fair eyes may never behold me again. This palace and thefe gardens, which muft difappear with me, will caufe your growing glory all to vanifh; you was not willing to believe me in the thing; and the fruit of this fcruple being cleared up is, that Deftiny, at which the heavens themfelves tremble, more powerful than my love and than all the gods together, will fhew its hatred to you, and banifh me from your fight.

[Cupid flies off, and the garden difappears.

S C E N E IV.

The Stage reprefents a defart, and wild banks of a river.

PSYCHE, and the RIVER-GOD fitting on a heap of flags, and leaning upon an urn.

PSYCHE.

CRUEL deftiny! deadly inquietude! fatal cufiofity! What! have you turned all my happinefs into a dreary defart? I loved a god, and was adored by him, my felicity redoubled every moment; and now I find myfelf alone, diffolved in tears, in the midft of a folitude, where, to overwhelm me quite, I find, to my confufion and defpair, my love increafed when bereft of my lover. The remembrance of it both charms and empoifons me, and tyrannizes over a miferable heart which my flame has condemned to the fharpeft anguifh. O heavens! When Cupid flew from me, why did he leave me the love he infpired me with? Thou fource of all pure and inexhauftible treafures, ruler of gods and men, thou dear author of the torments I endure, fhall I never fee thee more? I myfelf have indeed banifhed thee from me; in the height 'of love, and the extremity of happinefs, my heart was alarmed with a mean fufpicion; ungrateful heart, how dull was thy fight? when we love we fhould not entertain a wifh but what is agreeable to the object beloved.   Let me die, that is the only part that is now left me, after the lofs I have occafioned.   For whom, ye gods, would I defire to live, or for whom form a fingle wifh?   Thou river, whofe waters wafh thefe fands, let my ciime be buried in thy waves; and, to put an end to my deplorable ills, let me fecure my repofe in thy deepeft ftreams.

River-God. Heaven forbids thee, fair one, to do fo rafh a deed, and my ftreams would be polluted by it; perhaps after thefe profound forrows, a happier fate attends thee. Fly rather from the implacable wrath of Venus.   I fee her coming to feek you, and to inflict a punifhment on you; the love of the fon has occafioned the mother's hatred; fly, I can retain her.

Pfyche. I attend her revenging fury; what can fhe have in ftore for me but what is too gentle for me? one that wifhes for death, and fears neither gods nor goddeffes, but bids defiance to their utmoft efforts.

S C E N E V.

V E N U S, P S Y C H E, R I V E R - G O D.

V E N U S.

CAN you have the boldnefs, Pfyche, to appear before me, after you have bore off from me the honours done me upon earth, after your feducing charms have received that incenfe which is due to none but mine?   I have feen my| temples forfaken; I have feen mankind, feduced by your charms, idolize you as the fupreme beauty, and pay you homage till then' unknown, without fo much as confidering whether there was any other Venus or no; and I ftill fee you fo audacious as not to be afraid of being feverely punifhed, and to look me as boldly in the face as if you had nothing to fear from my refentment.

Pfyche. If I have been adored by any part of mankind, is it any crime in me to be poffeffed of charms? Or that their unthinking minds fhould yield to my attractions, when they had never the pleafure of beholding you. I am juft what heaven has made me. If the vows that have been paid me have proved difagreeable to you, you needed only to have fhewn yourfelf, to have had them brought back to you. As foon as you ceafed to conceal yourfelf, all would know their duty, fince you need only to be feen to be adored.

Venus. You ftand in need of a much better defence. This adoration, this incenfe ought to be refufed you; and the better to difabufe mankind, it is neceffary that you fhould pay them to me, even in their fighs. You have been in love with a crime which you ought to have abhorred; nay, you have gone ftill farther; your haughty temper, after having rejected feveral kings, has carried the extravagant ambition of its choice even to the immortals.

Pfyche. Did I, goddefs, carry my ambition to the immortals?

Venus. Your infolence is without example; to defpife all earthly monarchs, is not this to afpire at the gods themfelves?

Pfyche. If Cupid had made me infenfible to their addreffes with a defign to referve me for himfelf, am I to blame for that? And is it therefore neceffary that I fhould pay fo dearly for his agreeable paffion as to be for ever fubject to your refentment?

Venus. Pſyche, you ought to have known yourſelf, as well as the dignity of this god.

Pſyche. Did he leave me any time for this, he who in an inſtant became maſter of my whole heart?

Venus. You have ſuffered your heart to be charmed by him, and became enamoured with him as ſoon as he ſaid, *I love.*

Pſyche. Was it poſſible for me to avoid loving the god who inſpires with love, and who addreſſed me for himſelf? It is your ſon, whoſe power and merit you know.

Venus. He is indeed my ſon; but a ſon that provokes me, a ſon who renders me not what he is ſenſible he owes me, a ſon who cauſes every one to abandon me, and who, ſince he has been in love with you, the better to flatter his own unworthy amours, wounds not a ſingle mortal to come to my altars and implore my aid. You have made him a rebel to me, for which I ſhall fully revenge myſelf on you, and that highly too; and ſhall let you know if a mortal ought to ſuffer a god to ſigh at her feet. Follow me; you ſhall ſoon experience, to what a height of folly you carry this ambition. Come, and ſhew yourſelf as patient under your ſufferings as you have been ambitious.

END of the FOURTH ACT.

FOURTH INTERLUDE.

THE Scene repreſents hell. A ſea of fire appears, whoſe waves are in conſtant motion. This dreadful ſea is bordered with ruins of burnt buildings;

and in the midft of its rolling waves, acrofs its terrible gulph, appears Pluto's infernal palace.

F I R S T E N T R Y.

The Furies rejoice at the rage they have kindled in
Venus's breaft.

S E C O N D E N T R Y.

The Imps performing fome dangerous feats of activi-
ty, mingle with the Furies, and endeavour to frighten Pfyche; but the charms of her beauty caufe the
Furies and Imps to retire.

END of the FOURTH INTERLUDE.

A C T T H E F I F T H.

Pfyche appears paffing in a boat, with a box which
Venus had demanded of Proferpine.

S C E N E I.

PSYCHE.

IS there a pain equal to that which Venus condemns
my love, amongft your dreadful windings, ye infernal lakes, ye gloomy palaces, where Megera and her
fifters reign, eternal enemies of day; or amongft your
Ixion's, your Tantalus's, and your continual torments?
No, nothing can fatisfy her rage; and fince I find myfelf fubjected to her laws, fince fhe gives me over to

refentments, I am compelled, in thefe cruel moments, to have more than one life or one foul to fulfil her commands. I fhould chearfully fuffer every thing a-midft the rigours her hatred difplays, if I could but for one moment view that dear, that amiable lover. I dare not name him; my guilty lips, by having demanded too much of him, are rendered unworthy to mention him; and in this cruel affliction, the moft mortal anguifh I perpetually fuffer, is that of not feeing him. If his anger ftill continues, no misfortune can equal mine; but if he would have compaffion on a heart that adores him, whatever I muft undergo would be no fuffering at all to me. Yes, ye fates, if his juft indignation was but appeafed, all my misfortunes would be at an end; I want nothing but a kind look from the fon to make me infenfible to the mother's fury. I will no longer doubt of it; he undoubtedly fhares my forrows, he is fenfible of what I fuffer, and fuffers with me; all the torment that I endure an amorous law impofes on him. In fpite of Venus, and in fpite of my crime, it is he who fupports and reinftates me in the midft of the perils I am made to undergo; he preferves the tendernefs his flame infpired him with, and takes care to reftore life to me as often as I find myfelf near the point of death. But lo two ghofts approach me, acrofs the glimmerings of thefe gloomy manfions, I wonder what they can want.

PSYCHE.

WHAT, Cleomenes and Agenor, is it you that I now behold? Who has deprived you of life?

Cleomenes. The juſteſt grief that ever could furniſh matter of deſpair; that funeral pomp, where you waited the cruelleſt rigour of a diſmal fate, and the moſt ſupreme injuſtice..

Agenor. On that very rock where heaven in wrath had promiſed you, inſtead of a huſband, a dragon that ſhould ſuddenly deſtroy you, we ſtood prepared to repel his rage, or die with you. Princeſs, you are ſenſible of it; and as ſoon as you diſappeared, by being carried up into the air, tranſported both by grief and love, we threw ourſelves headlong from the rock to follow your charms, or rather to taſte the amorous joy of offering the firſt prey to the monſter for you.

Cleomenes. Happily deceived in the meaning of the oracle, we have found out the miracle, and diſcovered that the devouring dragon was the god of love; and who, though a god, adoring you himſelf, could not endure that any mortal, like us, ſhould dare to adore you.

Agenor. In recompence for having followed you, we here enjoy a very agreeable death. It is better to be dead than alive, if we cannot be yours? We here review your charms, which neither of us could ever have ſeen again in the other world. Happy, if you honour the misfortunes you have occaſioned us with the ſlighteſt tear.

C 6

Pfyche. Is it poffible I fhould have any tears remain-ing, after my own misfortunes have been carried to the higheft pitch? Let us join our fighs in this dire cala-mity, for fighs are never exhaufted. But you, princes, figh for an ungrateful creature. You would not furvive my misfortunes; but I, whatever troubles affault me, did not die for you.

Cleomenes. Did we merit that from you, we whofe flame has only tired you with an account of our mi-feries?

Pfyche. You might have merited my intire affec-tion, princes, had not you been rivals. Thofe in-comparable qualities which attended both your addref-fes rendered you both too amiable for either of you to be rejected.

Agenor. You might juftly, and without any cruel-ty, refufe us a heart which was referved for a god. But revifit Venus; we are called by deftiny, and obliged to leave you.

Pfyche. Will not it afford you fo much time as to tell me where your abode is in thefe regions?

Cleomenes. We dwell in verdant groves, where no-thing but love is breathed. Where, as foon as we die for love, we there again through love revive; there through love we figh under the gentleft laws of its hap-py empire; whence eternal night dare not chace the day which that love, which infpires us ghofts, fheds round us, and for which it erects a court even in the infernal fhades.

Agenor. Your envious fifters, after us defcended, feeking to deftroy you, are deftroyed themfelves, and each, in their turns, in reward for the counfel which coft them their lives, fuffer by the fides of Ixion and Tiryus fometimes the rack, and fometimes the vulture. Cupid, by the Zephyrs, took fwift vengeance for their

envenomed and jealous malice; thòfe winged mini-
fters of his juft wrath, under pretence of conveying
them once more to you, plunged them both together
down a precipice, where the difmal fpectacle of their
torn bodies difplays only the leaft and firft punifhment
for thofe counfels whofe artifice brought on the ills
you fuffer.

Pfyche. I greatly pity them.

Cleomenes. You are moft to be pitied. But we
ftay too long difcourfing with you; farewel, and may
we live in your remembrance! May Cupid foon exalt
you to the heavens, and rank you with the gods, and
rekindling a love never to be extinguifhed, refcue for
ever the luftre of your beautiful eyes to augment the
light of thofe abodes!

S C E N E III.

P S Y C H E alone.

WRETCHED youths! though dead, they ftill
admire me, notwithftanding I gave fo ill a
reception to their vows. It is not fo with thee, thou
who alone haft enchanted me, thou whom I ftill love
a thoufand times more than life itfelf, and who haft
broken thofe charming ties. No longer avoid me, but
give me hopes that thou wilt one day vouchfafe to caft
an eye on me; that by my fufferings I fhall be able to
appeafe thee, and recover thy plighted faith. But I
am too much disfigured by what I have fuffered, to entertain any fuch hope. An eye dejected, fad, de-
fpairing, languid, and difcoloured; what have I that
can poffibly prevail for me, unlefs by fome unexpected
miracle, my beauties, which once pleafed thee, fhould
be repaired. This treafure of divine beauty which Pro-

serpine has put into my hands for Venus, contains charms by which mine may be repaired; and the luftre of them muft certainly be great, fince Venus, Beauty's felf, requires them to adorn her. Would I be to blame, if I was to rob her of a few? Is not eveiy thing lawful that can render me pleafing in the eyes of a god, who voluntarily became my lover; and that can regain his heart, and put an end to my pain? Let me open it. What vapours opprefs my clouded brain? What is it that proceeds from this box I have opened? O Cupid! unlefs thy pity oppofes my deftruction, I muft defcend to the grave, never more to revive.   [Pfyche fwoons.

S C E N E IV.

CUPID, PSYCHE in a Swoon.

CUPID.

THY danger, Pfyche, difpels my wrath, or rather the ardour of my paffion has not ceafed; and though you have greatly difpleafed me, I am only interefted againft my mother's anger. I bave been witnefs to all thou haft fuffered, my fighs have every where accompanied thy tears; turn thy eyes towards me, I am ftill the fame. I fay it, and repeat it aloud, that I love thee, but you do not tell me, Pfyche, that you love me. Are thofe lovely eyes then clofed for ever? Will thofe lovely eyes never more be opened? O death, thou fhouldft not have been fo hardhearted. How could you, without any regard to my eternal being, make an attempt upon my own life? How often, ungrateful deity, have I enlarged thy gloomy empire by the contempt or cruelty of a proud and infolent beauty? How many faithful lovers, if I may fo fay, have I facrificed to thee by excefs of tranfport?

Go, I will wound no more fouls, I will pierce no more breafts but with darts dipt in the divine liquors which nourifh the immortal flames of heaven, and will never hurt them again but to prefent before thy eyes as many gods as lovers. And you, cruel mother, who forced it to fnatch away from me all I held the moft dear, dread, in your turn, the effect of my wrath. Will you make laws for me? You, who fo frequently receive them from me? You who have a heart as fenfible as another, do you envy mine the delight that your own enjoys? But I will pierce that heart with fuch a ftroke as fhall be followed by jealous anxieties alone; I will load you with fhameful furprizes, and every where look out for your tendereft wifhes, Adonis's and Anchifes's, who will only hate you.

S C E N E V.

V E N U S, C U P I D, P S Y C H E in a Swoon.

V E N U S.

WHAT a refpectful threat is this! fhall the prefumptuous anger of a revolted boy——

Cupid. I am no longer a boy, I have been too long fo; and I have juft caufe to be enraged.

Venus. You may remember, that to me you owe your birth, and ought therefore to reftrain your rage.

Cupid. And you fhould not forget that you have a heart and charms which are heightened by my power; that my bow is the only fupport of yours; that without my arrows it is of no value; and that if the braveft hearts have fuffered themfelves to be led in triumph by you, yet you have made none your flaves but whom I pleafed to fubject to your charms. Boaft no longer therefore of thofe laws of birth which tyrannize over

my defires; and if you would not lofe a thoufand
fighs, think of gratitude when you behold me; you,
whofe glory and pleafure depend upon my power a-
lone.

Venus. How have you maintained this glory you
fpeak of? How have you rendered it to me? And
when you have feen my altars deferted, my temples
violated, my honours diminifhed, if you have taken
part in fuch ignominy, in what manner has Pfyche,
who robbed me of them, been punifhed for it? I
commanded you to caufe her to be charmed with the
bafeft of mortals, who fhould not condefcend to anfwer
her inflamed heart with any thing but eternal repulfes,
and the moft cruel contempt; and you yourfelf have
fallen in love with her! you have feduced the immortal beings to be againft me; it was for you that the
Zephyrs hid her from my eyes; that Apollo himfelf
being fuborned, fo effectually bore her away from me
by a crafty oracle, that, if her own blind curiofity had
not furrendered her to my vengeance, fhe would have
efcaped my incenfed heart. See to what a condition
your love has reduced your Pfyche; fee, her foul is
departed, and if yours is ftill inflamed with love of
her, receive her laft figh. Menace and brave me in
the mean time that fhe expires, fuch infolence becomes
you well; and I ought to bear every thing you chufe
to fay, I, who can do nothing without the aid of your
arrows.

Cupid. You can only do too much, hard-hearted
goddefs, the fates abandon her to your difpleafure; but
be not fo inexorable to the prayers and tears of your
fupplicating fon. You muft now undoubtedly be pleafed, to fee with one eye Pfyche expiring, and your fon
with the other, defiring to hold all his happinefs from
you. Give me back my Pfyche, give her back all her

charms again, give her back, goddefs, to my flowing tears; give back to my love, give back to my grief the charm of my eyes, and the choice of my heart.

Venus. How greatly foever you love Pfyche, expect not the end of her misfortunes from me; if deftiny abandons her to me, I abandon her to deftiny. Trouble me no more, and let her, in this adverfity, triumph or perifh, without the interpofition of Venus.

Cupid. Forgive me if I am too troublefome, I would not be fo if I could but die.

Venus. This is an extreme grief indeed, that forces a deity to defire death.

Cupid. You may perceive, by the excefs of my paffi- on, how ftrong it is. Will you not be in the leaft fa- vourable to it?

Venus. I confefs your paffion does affect me, it difarms, it abates my rigour. Your Pfyche fhall yet live.

Cupid. How will I make you every where adored!

Venus. Yes, you fhall behold her in her priftine beauty; but I require the entire deference of your grate- ful vows. And that an unfeigned refpect fuffer my friend- fhip to chufe you another half.

Cupid. You could not confer a greater bleffing up- on me; and now I reaffume my former boldnefs, and defire Pyfche, I defire her faith, I defire that fhe may revive, and revive for me; I think it an indifferent thing, that your hatred being ended, ceafes in favour of another. Jupiter, whom I fee coming, will judge between us, both of my paffionate behaviour, and your wrath.

[After feveral flafhes of lightning, and claps of thun- der, Jupiter appears in the air upon an eagle, and defcends upon the earth.

SCENE THE LAST.

JUPITER, VENUS, CUPID, PSYCHE in a Swoon.

CUPID.

ALMIGHTY father of gods and men, you to whom nothing is impossible, abate the rigour of an hard-hearted mother, who without me, would have no altars. I have wept, I have prayed, sighed, threatened, and all to no purpose. She will not admit that on my displeasure depends the happy or melancholy aspect of the whole world; and that if Psyche ceases to live, and if she lives not for me, I shall be no longer the god of love. Yes, I will break my bow and my arrows in pieces; I will even quench my torch, and let nature languish in her tomb; or, if I condescend to pierce any hearts with these golden shafts that command obedience, I will wound you all above for mortals, and let no arrows fly at them but such as are blunted, and force them to hatred; and which will produce nothing but rebels, ingrates, and savages. By what tyrannic law shall I be obliged to keep my arms always in readiness to serve you, and make conquests after conquests upon all for you, if you will not allow me to make one for myself?

Jupiter to Venus.] Be more tender to him, my daughter, you have the destiny of Psyche in your hands, the fatal sisters, at the least word, will pursue your wrath; speak, and suffer thyself to be overcome with the tenderness of a mother, or dread an anger which I myself am afraid of. Will you deliver up the world a prey to hatred, to disorder, to confusion; and of a god of peace and delight, make him a god of bitter-efs and divifion? Let us confider who we are, and if we ought to be flaves to paffion. The more grateful revenge is to mortals, the more it becomes the gods to pardon.

Venus. I forgive my rebellious fon; but would you have me fubmit to the reproach that an infolent woman, the object of my anger, the haughty Pfyche, becaufe fhe is fomewhat handfome, fhould, by a marriage which I am afhamed at, fully my alliance, and my fon's bed?

Jupiter. Be not uneafy on that account, for I will make her immortal?

Venus. Then I have no longer a contempt nor hatred for her; I admit her the honour of this conjugal tie. Awake, Pfyche, never more to die. Jupiter has made your peace; and I lay afide the haughty difpofition which oppofed your wifhes.

Pfyche recovering from her fwoon.] Do you then pity me, great goddefs, and reftore life to this innocent heart?

Venus. Jupiter has procured you favour, and I am no longer angry. Live, Venus commands it; love, for fhe allows it.

Pfyche to Cupid.] Lovely object of my paffion, do I once more behold you?

Cupid to Pfyche.] Am I once more, joy of my foul, in poffeffion of thee?

Jupiter. We muft now afcend to heaven, to compleat fo happy and noble a wedding. You will no longer be an inhabitant of earth, lovely Pfyche, but an immortal goddefs.

END of the FIFTH ACT.

FIFTH INTERLUDE.

THE Stage reprefents heaven. The palace of Jupiter defcends, and the other palaces of the greateft of the celeftial gods are difcovered at a diftance. A cloud defcends, on which Cupid and Pfyche place themfelves, and are carried up in the air by a fecond cloud, which had, in defcending, joined itfelf to the firft. Jupiter and Venus crofs one another in the air, in their machines, and range themfelves near Cupid and Pfyche.

The deities who had been divided between Venus and her fon, unite again upon their agreement; and all together, by concerts, fongs, and dances, celebrate the marriage of Cupid and Pfyche.

JUPITER, VENUS, CUPID, PSYCHE,
a chorus of immortals.

APOLLO, the MUSES, the ARTS difguifed like fhepherds.

BACCHUS, SILENUS, SATYRS, MOMUS, PUNCHINELLO'S, PANTOMIMES, MARS, and a troop of warriors.

APOLLO.

IMMORTAL band, let difcord ceafe;
 Cupid enjoys his love in peace,
Venus her native fmiles puts on
In favour of her charming fon;

New croffes he no more fhall dread,
But joys eternal fhall fucceed.

A chorus of I M M O R T A L S.

LET us grace this joyful day
With fongs of mirth, and jocund play;
Songs that fhall bear the news around,
And make thofe bleft abodes refound.
Let each in tuneful ftrains declare
How powerful Love's attractions are,
That none fo rough or favage prove
But foon or late fubmit to Love.

B A C C H U S.

IF fometimes our rules
Make madmen or fools,
And reafon is loft in good wine,
In the fpace of a day
All the fumes will away
That did the bright regent confine:
But when Love's foft fmart
Bewitches the heart,
Perhaps all our life-time we pine.

M O M U S.

'TIS mine, fharp raillery to throw
At gods above and men below;
In fportive mood my darts I fling,
Nor fpare ev'n heav'n's imperial king;
On all but Love my fatires fall,
But he fpares none, his arrows fly at all.

M A R S.

MY fierceft foes o'ercome, or ftruck with dread,
Have always yielded, or inglorious fled;
None but Love can boaft that he
Has proudly triumph'd over me.

Chorus of I M M O R T A L S.

LET our joyous fongs declare
The raptures of the happy pair;
In hafte is each Olympian power
To hail their foft, their blifsful hour.
Let us celebrate the day
With various mirth and wanton play;
And while the hours too fleeting move
Let our ftrains be all of love.

F I R S T   E N T R Y.

A T T E N D A N T S   O N   A P O L L O

A dance of the ARTS difguifed like Shepherds.

A P O L L O.

THE god to whom we make our court
   Forbids us to be overwife;
Diverting play, and am'rous fport,
   We in our turn fhould learn to prize.
At night, at leaft, we all fhould prove
The foft delights of fports and love.

'Tis pity in this fweet fojourn
   Any a favage heart fhould bear:
Pleafures fhould have their foft return,
   And end the day's diftracting care.
At night, at leaft, we all fhall prove
The foft delights of fports and love.

T W O   M U S E S.

BEWARE, ye charmers all, beware,
Love is full of anxious care;
Guard with diligence your heart,
Left it feel an am'rous fmart.

The paffion you with eafe may gain;
      But to reveal
      The pain you feel,
Is by far the greateft pain.

Torments ftill on love await,
  Its chains are oft too hard to bear;
Alarms inceffant are the fate
  Of ev'ry yielding, fighing fair.
The paffion you with eafe may gain;
      But to reveal
      The pain you feel,
Is by far the greateft pain.

SECOND ENTRY.

BACCHUS'S TRAIN.

A dance of Pantomimes.

BACCHUS.

OF wine let our praifes ne'er ceafe,
  Its charms how engaging they are!
'Tis ufeful in times of foft peace,
  And always does wonders in war;
But when we to love are inclin'd,
Its greateft affiftance we find.
  SILENUS mounted upon an afs.
  Of Bacchus, 'tis the chief defign
  That we fhould oft caroufe with wine;
His reign is delightful, we can't but confefs,
For we laugh all the day, and at night fleep in peace.
  This god, propitious to our vows,
  Whate'er our heart can wifh allows.

Of the charms of his court may our praises ne'er cease.
For we drink all the day, and at night sleep in peace.
      SILENUS and TWO SATYRS together.
      Would you have sweets without allay,
      Full bumpers will your wish repay.

I. SATYR.

Greatness we pursue in vain,
It always brings a secret pain.

2. SATYR.

And rest will fly if love should reign.

ALL THREE TOGETHER.

Would you have sweets without delay?
Full bumpers will your wish repay.

I. SATYR.

Hence laughter, sport, and each gay song,

2. SATYR.

And merry jokes to wine belong.

ALL THREE TOGETHER.

Would you have sweets without allay?
Full bumpers will your wish repay.

THIRD ENTRY.

Two other Satyrs take Silenus from his ass, which
serves them to vault upon, and perform several a-
greeable and surprizing feats.

FOURTH ENTRY.

MOMUS'S TRAIN.

A dance of Punchinello's and Mimics.

MOMUS.

LET mirth and satire now prevail,
  Let none the poignant joke refuse;

Becaufe 'tis always good to rail,
  However mild the fport we ufe.
Whenever the pleafure of railing we flight,
  'Gainft fadnefs there is no defence,
For in laughing we find the fupremeft delight,
  If we laugh at another's expence.

With the faults of a neighbour be fure let us play,
  'Tis modifh an error to blaze;
There is nothing fo tirefome at this time o' day,
  As to clog one's difcourfe with dull praife.

Whenever the pleafure of railing we flight,
  'Gainft fadnefs there is no defence;
For in laughing we find the fupremeft delight,
  If we laugh at another's expence.

FIFTH ENTRY.

ATTENDANTS ON MARS.

MARS.

LET's leave the world without alarms;
  And feek amufement's gentler charms;
Amidft the pleafures of the court,
Let's add war's image to the fport.

Four warriors bearing maces and bucklers, four others
armed with pikes, and four more with colours, perform a kind of exercife in dancing.

SIXTH and laſt ENTRY.

The four ſeveral companies that attend Apollo, Bacchus, Momus, and Mars, unite and mix with one
another.

Chorus of IMMORTALS.

LET our joyous ſongs declare
　The raptures of the happy pair;
Trumpets, timbals, tender lutes,
Rattling drums, and warbling flutes,
All in joyful concert move,
Whilſt our pleaſing ſtrain is Love.

THE END.

THE

GENTLEMAN CIT.

A

COMEDY.

The GENTLEMAN CIT, *a Comedy of Five Acts, performed at Chambord in October 1670, and at Paris
at the Theatre of the Palace-Royal the 29th of No-
vember the same Year.*

THIS comedy was very unfavourably received by
the court, and was ranked amongst the number
of those whose only merit was in making the people
laugh. However, Lewis XIV. judged more favourably
of it, and gave encouragement to the author, who was
very much alarmed at the bad reception it met with.
All Paris was struck with the truth of the portrait
which he had given them, and the town soon silenced
the critics. They saw in Mr. Jordain a folly common
to mankind in every condition of life, namely, the vanity of endeavouring to appear greater than what they
really are. This ridicule would not have been striking
in a person of too high a rank; nor would it have appeared with grace in one of a rank too low; but to
have a proper effect in the comic scene, it was necessary that in the choice of the character there should
be a distance between his real condition and that to
which he aspired, sufficient to make the bare contrast
of the manners proper to the two conditions strongly
paint out in one single point, and in one and the same
subject, the excess of the general folly that was intended to be corrected. The GENTLEMAN CIT answers
this compleatly; for we at once behold the man and
the character, the mask and the face placed in such an
opposition of light and shade, that we always perceive
what he is, as well as what he would appear to be.
The good sense of Mrs. Jordain, the interested complaisance of Dorantes, the witty gayety of Nicola, the
happy turn of wit in Lucilia, the noble frankness of

Cleontes, the pregnant subtilty of Coviel, and the burlesque vanity of the different masters of arts and sciences, cast still a new light on the character of Mr. Jordain, and he receives from every thing about him a new kind of ridicule which rebounds on him, and from him, on all the conditions of life. The Turkish ceremony, which Cleontes should not have been accessary to, or assisting in, past pretty well, by means of the oddness of the scenery, and the exquisite music.

ACTORS.

Mr. JORDAIN, the Cit.
Mrs. JORDAIN.
LUCILIA, daughter to Mr. Jordain.
CLEONTES, in love with Lucilia.
DORIMENE, a marchioness.
DORANTES, a count, Dorimene's lover.
NICOLA, a maid-servant to Mr. Jordain.
COVIEL, servant to Cleontes.
MUSIC-MASTER.
MUSIC-MASTER's SCHOLAR.
DANCING-MASTER.
FENCING-MASTER.
PHILOSOPHY-MASTER.
TAILOR.
TAILOR's MAN.
TWO FOOTMEN.

T H E

GENTLEMAN CIT.

ACT I. SCENE I.

MUSIC-MASTER, A SCHOLAR to the music-master, composing at a table in the middle of the Stage, A WOMAN SINGER, AND TWO MEN SINGERS, A DANCING-MASTER, AND DANCERS.

MUSIC-MASTER to the muficians.

HIS worſhip will be here preſently, do you therefore retire into that room till he comes.

Dancing-maſter to his people.] Do you alſo retire into that other apartment.

Muſic-maſter to his ſcholar.] Have you done?

Scholar. Yes, Sir.

Muſic-maſter. Shew it me—Hum! this is very well

Dancing-maſter. Pray have you got any thing new there?

D 4

Music-master. Yes, I ordered him to compose a song for a serenade till our genius comes down.

Dancing-master. Pray let me see it.

Music-master. Why he will soon be here, and then you will hear it with the dialogue.

Dancing-master. I think we have no reason to complain at present, we have pretty good business.

Music-master. It is true. Your capers and my fiddle would have a rare time of it, if every one were like this same Mr. Jordain; for those whims of gallantry and nobility which have taken possession of his brain are as good as an estate to us. In short, he is just such a person as we wanted.

Dancing master. I am of a different opinion from you, I wish he was more ready in learning what we teach him.

Music-master. Why he is certainly a most abominable dunce, and doth not understand what we endeavour to teach him; but the principal thing we regard in scholars is to pay for what they do not understand.

Dancing-master. I really differ from you on that head, for I think the approbation of the public is the most exquisite of all pleasures, and the grand reward for all our toils. I am pleased with applause as well as profit, and I think it degrades a professor of the polite arts to be obliged to expose his compositions to blockheads who are as stupid as asses.

Music-master. Why what you say is certainly right; yet, notwithstanding this ignorant vain cit, who has no understanding, talks of things in the most ridiculous manner imaginable, yet he is of more use to us than the most knowing noblemen of them all. His purse and praises are current coin; for praise of itself is too thin a diet to live upon; something that will make a man eafy in his circumftances is more folid and lafting.

Dancing-mafter. Why I think you lay rather too much ftrefs upon this; a fordid love of gain is a mean groveling paffion, which does not become a man of honour.

Mufic-mafter. But notwithftanding this, you always readily take whatever he is pleafed to give you.

Dancing-mafter. Moft certainly. But it would give me great pleafure if I faw his liberality were joined with a good tafte.

Mufic mafter. I really wifh the fame; and as by his means we fhall become well known, let us join in ufing all our endeavours to infpire him with a good tafte.

Dancing-mafter. Here he comes.

SCENE II.

MR. JORDAIN in a night-gown and cap, MUSIC-MASTER, DANCING-MASTER, SCHOLAR to the MUSIC-MASTER, VIOLINS, MUSICIANS, DANCERS, two Footmen.

MR. JORDAIN.

ARE you there, gentlemen? fhall we fee a little of your drollery? have you any thing new?

Dancing-mafter. Our drollery, Sir? what do you mean?

Mr. Jordain. Why, I mean your——What do you call it, your prologue or dialogue of finging and dancing.

Dancing-mafter. Oh! do you mean that, Sir?

Mufic-mafter. You fee we are all ready, Sir.

Mr. Jordain. I am afraid I have made you wait a little, but I have been dreffing according to the fafhion this morning, and my hosier sent me a pair of silk stockings which I thought I should never have been able to draw on.

Music-master. We wait your leisure here, Sir,

Mr. Jordain. My tailor has just brought me a suit of cloaths, pray do not go till I see how I look in them.

Dancing-master. As you please.

Mr. Jordain. You shall see me most exactly equipped from head to foot.

Music-master. We do not doubt it.

Mr. Jordain. I have had this Indian thing made up for me.

Dancing-master. It is very handsome.

Mr. Jordain. My tailor tells me that people of quality go thus in a morning.

Music-master. It fits you to a miracle.

Mr. Jordain. Why, hoh! Fellow there! both my fellows!

1. Footman. Your pleasure, Sir?

Mr. Jordain. Nothing: it is only to try whether you hear me readily. [To the two masters] What say you of my liveries?

Dancing-master. They are magnificent.

Mr. Jordain half opens his gown and discovers a strait pair of breeches of scarlet velvet, and a green velvet jacket which he has on.] Here again is a kind of dishabille to perform my exercises in a morning.

Music-master. It is gallant.

Mr. Jordain. Footman?

1. Footman. Sir?

Mr. Jordain. The other footman!

2. Footman. Sir?

Mr. Jordain taking off his gown.] Hold my gown. [to the music and dancing-masters.] Do you like me so?

Dancing-master. Mighty well; nothing can be better.

Mr. Jordain. Now let me fee your affair.

Mufic-mafter. I fhould be glad firft to let you hear an air [pointing to his fcholar] he has juft compofed for the ferenade, which you gave me orders about. He is one of my fcholars, who has an admirable talent for thefe fort of things.

Mr. Jordain. It may be fo; but I hope you were not too good to do it yourfelf; you ought not to leave thofe things to be done by your fcholars.

Mufic-mafter. By no means, dear Sir, it is a fine air, if you will pleafe to hear it. I hope the name of fcholar will not prejudice you; for thefe kind of fcholars frequently know more than the beft mafters.

Mr. Jordain to his footman.] Give me my gown that I may hear the better—Stay, I believe I fhall be better without the gown.—No, give it me again, it will do better.

M U S I C I A N.

" I languifh night and day, nor fleeps my pain,
" Since thofe fair eyes impos'd the rigorous chain;
" But tell me, Iris, what dire fate attends
" Your enemies, if thus you treat your friends?"

Mr. Jordain. This fong feems to me a little upon the melancholy ftrain; it inclines one to fleep; I fhould be glad you could enliven it a little in fome parts.

Mufic-mafter. It is neceffary, Sir, that the mufic fhould be fuited to the words.

Mr. Jordain. I was taught one perfectly pretty fome time ago. Stay——Um——How is it?

Dancing-mafter. Truly, Sir, I do not know.

Mr. Jordain. There is fomething about mutton or lamb in it?

D 6

Dancing-mafter. Mutton or lamb in it?

Mr. Jordain. Yes——I have it! [He fings.

" I thought my dear Namby
" As gentle as fair-o:
" I thought my dear Namby
" As mild as a lamb-y.
　" Oh dear! oh dear! oh dear-o!
" For now the fad fcold, is a thoufand times told,
　" More fierce than a tiger or bear-o." ...

Is not it pretty?

Mufic-mafter. Nothing can be prettier.

Dancing-mafter. And you fing it well.

Mr. Jordain. Yet I never learned mufic.

Mufic-mafter. You ought to learn it, Sir, as you do dancing. They are two arts which are ftrictly related to each other.

Dancing-mafter. And which open the human mind to fee the beauty of things.

Mr. Jordain. What! do people of quality learn mufic too?

Mufic-mafter. Yes, Sir.

Mr. Jordain. Then to be fure I muft learn it, but how to find time for all thefe things I know not, for I have agreed with a mafter of philofophy befides my fencing-mafter.

Mufic-mafter. Philofophy is fomething; but mufic, Sir, mufic——

Dancing-mafter. Mufic and dancing—Mufic and dancing are every thing.

Mufic-mafter. There is nothing of fo much ufe in a ftate, as mufic.

Dancing-mafter. There is nothing fo neceffary for men, as dancing.

Mufic-mafter. A ftate cannot fubfift without mufic.

Dancing-mafter. Without dancing, a man can do nothing.

Mufic-mafter. All the diforders, all the wars one fees in the world, happen only for not learning mufic.

Dancing-mafter. All the difafters of mankind, all the fatal misfortunes that hiftories are replete with, the blunders of politicians, the mifcarriages of great commanders, all this comes from not knowing how to dance.

Mr. Jordain. How fo?

Mufic-mafter. Does not war proceed from want of harmony among mankind?

Mr. Jordain. That is true.

Mufic-mafter. And if all men learned mufic, would not that be a means of keeping them better in tune, and of feeing univerfal peace in the world?

Mr. Jordain. You are in the right.

Dancing-mafter. When a man has been guilty of a defect in his conduct, be it in the affairs of his family, or in the government of the ftate, or in the command of an army; do not we always fay, fuch a one has made a falfe ftep in fuch an affair?

Mr. Jordain. It is faid fo to be fure.

Dancing-mafter. And can making a falfe ftep proceed from any other caufe but the want of knowing how to dance?

Mr. Jordain. It is true, you are both in the right.

Dancing-mafter. This is to let you fee the excellence and advantage of dancing and mufic.

Mr. Jordain. I now comprehend it.

Mufic-mafter. Will you fee each of our compofitions?

Mr. Jordain. With all my heart.

Mufic-mafter. I have told you already, that this is a

flight effay which I formerly made upon the different paffions that may be expreffed by mufic.

Mr. Jordain. Very well.

Mufic-mafter to the muficians.] Here, come forward. [*to Mr. Jordain.*] You are to fuppofe them dreffed in the characters of fhepherds and fhepherdeffes.

Mr. Jordain. Why always fhepherds? one fees nothing but fuch ftuff every where.

Mufic-mafter. The reafon is, Sir, that when mufical performances are to be introduced, it is neceffary to probability that we give into the paftoral way. Singing has always been peculiar to fhepherds; and it would be unnatural in dialogue, that princes or citizens fhould fing their paffions.

Mr. Jordain. Well, well. Let us fee.

D I A L O G U E in M U S I C between one Woman and two Men.

W O M A N.

THE heart that muft tyrannic love obey,
  A thoufand fears and cares opprefs.
Sweet are thofe fighs and languifhments, they fay;
 Say what they will for me,
 Nought is fo fweet as liberty.

1. *Man.* Nothing fo fweet as love's foft fire,
 Which can two glowing hearts infpire
 With the fame life, the fame defire.
The lovelefs fwain no happinefs can prove.
 From life take foothing love,
 All pleafure you remove.

2. *Man.* Sweet were the wanton archer's fway,
 Would all with conftancy obey:
  But, cruel fate!

No nymph is true:
The faithlefs fex more worthy of our hate,
To love fhould bid eternally adieu.
      1. Man. Pleafing hates!
      Woman. Freedom bleft!
      2. Man. Fair deceit!
    1. Man. O how I love thee!
    Woman. How I approve thee!
    2. Man. I deteft!
1. Man. Againft love's ardour quit this mortal hate.
Woman. Shepherd myfelf I bind here,
    To fhow a faithful mate.
2. Man. Alas! but where to find her?
Woman. Our glory to retrieve,
    My heart I here beftow.
2. Man. But, nymph, can I believe
    That heart no change will know?
Woman. Let experience decide,
    Who loves beft of the two.
2. Man. And the perjured fide
    May vengeance purfue.
All Three. Then let us kindle foft defire,
    Let us fan the amorous fire.
    Ah! How fweet it is to love,
    When hearts united conftant prove!

Mr. Jordain. Is this all?

Mufic-mafter. Yes, Sir.

Mr. Jordain. Really I think it very prettily fet off, and there are fome good fayings enough in it.

Dancing-mafter. You have here, for my compofition, a little effay of the fineft movements, and the moft beautiful attitudes with which a dance can poffibly be varied.

Mr. Jordain. Are they fhepherds too?

Dancing-master. They are what you please. [to the dancers.] Come, begin.

[Several dancers enter, and perform various movements and steps.]

ACT II. SCENE I.

MR. JORDAIN, MUSIC-MASTER, DANCING-MASTER.

MR. JORDAIN.

THESE are clever fellows, and perform dexterously.

Mufic-mafter. When the dance is mixed with the mufic, it will have a greater effect ftill, and you will fee fomething gallant in the little entertainment we have prepared for you.

Mr. Jordain. That is however for by and by; and the perfon for whom I have ordered all this, is to do me the honour of dining with me here.

Dancing-mafter. Every thing is ready.

Mufic-mafter. But a fingle entertainment is not enough, Sir, it is neceffary fuch a perfon as you, who live great, and have an inclination to things that are handfome, fhould have a concert of mufic at your houfe once a week at leaft.

Mr. Jordain. Have people of quality them fo often?

Mufic-mafter. Yes, Sir.

Mr. Jordain. I will have one of them. Will it be fine?

Mufic-mafter. Without doubt. You muft have three voices, a treble, a counter-tenor, and bafs, which muft be accompanied with a bafs-viol, a theorbo-lute, and a harpficord for the thorough-bafs, with two violins to play the fymphonies.

Mr. Jordan. Pray let there be a trumpet-marine too. The trumpet-marine is an inftrument that pleafes me, and is very harmonious.

Mufic-mafter. Leave us to manage matters.

Mr. Jordain. However, do not forget by and by to fend the muficians to fing while I am at dinner.

Mufic-mafter. You fhall have every thing that is neceffary.

Mr. Jordain. I beg that you would let the entertain-ment be fine.

Mufic-mafter. You fhall have no reafon to complain, and amongft other things you fhall fee fome minuets in it.

Mr. Jordain. Ay, the minuets are my favourite dance; and I have a mind you fhould fee me dance one. Come, mafter.

Dancing-mafter. Your hat, Sir, if you pleafe. [Mr. Jordain takes off his foot-boy's hat, and puts it on over his own night-cap; upon which his mafter takes him by the hand, and makes him dance to a minuet-air which he fings.] Tol, lol, lol, lol, lol, lol; tol, lol, lol, twice; tol, lol, lol; tol, lol. Keep time, Sir, if you pleafe. Tol, lol, the right leg forward. Tol, lol, lol. Do not fhake your fhoulders fo much. Tol, lol, lol, lol, lol. Why, your arms hang as if they were bro-ken. Tol, lol, lol, lol, lol. Hold up your head. Turn out your toes. Tol, lol, lol. Your body erect.

Mr. Jordain. There, that is enough for this day.

Mufic-mafter. Exceedingly well performed.

Mr. Jordain. Now I think on it, teach me how I muft bow to pay my compliments to a marchionefs; I fhall foon have occafion for it.

Dancing-mafter. You want to know how to accoft a marchionefs?

Mr. Jordain. Yes, a marchionefs; her name is Dorimene.

Dancing-mafter. Give me your hand.

Mr. Jordain. No. You need only to do it, I fhall remember it eafily.

Dancing-mafter. If you would falute her with a great deal of refpect, you muft firft of all make a bow and fall back, then advancing towards her, bow thrice, and at the laft bow, bend yourfelf almoft to the ground.

Mr. Jordain. Do it a little yourfelf. [After the dancing-mafter has made three bows.] Enough, enough.

SCENE II.

MR. JORDAIN, MUSIC-MASTER, DANCING-MASTER, FOOTMAN.

FOOTMAN.

SIR, your fencing-mafter is here.

Mr. Jordain. Bid him come in that he may give me a leffon. [To the mufic and dancing-mafters.] Now you fhall fee how I will perform.

S C E N E III.

MR. JORDAIN, FENCING-MASTER, MUSIC-
MASTER, DANCING-MASTER, FOOTMAN
holding two foils.

FENCING-MASTER taking the two foils out of the footman's hand, and presenting one to Mr. Jordain. COME, Sir, your salute. Your body straight. A little bearing upon the left thigh. Do not straddle so. Your feet both on a line. Your wrist opposite to your hip. The point of your sword opposite your shoulder. Your arm not quite so much extended. Your left hand on a level with your eye. Your left shoulder more square. Hold up your head. Your look bold. Advance. Your body steady. Beat quarte, and push quarte. One, two. Recover. Again with it, your foot firm. One, two. Leap back. When you make a pass, Sir, it is necessary your sword should disengage first, and your body make as small a mark as possible. One, two. Come beat tierce, and push the same. Advance. Your body firm. Advance. Quit after that manner. One, two. Recover. Repeat the same. One, two. Leap back. Parry, Sir, parry.

[The Fencing-master gives him two or three home-thrusts, crying, parry.

Mr. Jordain. Ugh!

Music-master. You do wonders.

Fencing-master. I have told you already, that the whole science of defence consists but in two things, in giving and not receiving: and as I shewed you the other day by demonstrative reason, it is impossible you should receive, if you know how to turn your adversary's sword from the line of your body; which depends only upon a small motion of your wrist, either inward, or outward.

Mr. Jordain. Why then a man, if he is ever such a coward, is sure to kill his adversary, and not to be killed.

Fencing-master. Certainly, Do not you see it plainly demonstrated?

Mr. Jordain. Yes.

Fencing-master. By this one may see of what confideration such persons as we should be esteemed in a state, and how highly the science of arms exceeds all the other useless sciences, such as dancing, music, and—

Dancing-master. Soft and fair, Mr. Quarte and Tierce, Do not speak of dancing but with respect.

Music-master. Pray learn to treat the excellence of music in a handsomer manner.

Fencing-master. You are merry fellows, to pretend to compare your sciences with mine.

Music-master. Do but see the importance of the creature!

Dancing-master. The droll animal there, with his buff breast-plate!

Fencing-master. My little master skipper, I shall make you skip in another manner. And you, my little master scraper, I shall make you change your tune.

Dancing master. Mr. Tick-Tack, I shall teach you better manners.

Mr. Jordain to the Dancing-master.] Are you bewitched to quarrel with him, who understands tierce and quarte, who knows how to kill a man by demonstrative reason?

Dancing-master. I laugh at his demonstrative reason, and his tierce and his quarte.

Mr. Jordain to the Dancing-master.] Be quiet, I tell you.

Fencing-master to the Dancing-master.] How? Mr. impertinence!

Mr. Jordain. Nay, my dear Fencing-master!

Dancing-master to the Fencing-master.] How? You great dray-horse!

Mr. Jordain. Nay, my Dancing-master.

Fencing-master. If I lay my————

Mr. Jordain to the Fencing-master.] Gently.

Dancing-master. I will make you dance to such a tune————

Mr. Jordain. Nay, for heaven's sake!

Fencing-master. I shall curry you with such an air—

Mr. Jordain to the Fencing-master.] For goodness sake.

Dancing-master. I shall drub you after such a manner————

Mr. Jordain to the Dancing-master.] I beseech you.

Music-master. We will teach him how to speak.

Mr. Jordain to the Music-master.] Pray be quiet.

SCENE IV.

PHILOSOPHY-MASTER, MR. JORDAIN, MU-SIC-MASTER, DANCING-MASTER, FEN-CING-MASTER, FOOTMAN.

MR. JORDAIN.

OH! Mr. Philosopher, you are come in the nick of time with your philosophy. Come and make peace amongst these people.

Philosophy-master. What is the matter, gentlemen?

Mr. Jordain. Why they have gone together by the ears about the preference of their professions, abused each other, and would come to blows.

Philosophy-master. O fy, gentlemen! what need

was there of all this fury? Have you not read Seneca's excellent treatife upon Anger? Is there any thing more bafe and fhameful than this paffion, which redu-ces us to a level with beafts? and fhould not reafon guide all our actions?

Dancing-mafter. How, Sir? Why he has juft now been abufing us both, in defpifing dancing, which fci-ence I have the honour to teach, and mufic which is his profeffion.

Philofophy-mafter. A wife man is above all injurious language, and the only anfwer one fhould make to all affronts, is moderation and patience.

Fencing-mafter. They had both the affurance to compare their profeffions to mine.

Philofophy-mafter. Should this difturb you? Men fhould not difpute about vain-glory and rank; that which perfectly diftinguifhes one from another, is wif-dom and virtue.

Dancing-mafter. I mantained, that dancing was a fcience, which cannot be fufficiently honoured.

Mufic-mafter. And I, that mufic has always been revered.

Fencing-mafter. And I maintained againft them both, that the fcience of defence is the fineft and moft neceffary of all fciences.

Philofophy-mafter. And what becomes of philofophy then? You are all three very impertinent fellows, me-thinks, to talk in this manner in my prefence; and im-pudently to give the name of fcience to things that do not even deferve the name of art, that cannot be com-prized under any thing but the names of the pitiful trades of gladiator, ballad-finger, and morrice-dancer.

Fencing-mafter. Out, ye dog of a philofopher.

Mufic-mafter. Hence, ye fcoundrel of a pedant.

Dancing-mafter. Begone, ye arrant pedagogue.

Philofophy-mafter. How? you faucy impertinent varlets, do you——[The philofopher falls upon them, they all three belabour him.

Mr. Jordain. Mr. Philofopher!

Philofophy-mafter. Infamous dogs! rogues! infolent curs!

Mr. Jordain. Mr. Philofopher!

Fencing-mafter. Plague on the animal!

Mr. Jordain. Gentlemen!

Philofophy-mafter. Impudent villains!

Mr. Jordain. Mr. Philofopher!

Dancing-mafter. Duce take the loobily afs.

Mr. Jordain. Gentlemen!

Philofophy-mafter. Profligate vermin!

Mr. Jordain. Mr. Philofopher!

Mufic-mafter. Impertinent puppy!

Mr. Jordain. Gentlemen!

Philofophy-mafter. Knaves! fcoundrels! traitors! impoftors!

Mr. Jordain. Mr. Philofopher! Gentlemen! Mr. Philofopher! Gentlemen! Mr. Philofopher!

[They leave the ftage beating each other.

S C E N E V.

MR. JORDAIN, FOOTMAN.

MR. JORDAIN.

FAITH, gentlemen, you may fight as long as you pleafe, I fhall not meddle with you, I fhall not fpoil my gown to part you. I fhould be a great fool to thurft myfelf among them, and receive fome blow that I might never recover.

SCENE VI.

PHILOSOPHY-MASTER, MR. JORDAIN, FOOTMAN.

PHILOSOPHY-MASTER *setting his band right.*

NOW to our lesson.

Mr. Jordain. Ah! Sir, I am sorry for the blows they have given you.

Philosophy-master. It is nothing at all. A philosopher knows how to receive things in a proper manner; and I shall immediately write a satire against them, in the manner of Juvenal, that shall cut them most gloriously. Let that pass. What are you desirous of learning?

Mr. Jordain. All that I can, for I have a great desire to be a scholar, and it vexes me that my father and mother had not made me study all the sciences, when I was young.

Philosophy-master. This is a very rational sentiment. *Nam, sine doctrina, vita est quasi mortis imago.* You understand that, and are acquainted with Latin, I suppose?

Mr. Jordain. Yes; but not very well. Explain me the meaning of that.

Philosophy-master. The meaning of it is, that "without learning, life is as it were an image of death."

Mr. Jordain. That same Latin is in the right.

Philosophy-master. Have you not some principles, some rudiments of the sciences?

Mr. Jordain. Oh! Yes, I can read and write.

Philosophy-master. Where would you please to have us begin? Would you have me teach you Logic?

Mr. Jordain. Logic: what is that?

Philofophy-mafter. It is that which teaches us the three operations of the mind.

Mr. Jordain. And what are they?

Philofophy-mafter. The firft, the fecond, and the third. The firft is to conceive well, by means of univerfals. The fecond, to judge well, by means of categories. The third, to draw the conclufion right, by means of figures: *Barbara, Celarent, Darii, Ferio, Baralipton*, &c.

Mr. Jordain. Thefe words are too crabbed. This logic does not fuit me by any means. Let us learn fomething elfe that is prettier.

Philofophy-mafter. Will you learn morality?

Mr. Jordain. Morality!

Philofophy-mafter. Yes.

Mr Jordain. What means morality?

Philofophy-mafter. It treats of happinefs; teaches men to moderate their paffions, and————

Mr. Jordain. No, no, I will have nothing to do with that. I am as choleric as the devil, and there is no morality holds me; I will have my bellyfull of paffion, whenever I have a mind to it.

Philofophy-mafter. Would you learn natural philofophy?

Mr. Jordain. What is natural philofophy?

Philofophy-mafter. Natural philofophy explains to us the principles of things natural, and the properties of bodies; it difcourfes of the nature of elements, of metals, of minerals, of ftones, of plants, and animals, and teaches us the caufe of all the meteors; the rainbow, *ignes fatui*, comets, lightnings, thunder, thunder-bolts, rain, fnow, hail, winds, and whirl-winds.

Mr Jordain. There is too much hurly-burly in this; too much confufion.

Philofophy-mafter. What muft I teach you then?

Mr. Jordain. Teach me orthography.

Philofophy-mafter. With all my heart.

Mr. Jordain. Afterwards you may teach me the almanack, to know when there is a moon, and when not.

Philofophy-mafter. Be it fo. To purfue this thought of yours right, and treat this matter like a philofopher, we muft begin, according to the order of things, with an exact knowledge of the nature of letters, and the different manner of pronouncing them. And on this head I muft obferve to you, that letters are divided into vowels, fo called, becaufe they exprefs the voice: and into confonants, fo called becaufe they found with the vowels, and only mark the different articulations of the voice. There are five vowels or voices, A, E, I, O, U.

Mr. Jordain. I underftand all that.

Philofophy-mafter. The vowel A is formed by bringing the under-jaw near to the upper.

Mr. Jordain. A, A. Yes.

Philofophy-mafter. The vowel E is formed by drawing the under-jaw a little nearer to the upper, A, E.

Mr. Jordain. A, E. A, E. Faith it is fo. How pretty that is!

Philofophy-mafter. And the vowel I, by opening the mouth pretty wide. A, E, I.

Mr. Jordain. A, E, I, I, I, I. It is true. Learning is a noble thing!

Philofophy-mafter. The vowel O is formed by keeping the jaws open, and drawing the lips near at the two corners, the upper and the under, O.

Mr. Jordain. O, O. There is nothing more juft, A, E, I, O, I, O. It is admirable! I, O, I, O.

Philofophy-mafter. The opening of the mouth forms a little circle, which refembles an O.

Mr. Jordain. O, O, O. You are in the right, O. How fine a thing it is but to know fomething!

Philofophy-mafter. The vowel U is formed by pufhing out both lips, bringing them alfo near together without abfolutely joining them, U.

Mr. Jordain. U, U. There is nothing more true, U. Ah! why did I not ftudy fooner, that I might have known all this!

Philofophy-mafter. To-morrow we fhall confider the other letters, which are the confonants.

Mr. Jordain. Is there any thing as curious in them, as in thefe?

Philofophy-mafter. Yes, yes. The confonant D, for example, is pronounced by ftriking the tip of your tongue above the upper teeth, D, E.

Mr. Jordain. DE, DE. It is fo. Oh! charming things! charming things!

Philofophy-mafter. The F, in leaning the upper-teeth upon the lower-lip, EF.

Mr. Jordain. EF, EF. Perfectly right! Ah! father and mother of mine, how vexed I am at you!

Philofophy-mafter. And the R, in carrying the tip of the tongue up to the roof of your mouth; fo that being grazed upon by the air which burfts out with a force, it yields to it, and returns always to its place, making a kind of undulatory found. R, ra.

Mr. Jordain. R, r, ra. R, r, r, r, r, ra. That is true. What a clever man you are! How much time have I loft! R, r, r, ra.

Philofophy-mafter. I will thoroughly explain to you all thefe curiofities.

Mr. Jordain. Pray do: but now I muft make you my confident in a little affair. I am in love with a perfon of great quality, and I fhould be glad you would help me to write fomething to her in a fhort Billet-doux, which I will drop at her feet.

Philofophy-mafter. Very well.

Mr. Jordain. Will not that be very gallant?

Philofophy-mafter. Without doubt. Is it verfe that you would write to her?

Mr. Jordain. No, no, none of your verfe.

Philofophy-mafter. You would only have profe?

Mr. Jordain. No, I would neither have verfe nor profe.

Philofophy-mafter. It muft be one of the two.

Mr. Jordain. Why fo?

Philofophy-mafter. Becaufe, Sir, there is no other way of expreffing ourfelves but by profe, or verfe.

Mr. Jordain. Is there nothing then but profe, or verfe?

Philofophy-mafter. No, Sir, whatever is not profe, is verfe; and whatever is not verfe, is profe.

Mr. Jordain. And when one talks, what may that be then?

Philpfophy-mafter. Profe.

Mr. Jordain. How? When I fay, Nicola, bring me my flippers, and give me my night-cap, is that profe?

Philofophy-mafter. Yes, Sir.

Mr. Jordain. Faith then, I have fpoke profe above thefe forty years, without knowing any thing of the matter; and I am greatly obliged to you, for informing me of this. I would therefore put into a letter to her; " Beautiful marchionefs, your bright eyes make me die " with love;" but I would have this placed in a gallant manner; and have a genteel turn.

Philofophy-mafter. Why, add that the fire of her eyes has reduced your heart to afhes: that you con-ftantly fuffer fuch torments that——   .

Mr. Jordain. No, no, no, I will not have all that——

I will have nothing but what I told you: "Beautiful
"marchionefs, your fair eyes make me die with love."

Philofophy-mafter. But you muft lengthen it out a
little.

Mr. Jordain. No, I tell you, I will have none but
thofe very words in the letter: but turned in a modifh
quality-like manner. I defire you would fhew me how
many different manners they may be put in.

Philofophy-mafter. One may place them firft of all as
you faid: "Beautiful marchionefs, your fair eyes make
"me die for love:" Or fuppofe; "For love die me
"make, beautiful marchionefs, your fair eyes." Or,
"Your eyes fair, for love me make, beautiful marchi-
"onefs, die." Or fuppofe: Die your fair eyes, beauti-
"ful marchionefs, for love me make." Or, "Me make
"your eyes fair die, beautiful marchionefs, for love."

Mr. Jordain. But which is the wittieft of all thefe
ways?

Philofophy-mafter. That which you faid: "Beau-
"tiful marchionefs, your fair eyes make me die for-
"love."

Mr. Jordain. Yet at the fame time, I never ftudied
it, and I made the whole of it at the firft touch. I
heartily thank you, and defire you would come foon to-
morrow.

Philofophy-mafter. I fhall not fail.

SCENE VII.

MR. JORDAIN, A FOOTMAN.

MR. JORDAIN to his Footman.

WHAT! Are my clothes not come yet?
Footman. No, Sir.
Mr. Jordain. This damned rafcal of a tailor! to make

E 3

me wait on a day that I have so much business to do.

I shall go mad! A quartan ague wring this villain of a tailor! Devil take the tailor! A plague choke the tailor! If I had him but here now, this detestable tailor, this dog of a tailor, this traitor of a tailor: I——

SCENE VIII.

MR. JORDAIN, TAILOR, his MAN, bringing a suit of clothes for Mr. Jordain, FOOTMAN.

MR. JORDAIN.

OH! You are there. I was going to be in a passion with you.

Tailor. I could not possibly come sooner; I have employed no less than twenty journeymen at your clothes.

Mr. Jordain. You have sent me a pair of silk stockings so strait, that I had all the difficulty in the world to get them on, and there are two stitches broke in them.

Tailor. They will stretch, Sir.

Mr. Jordain. Yes, if I break every day a loop or two. You have made me a pair of slippers too, that pinch me execrably.

Tailor. Not at all, Sir.

Mr. Jordain. How, not at all?

Tailor. No, they do not pinch you at all.

Mr. Jordain. I tell you they do hurt me.

Tailor. You fancy so.

Mr. Jordain. I fancy so, because I feel it. There is a fine reason indeed!

Tailor. Look here, Sir; I have brought you one of the handsomest suits at court, and the best-matched. It is a masterly work to invent a grave suit of clothes, that is not black; and I will give the cleverest tailor in town six trials to equal it.

Mr. Jordain. What a duce have we here? you have put the flowers downwards.

Tailor. Why, you did not tell me you would have them upwards.

Mr. Jordain. Must one tell you every thing?

Tailor. Yes certainly. All the people of quality wear them in that way.

Mr. Jordain. Do people of quality wear the flowers downwards?

Tailor. Yes, Sir.

Mr. Jordain. Oh! it is very well then.

Tailor. If you pleafe I shall turn them the other way.

Mr. Jordain. No, no.

Tailor. You need only fay the word.

Mr. Jordain. No, I tell you, you have done right. Do you think my clothes will fit me?

Tailor. A pretty queftion! I defy a painter with his pencil to make any thing more exact. I have a fellow at home, who is the greateft genius in the world for cutting out; and another, who is the hero of the age at making a button-hole.

Mr. Jordain. Are the peruque and feather as they should be?

Tailor. Every thing is well.

Mr. Jordain looking earnestly at the tailor's clothes.] Ah, hah! Mr. Tailor, here is fome of the cloth of the laft fuit you made for me. I know it very well.

Tailor. The ftuff appeared to me fo handfome, that I muft confefs I cabbaged a fuit of it for myfelf.

Mr. Jordain. But was that acting honeftly?

Tailor. Will you put on your clothes?

Mr. Jordain. Yes, give me them.

Tailor. Have a little patience, Sir, if you please; thefe things are always done with ceremony; I have brought men along with me, to drefs you to mufic. Soho, come in there.

S C E N E IX.

MR. JORDAIN, TAILOR, his MAN, JOURNEY-MEN-TAILORS dancing, a FOOTMAN.

TAILOR to his Journeymen.

DRESS the gentleman in the manner you do peo-ple of quality. [Enter four Journeymen-tailors, two of which pull off his ftrait breeches made for his exercifes, and two others his waiftcoat; then they put him on his new fuit to mufic; and Mr. Jordain walks amongft them to fhew them his clothes to fee whether they fit or no.

Journeyman-tailor. Good your worfhip give us fomething to drink.

Mr. Jordain. How do you call me?

Journeyman-tailor. Good your worfhip remember us.

Mr. Jordain. Good your worfhip! See what it is to drefs like people of quality. You may go clothed like a cit all your days, and they will never call you, good your worfhip. [Gives them fomething.] Stay, there is fomething for good your worfhip.

Journeyman tailor. My lord, we are infinitely obli-ged to you.

Mr. Jordain. My lord! Oh, hoh! my lord! Stay, friend, my lord deferves fomething, my lord is a word not to be forgotten. Hold, there my lord gives you that.

Journeyman-tailor. My lord, we shall go drink your grace's health.

Mr. Jordain. Your grace! Stay, stay, do not go till I have given you something more. Your grace, to me! [aside.] I'faith if he goes as far as highnefs, he will empty my purfe. [aloud.] Hold, there is for my grace.

Journeyman-tailor. My lord, we moft humbly thank your grace for your liberality.

Mr. Jordain. If they had gone on much longer they would have got all my money.

ACT III. SCENE I.

MR. JORDAIN, and his two FOOTMEN.

MR. JORDAIN.

I Am going about the town to fhew my clothes, and do you walk behind me, and efpecially take care, both of you, to walk immediately at my heels, that people may plainly fee you belong to me.

Footmen. Yes, Sir.

Mr. Jordain. Call Nicola to me that I may give her fome directions. Stay, here fhe comes.

SCENE II.

MR. JORDAIN, NICOLA, two FOOTMEN.

MR. JORDAIN.

NICOLA.

Nicola. Your pleafure, Sir?

Mr. Jordain. Come hither.

Nicola laughing.] Ha, ha, ha, ha, ha!

Mr. Jordain. Who do you laugh at?

Nicola. Ha, ha, ha, ha, ha, ha!

Mr. Jordain. What ails the flut?

Nicola. Ha, ha, ha! How you are bedizoned! Ha, ha, ha!

Mr. Jordain. Why, what——

Nicola. Oh! oh! my stars! ha, ha, ha, ha, ha!

Mr. Jordain. What a baggage this is! What, do you make a jest of me?

Nicola. No, no, Sir, I should be very sorry to do any such thing. Ha, ha, ha, ha, ha, ha!

Mr. Jordain. I shall give you a slap on the chops, if you laugh any more.

Nicola. Sir, I cannot help it. Ha, ha, ha, ha, ha, ha!

Mr. Jordain. Will not you have done?

Nicola. Sir, I ask your pardon; but you are such a figure, that I cannot help laughing. Ha, ha, ha!

Mr. Jordain. Do but see the insolence!

Nicola. You are so thoroughly droll there! Ha, ha!

Mr. Jordain. I shall——

Nicola. I beg you would excuse me. Ha, ha, ha, ha!

Mr. Jordain. Hold, if you laugh again the least in the world, I protest and swear, I will give you the heartiest blow on the ear you ever had in your life.

Nicola. Well, Sir, I have done; I will not laugh any more.

Mr. Jordain. Take care you do not. I would have you go immediately and clean——

Nicola. Ha, ha!

Mr. Jordain. You must clean out as it should be——

Nicola. Ha, ha!

Mr. Jordain. I fay, you muft go clean out the hall, and——

Nicola. Ha, ha!

Mr. Jordain. Again?

Nicola falls down with laughing.] Hold, Sir, beat me rather, and let me laugh my bellyfull, that will do me more good. Ha, ha, ha, ha!

Mr. Jordain. I fhall run mad!

Nicola. For goodnefs fake, Sir, let me laugh. Ha, ha, ha!

Mr. Jordain. If I take you in hand————

Nicola. Si--r, I fhall bu--urft, if I do not laugh. Ha, ha, ha!

Mr. Jordain. Was there ever fuch an impertinent flut as that! fhe laughs in my face when I give her orders.

Nicola. What would you have me do, Sir?

Mr. Jordain. Why, take care to get ready my houfe, for the company who are to be here to day.

Nicola getting up.] Faith, I have no more inclination to laugh now, all your company makes fuch a litter here, that the very word company is enough to put one in an ill humour.

Mr. Jordain. What! I ought to fhut my door againft every body to pleafe you?

Nicola. You ought at leaft to fhut it againft certain people.

SCENE III.

MRS. JORDAIN, MR. JORDAIN, NICOLA,
TWO FOOTMEN.

MRS. JORDAIN.

HEY-DAY, hufband, what fine drefs is this you have got now ? Do you defpife the world, that you harnefs yourfelf out in this manner? Have you a mind to make yourfelf a laughing-ftock wherever you go?

Mr. Jordain. None but fools, wife, will laugh at me.

Mrs. Jordain. Nay, people have not ftaid thus long to laugh, your ridiculous manners have long been the jeft of the town.

Mr. Jordain. And who is this town, pray?

Mrs. Jordain. Why, every one that has any reafon in them, and are not as great fools as yourfelf. For my part, I am fhocked at the life you lead. I do not know what to call our houfe. One would fwear there was a continual mafquerade in it; and from break of day, for fear there fhould be any refpite, there is nothing to be heard here, but an uproar of fiddlers and fongfters, which difturb the whole neighbourhood.

Nicola. This is every word truth. I fhall never fee my things fet to rights again for that gang of folks that you bring to the houfe. They ranfack every quarter of the town with their feet for dirt to bring here; and I, poor huffy! am almoft flaved off my legs with fcrubbing the floors, which your pretty mafters come to daub as regularly as the day comes.

Mr. Jordain. Hey-day! our maid Nicola! you have

a pretty nimble tongue of your own, for a country wench.

Mrs. Jordain. Nicola is in the right, and she has more sense than you have. I should be glad to know what you think to do with a dancing-master at your age?

Nicola. And with a lubberly fencing-master, that comes here with his stamping to shake the whole house: I am sure he has broke half a dozen boards already.

Mr. Jordain. Peace both of you.

Mrs. Jordain. What! will you learn to dance that you may go capering to your grave?

Nicola. Or have you a mind to murder somebody?

Mr. Jordain. Hold your prate, I tell you, you are ignorant creatures, both of you, and do not know the advantage of all this.

Mrs. Jordain. You ought much rather to think of marrying your daughter, who is of an age now to be settled in the world.

Mr. Jordain. I shall think of marrying my daughter when a suitable match presents itself; but in the mean time, I shall endeavour to improve myself in the arts and sciences.

Nicola. I have heard say farther, madam, that to pin the basket he has got a flossophy-master to day.

Mr. Jordain. Very well, and what then? I have a mind to have wit, and to know how to reason upon things with your people of quality.

Mrs. Jordain. Will you not go to school one of these days, and be whipt at your age?

Mr. Jordain. Why not? I would willingly be whipt this very instant before all the world, so I did but know what they learn at school.

Nicola. Yes, forsooth, that would be a mighty advantage to you.

Mr. Jordain. Indeed it would.

Mrs. Jordain. No doubt, this is all very neceſſary to the management of your houſe.

Mr. Jordain. Certainly. You talk, both of you like aſſes, and I am aſhamed of your ignorance. [to Mrs. Jordan.] For example, do you know, you, what it is you now ſpeak?

Mrs. Jordain. Yes, I know that what I ſpeak is nothing but the truth, and that you ought to think of living in another manner.

Mr. Jordain. I do not talk of that; I aſk you what the words are that you now ſpeak?

Mrs. Jordain. They are words that have a good deal of ſenſe in them, and your conduct is quite the contrary.

Mr. Jordain. I do not talk of that, I tell you: I aſk you, what is that I now ſpeak to you, which I ſay this very moment?

Mrs. Jordain. Nonſenſe.

Mr. Jordain. Pſhaw, no, it is not that. That which we both of us ſay, the language we ſpeak this inſtant?

Mrs. Jordain. Well?

Mr. Jordain. How do you call it?

Mrs. Jordain. Call it? Why call it what you pleaſe.

Mr. Jordain. It is proſe, you ignorant creature.

Mrs. Jordain. Proſe?

Mr. Jordain. Yes, proſe. Whatever is proſe, is not verſe; and whatever is not verſe, is proſe. There now, I learnt this by ſtudying. And you, [to Nicola.] do you know how you muſt do to form an U?

Nicola. How?

Mr. Jordain. Yes. What is it you do when you form an U?

Nicola. What?

Mr. Jordain. Say U only.

Nicola. Well, U.

Mr. Jordain. What is it you do?

Nicola. I fay U.

Mr. Jordain. Yes, but when you fay U, what is it you do?

Nicola. Why I do what you bid me.

Mr. Jordain. O! what a ftrange thing it is to have to do with ignorant people! You pout out your lips, and bring your under-jaw to your upper, U; do you fee? I make a mouth, U.

Nicola. Yes, that is fine.

Mrs. Jordain. It is admirable!

Mr. Jordain. Yes, but what would you have faid had you feen O, and DEE, DEE, and EF, EF.

Mrs. Jordain. What ridiculous ftuff!

Nicola. What are we the better for all this?

Mr. Jordain. It makes one mad to fee thefe ignorant women.

Mrs. Jordain. For fhame! you fhould fend all thefe folks a packing with their filly ftuff.

Nicola. And efpecially that great lubberly fencing-mafter, who fills the whole houfe with dirt.

Mr. Jordain. Hey-day! This fencing-mafter fticks ftrangely in thy ftomach. I will let thee fee thy igno-rance prefently. [He orders the foils to be brought, and gives one to Nicola.] Stay, reafon demonftrative, the line of the body: when they pufh quarte one needs only do fo; and when they pufh in tierce, fo. This is the way never to be killed; and is not that clever to be upon fure grounds, when one fights with any bo-dy? There, pufh at me a little, to try.

Nicola. Well, and how then? [Nicola gives him fe-veral thurfts.

Mr. Jordain. Gently! Hold! Oh! feftly; ducc take the huffy.

Nicola. You bid me pufh.

Mr. Jordain. Yes, but you puſh me in tierce, before you puſh in quarte; and you do not give me time to parry.

Mrs. Jordain. You are a fool, huſband, with all theſe whims, and this is come to you ſince you have taken upon you to keep company with people of quality, as you call them.

Mr. Jordain. In keeping company with people of quality, I ſhew my judgment; and that is much better than herding with your cits.

Mrs. Jordain. Yes, truly, there is a great deal to be got by keeping company with your nobility; and you have made fine work with that count you are ſo bewitched with.

Mr. Jordain. Peace, take care what you ſay: do you know, wife, whom you ſpeak of, when you mention him? He is a man of more importance than you imagine; a nobleman of conſideration at court, who ſpeaks to the king juſt as freely as I ſpeak to you. Is it not a thing that does me great honour, to ſee a perſon of that quality come ſo often to my houſe, who calls me his dear friend, and treats me as if I were his equal? He has more kindneſs for me than one would ever imagine; and he careſſes me in ſuch a manner before company, that I myſelf am perfectly confounded at it.

Mrs. Jordain. Yes, he is very kind to you truly! and careſſes you; but it is only to borrow your money of you.

Mr. Jordain. Well, and is it not a great honour to me to lend money to a man of that rank? And can I do leſs for a lord who calls me his dear friend?

Mrs. Jordain. And pray what is it this lord does for you?

Mr. Jordain. Things that would aſtoniſh you, if you did but know them.

Mrs. Jordain. And what may they be?

Mr. Jordain. No, hold there, wife. It is sufficient that if I have lent him money, he will pay it me honestly, and that before it is long.

Mrs. Jordain. Yes, trust you to that.

Mr. Jordain. Certainly: did he not tell me so?

Mrs. Jordain. I dare say he has, and he will not fail to disappoint you.

Mr. Jordain. He swore to me on the honour of a gentleman.

Mrs. Jordain. All that is nothing.

Mr. Jordain. Heh! You are mighty obstinate, wife of mine; I tell you he will keep his word with me, I am sure of it.

Mrs. Jordain. And I am sure that he will not; and all the great kindness he shews you is only to make a dupe of you.

Mr. Jordain. Hold your tongue. Here he comes.

Mrs. Jordain. Yes, he comes I suppose to do you the honour of borrowing something more of you; I hate the very sight of him.

Mr. Jordain. Peace, once more.

SCENE IV.

DORANTES, MR. JORDAIN, MRS. JORDAIN, NICOLA.

DORANTES.

MY good friend, Mr. Jordain, how do you do?

Mr. Jordain. Very well, Sir, at your service.

Dorantes. And madam Jordain there, how does she do?

Mrs. Jordain. Madam Jordain does as well as she can.

Dorantes. Hah! Mr. Jordain, you are dreſt the moſt genteelly in the world!

Mr. Jordain. As you ſee.

Dorantes. I declare you have quite the quality air, and we have never a young fellow at court that looks better than you.

Mr. Jordain. He! he! Sir, you are pleaſed to compliment me.

Mrs. Jordain aſide.] He ſcratches him where it itches.

Dorantes. Turn about. It is moſt gallant.

Mr. Jordain aſide.] Yes, as much of the fool behind as before.

Dorantes. 'Faith, Mr. Jordain, I was ſtrangely impatient to ſee you. You are the man in the world I moſt eſteem, and I was talking of you but this morning at the king's Levee.

Mr. Jordain. You do me a great deal of honour, Sir. [to Mrs. Jordain.] At the king's Levee!

Dorantes. Pray be covered.

Mr. Jordain. Sir, I know the reſpect I owe you.

Dorantes. I beg that you would be covered; no ceremony pray between us two.

Mr. Jordain. Sir.

Dorantes. Put on your hat, I tell you, Mr. Jordain, you are my friend.

Mr. Jordain. Sir, I am your humble ſervant.

Dorantes. I will not be covered, if you will not.

Mr. Jordain puts on his hat.] I had rather be unmannerly than troubleſome.

Dorantes. I am your debtor, you know.

Mrs. Jordain aſide.] Yes, faith, we know it but too well.

Dorantes. You have generouſly lent me money upon

several occasions; and have obliged me, most certainly, with the best grace in the world.

Mr. Jordain. You jest, Sir.

Dorantes. But I know how to acknowledge favours.

Mr. Jordain. I do not doubt it, Sir.

Dorantes. I am willing to get out of your books, and came hither to make up our accounts together.

Mr. Jordain aside to Mrs. Jordain.] Well, wife, you see your impertinence.

Dorantes. I am one who love to pay every one as soon as possible.

Mr. Jordain aside to Mrs. Jordain.] I told you so.

Dorantes. Pray how much do I owe you?

Mr. Jordain aside to Mrs. Jordain.} Now, what are come of your ridiculous suspicions?

Dorantes. Do you remember right all the sums you have lent me?

Mr. Jordain. I believe so. I made a little memorandum of it. Here it is. Let you have at one time two hundred louis d'ors.

Dorantes. Right.

Mr. Jordain. Another time, six score.

Dorantes. Yes.

Mr. Jordain. And another time a hundred and forty.

Dorantes. You are right.

Mr Jordain. These three articles make four hundred and sixty louis d'ors, which come to five thousand and sixty livres.

Dorantes. The account is very right. Five thousand and sixty livres.

Mr. Jordain. One thousand eight hundred and thirty two livres to your plume-maker.

Dorantes. Just.

Mr. Jordain. Two thousand seven hundred and fourscore livres to your tailor.

Dorantes. True.

Mr. Jordain. Four thoufand three hundred and feventy nine livres, twelve fols and eight deniers to your merchant.

Dorantes. Very well. Twelve fols, eight deniers. The account is juft.

Mr. Jordain. And a thoufand feven hundred and forty eight livres feven fols four deniers to your faddler.

Dorantes. Exactly. What does that amount to?

Mr. Jordain. Sum total, fifteen thoufand eight hundred livres.

Dorantes. It is all right. Fifteen thoufand and eight hundred livres. To which add two hundred piftoles, which you are going to lend me, that will make exactly eighteen thoufand franks, which I fhall pay you the firft opportunity.

Mrs. Jordain afide to Mr. Jordain.] Well, did I not guefs how it would be?

Mr. Jordain afide to Mrs. Jordain.] Peace.

Dorantes. If it is not convenient to you, I fhall apply fomewhere elfe.

Mr. Jordain. Oh! no.

Mrs. Jordain afide to Mr. Jordain.] This man will certainly ruin you.

Mr. Jordain afide to Mrs. Jordain.] Hold your tongue.

Dorantes. If this will incommode you, I will feek it elfewhere.

Mr. Jordain. No, Sir.

Mrs. Jordain afide to Mr. Jordain.] He is a true leech.

Mr. Jordain afide to Mrs. Jordain.] Hold your tongue, I tell you.

Dorantes. You need only tell me if this puts you to any ſtraits.

Mr. Jordain. Not at all, Sir.

Mrs. Jordain aſide to Mr. Jordain.] He is a true wheedler.

Mr. Jordain aſide to Mrs. Jordain.] Hold your tongue then.

Mrs. Jordain aſide to Mr. Jordain.] He will drain you to the laſt farthing.

Mr. Jordain aſide to Mrs. Jordain.] What, again?

Dorantes. I have a good many people would be glad to lend it me, but as you are my very good friend, I thought I ſhould wrong you if I applied to any other perſon.

Mr. Jordain. It is too much honour, Sir, you do me. I will go fetch what you want.

Mrs. Jordain aſide to Mr. Jordain.] What! going to lend him ſtill more?

Mr. Jordain aſide to Mrs. Jordain.] What can I do? Would you have me refuſe a man of that rank, who ſpoke of me this morning at the king's Levee?

Mrs. Jordain aſide to Mr. Jordain.] Go, you are a downright dupe.

SCENE V.

DORANTES, MRS. JORDAIN, NICOLA.

DORANTES.

YOU ſeem very melanchcly, Madam Jordain, What ails you?

Mrs. Jordain. My head is bigger than my fiſt, unlefs it is ſwelled.

Dorantes. Where is mifs your daughter, that I have not the pleaſure of ſeeing her?

Mr. Jordain. Miſs my daughter is pretty well where ſhe is.

Dorantes. How does ſhe go on?

Mr. Jordain. She goes on hér two legs.

Dorantes. Will not you come with her, one of theſe days, and ſee the ball, and the play that is acted at court?

Mrs. Jordain. Yes truly, we have a great inclination to laugh, a great inclination to laugh indeed!

Dorantes. I fancy, Madam Jordain, you had a vaſt many ſparks in your younger years, being ſo handſome and good-humouréd as you certainly were then?

Mrs. Jordain. What, Sir, is Madam Jordain grown decrepit? and does her head totter already with a palſy?

Dorantes. I aſk your pardon, Madam Jordain, I did not conſider that you were yet in your bloom. I am very often abſent. Pray excuſe my impertinence.

SCENE VI.

MR. JORDAIN, MRS. JORDAIN, DO-
RANTES, NICOLA.

Mr. JORDAIN to Dorantes.

HERE are two hundred pieces for you.

Dorantes. I do aſſure you, Mr. Jordain, I am greatly obliged to you; and I long to do you ſervice at court.

Mr. Jordain. I am infinitely obliged to you.

Dorantes. If Madam Jordain has a mind to ſee the royal diverſion, ſhe ſhall have the beſt place in the drawing-room.

Mrs. Jordain. Madam Jordain is your humble ſervant.

Dorantes afide to Mr. Jordain.] Our pretty marchi-enefs, as I informed you in my letter, will be here prefently to honour your mufical entertainment; I brought her, at laft, to confent to accept of the treat you defign to give her.

Mr. Jordain. Let us draw afide a little, for a certain reafon.

Dorantes. It is eight days fince I faw you, and I gave you no tidings of the diamond you put into my hands to make her a prefent of as from you; but the reafon was, I had all the difficulty in the world to con-quer her fcruples, and it was not till this very day that I could prevail on her to accept of it.

Mr. Jordain. How did fhe like it?

Dorantes. Greatly; and I am much deceived if the beauty of this diamond has not an admirable effect up-on her.

Mr. Jordain. Grant it, kind heaven!

Mrs. Jordain to Nicola.] When they get together, there is no parting of them.

Dorantes. I made her fenfible in a proper manner, of the richnefs of the prefent, and the greatnefs of your love.

Mr. Jordain. You perfectly overwhelm me with fa-vours; I am in the greateft confufion in the world to fee a perfon of your quality condefcend to do what you do for me.

Dorantes. You jeft fure. Does one ever ftop at fuch fort of fcruples among friends? And would not you do the fame thing for me upon fuch an occafion?

Mr. Jordain. Oh! certainly I would.

Mrs. Jordain afide to Nicola.] I hate the fight of him.

Dorantes. For my part, I ftop at nothing to ferve a friend; and when you imparted to me the ardent paffion you had entertained for the agreeable marchionefs, with whom I was acquainted, you fee that I made an immediate offer of my fervice.

Mr. Jordain. It is true. I am quite afhamed of fo many favours.

Mrs. Jordain to Nicola.] What! will he never be gone?

Nicola. They are mighty fond of each other.

Dorantes. You have took the right way to touch her heart. Women, above all things, love the expence we are at on their account; and your frequent fere-nades, your entertainments; that elegant fire-work on the water, the diamond fhe received by way of prefent from you, and the banquet you are now preparing; all this fpeaks much better in favour of your paffion than any thing you yourfelf could poffibly have faid to her.

Mr. Jordain. I fhould grudge no expence to gain her affection. A woman of quality has powerful charms for me, and it is an honour I would purchafe at any rate.

Mrs. Jordain afide to Nicola.] What can they be talking of fo long? Go foftly, and liften.

Dorantes. You will foon have the pleafure of fee-ing and entertaining her without any reftraint.

Mr. Jordain. To be at full liberty, I have ordered matters fo, that my wife fhall dine with my fifter, where fhe will pafs the whole afternoon.

Dorantes. You have done wifely, for your wife's prefence might have been troublefome to us. I have given the proper orders for you to the cook, and for e-very thing neceffary for the ball. It is of my own in-vention; and provided the execution anfwers the plan, I am certain————

Mr. Jordain perceives that Nicola liftens, and gives

her a box on the ear.] What do you want, Mrs. Sly-boots? [to Dorantes.] Let us retire, if you pleafe.

SCENE VII.

MRS. JORDAIN, NICOLA.

NICOLA.

YOU fee, madam, what I have got for my curio-fity, but I believe there is a fnake in the grafs; for they were talking of fome affair, which they were not willing you fhould be prefent at.

Mrs. Jordain. This is not the firft time, Nicola, that I have fufpected my hufband's fidelity. I am the moft deceived perfon in the world, or there is fome amour in agitation, and I am labouring to difcover what it fhould be. But let us think of my daughter. You know how greatly Cleontes loves her. He is a man who hits my fancy, and I am determined to ufe my utmoft efforts to have him for my fon-in-law.

Nicola. In truth, madam, I am rejoiced to find you in this mind; for if the mafter hits your tafte, the man hits mine no lefs; and I could wifh our marriage might be concluded under favour of theirs.

Mrs. Jordain. Go, and talk with him about it, as from me, and tell him to come to me immediately, that we may join in afking my hufband's confent.

Nicola. I fly, madam, with joy, and could not have received a more agreeable commiffion. [alone.] I be-lieve this meffage will be very agreeable to them both.

SCENE VIII.

CLEONTES, COVIEL, NICOLA.

NICOLA to Cleontes.

HAH, well met. Rare tidings! I come——

Cleontes. Begone, ye perfidious flut, and do not come to amufe me with thy falfe fpeeches.

Nicola. Do you receive in this manner——

Cleontes. Begone, I tell thee, and go directly and inform thy traiterous miftrefs, that fhe fhall no longer impofe upon the too fond and credulous Cleontes.

Nicola. What whim is this? My dear Coviel, tell the meaning of all this.

Coviel. Thy dear Coviel, wicked minx? Away quickly out of my fight, huffy, and leave me at quiet.

Nicola. What! doft thou too——

Coviel. Begone, I fay, and talk not to me, for thy life.

Nicola afide.] Hey-day! I wonder what has poffeffed them both. Well, I muft go and inform my miftrefs of this affair.

SCENE IX.

CLEONTES, COVIEL.

CLEONTES.

WHAT! to ufe a lover in this manner! and a lover the moft conftant, the moft paffionate of all his fex!

Coviel. Never were two lovers fo terribly duped.

Cleontes. I difcover all the ardour for her, all the tendernefs one can imagine: I love nothing in the world but her, have nothing in my thoughts befides her. She has all my care, all my defire, all my joy. I fpeak of nought but her, think of nought but her, dream of nought but her, I breathe only for her, my heart lives wholly in her; and this is the worthy recompenfe of fuch a love! After an abfence of two tedious days, which are to me as many ages, I meet her accidentally, my heart feels all tranfported at the fight; joy fparkles in my face; I fly to her with extafy, and the faithlefs creature turns away her eyes, and brufhes haftily by me, as if fhe had never feen me in her life!

Coviel. I may fay the fame as you do.

Cleontes. Is it poffible to fee any thing, Coviel, equal to this perfidy of the ungrateful Lucilia?

Coviel. Or that, Sir, of the treacherous flut Nicola?

Cleontes. After fo many ardent facrifices of fighs and vows that I have breathed to her charms!

Coviel. After fo many affiduous fneaking cares, and fervices that I have paid her in the kitchen!

Cleontes. So many tears that I have fhed at her feet!

Coviel. So many buckets of water that I have drawn for her!

Cleontes. Such fervency as I have fhown, in loving her more than myfelf!

Coviel. So much heat as I have endured, in turning the fpit in her place!

Cleontes. She avoids me with contempt!

Coviel. She turns her back upon me with impudence!

Cleontes. Such an infult deferves the greateft punifhment!

Coviel. This is a treachery that deferves a thoufand boxes on the ear.

Cleontes. I charge thee never to speak to me once more in her favour.

Coviel. I, Sir? heaven forbid.

Cleontes. Never come to excuse the actions of this false woman.

Coviel. Not I, truly.

Cleontes. Do not, I say; all discourses in her defence will signify nothing.

Coviel. Who dreams of such a thing?

Cleontes. I am determined to continue my resentment against her, and part with her for ever.

Coviel. I give my consent.

Cleontes. This same count that visits her, has, I suppose, dazzled her eye; and her fancy, I see plainly, is touched with his quality. But I must, for my own honour, prevent the triumph of her inconstancy: I will make as sudden a change as herself, and will not leave her all the glory of having cast me off.

Coviel. It is very well said, and for my share, I enter into all your sentiments.

Cleontes. Second my resentments, and support my resolutions against all the remains of love, that may yet plead for her. I conjure thee, set all her faults before my eyes; paint her person so as to make her despicable.

Coviel. She, Sir? A fine piece indeed to be so much enamoured with! I see nothing in her, but what is very indifferent, and you might find a hundred persons more deserving of you. First of all, she has little eyes.

Cleontes. It is true, she has little eyes; but they are full of fire, the most sparkling, piercing, striking, that ever——

Coviel. She has a wide mouth also.

Cleontes. Yes; but one sees such graces in it, as one

does not fee in other mouths, and the fight of that mouth infpires defire: it is the moft attractive, the moft amorous in the world.

Coviel. As to her height, fhe is not tall.

Cleontes. No; but fhe is eafy, and well-fhaped.

Coviel. She affects a negligence in her fpeech and actions.

Cleontes. It is true; but all this has a gracefulnefs in her, and her ways are engaging; they have I do not know what charms, that infinuate into our hearts.

Coviel. As to her wit——

Cleontes. Ah! Coviel, fhe has the moft refined, the moft delicate turn of wit.

Coviel. And her converfation——

Cleontes. Is charming.

Coviel. She is always furly.

Cleontes. Would you have her always laughing? Do you fee any thing more impertinent than thofe women who are always upon the giggle?

Coviel. In fhort, fhe is the moft capricious creature I ever beheld.

Cleontes. Yes, I own fhe is capricious; but every thing fits well upon fine women; we bear with every thing from the fair.

Coviel. Well, well, I fee plainly you defire always to love her.

Cleontes. I! I fhould love death fooner; and I am now going to hate her as much as ever I loved her.

Coviel. How can that be, when you think her fo perfect?

Cleontes. That will make my revenge the more confpicuous; in that I fhall better difplay the force of my refolution in hating her, quitting her, moft beautiful as fhe is; moft charming, moft amiable, as I think her. But here fhe comes.

SCENE X.

LUCILIA, CLEONTES, COVIEL, NICOLA.

NICOLA to Lucilia.

FOR my part, I am quite ashamed of your behaviour.

Lucilia. It can proceed from nothing else, Nicola, but what I said. But there he comes.

Cleontes to Coviel.] I will not condescend to speak to her.

Coviel. I will follow your example.

Lucilia. What means this, Cleontes, what is the matter with you?

Nicola. What ails thee, Coviel?

Lucilia. What is the reason of this uneasiness?

Nicola. What cross humour possesses thee?

Lucilia. Are you dumb, Cleontes?

Nicola. Have you lost your speech, Coviel?

Cleontes. Was ever such baseness?

Coviel. Oh! the Judas in petticoats.

Lucilia. I see very well that the late meeting has enraged you.

Cleontes to Coviel.] You see she is sensible of what she has done.

Nicola. The reception you met with this morning I suppose has put you in a pet.

Coviel to Cleontes.] She has guessed where the shoe pinches.

Lucilia. Is it not true, Cleontes, that this is the reason of your being angry?

Cleontes. Yes, perfidious maid, that is it, since I must speak; and I must tell you, that you shall not tri-

umph, as you imagine, by your unfaithfulnefs. I am
refolved to be the firft to break off all connections between us, and you will not have the credit of difcard-
ing me. I fhall, doubtlefs, have fome difficulty in con-
quering the paffion I have for you: it will caufe me
uneafinefs; I fhall. fuffer for a while; but I fhall com-
pafs my point, and I would fooner ftab myfelf to the
heart than have the weaknefs of returning to you.

Coviel to Nicola.] Like mafter, like man.

Lucilia. Here is a noife indeed about nothing: I will
tell you, Cleontes, the reafon that made me avoid joining you this morning.

Cleontes endeavouring to go to avoid Lucilia.] No,
I will hear nothing.

Nicola to Coviel.] I will tell you what made us leave
you fo fuddenly.

Coviel endeavouring to go to avoid Nicola.] I will
hear nothing.

Lucilia following Cleontes.] You muft know that
this morning——

Cleontes walks about without regarding Lucilia.]No,
I tell you.

Nicola following Coviel.] Know that——

Coviel walks about likewife without regarding Nicola.] No, traitrefs.

Lucilia. Hear me.

Cleontes. No.

Nicola. Let me fpeak.

Coviel. I am deaf.

Lucilia. Cleontes.

Cleontes. No.

Nicola. Coviel.

Coviel. No.

Lucilia. Stay.

Cleontes. Idle ftuff.

Nicola. Hear me.

Coviel. No such thing.

Lucilia. One moment.

Cleontes. Not at all.

Nicola. A little patience.

Coviel. A fiddle-stick.

Lucilia. Two words.

Cleontes. No, it is over.

Nicola. One word.

Coviel. I have done with you.

Lucilia stopping.] Well, since you will not hear me, remain in your present way of thinking, and do what you please.

Nicola stopping likewise.] Since that is thy way, you may do as you will for me.

Cleontes. Let us know the subject then of this strange behaviour.

Lucilia going in her turn to avoid Cleontes.] I do not chuse to speak any more to you.

Coviel. Let us a little into this story.

Nicola going likewise in her turn to avoid Coviel.] I will not inform thee now, not I.

Cleontes following Lucilia.] Tell me——

Lucilia. No, I will tell you nothing.

Coviel following Nicola.] Say——

Nicola. No, I will say nothing.

Cleontes. Pray now do.

Lucilia. No, I tell you.

Coviel. For heaven's sake.

Nicola. I have no more to say to you.

Cleontes. I beseech you.

Lucilia. Let me alone.

Coviel. I conjure thee.

Nicola. Away with thee.

Cleontes. Lucilia!

Lucilia. No.

Coviel. Nicola!

Nicola. Not at all.

Cleontes. For heaven's fake.

Lucilia. I will not.

Coviel. Speak to me.

Nicola. Not a word.

Cleontes. Clear up my doubts.

Lucilia. No, I will not concern myfelf about you.

Coviel. Do but make me eafy.

Nicola. No, it is not my pleafure.

Cleontes. Well, fince you are fo indifferent about making me eafy, or juftifying yourfelf as to the unworthy treatment my paffion has received from you, ungrateful creature, it is the laft time you fhall fee me, and I am going far from you to die of grief and love.

Coviel to Nicola.] And I fhall do the fame.

Lucilia to Cleontes who is going:] Cleontes!

Nicola to Coviel, who follows his mafter.] Coviel!

Cleontes ftopping.] Well?

Coviel likewife ftopping.] Your pleafure?

Lucilia. Whither are you going?

Cleontes. Where I told you.

Coviel. We go to die.

Lucilia. Do you go to die, Cleontes?

Cleontes. Yes, hard-hearted fair one, fince you will have it fo.

Lucilia. I? I have you die?

Cleontes. Yes, you wifh it.

Lucilia. Who told you fo?

Cleontes going up to Lucilia.] Would you not have it fo, fince you would not clear up my fufpicions?

Lucilia. Is that my fault? If you had but given me the hearing, fhould I not have told you that the adventure you complain so much of, was occasioned this morning by the presence of an old aunt who will absolutely have it, that the mere approach of a man is a dishonour to a girl; who is perpetually lecturing us upon this head, and represents all your sex as so many devils, whom every woman who would maintain her virtue ought to avoid.

Nicola to Coviel.] There is the whole secret of the affair.

Cleontes. Do not you deceive me, Lucilia?

Coviel to Nicola.] Dost thou not put a trick upon me?

Lucilia to Cleontes.] Is it nothing but the truth?

Nicola to Coviel.] It is just as you have heard.

Coviel to Cleontes.] Well, Sir, shall we surrender?

Cleontes. Ah, Lucilia! what art you have to calm my passions with a single word! How easily do we suffer ourselves to be persuaded by those we love!

Coviel. Those bewitching devils can turn us any way they think proper.

SCENE XI.

MRS. JORDAIN, CLEONTES, LUCILIA, COVIEL, NICOLA.

MRS. JORDAIN.

I HAVE just been seeking you, Cleontes, and am glad I have found you. My husband is a coming, catch your opportunity, and demand Lucilia in marriage.

Cleontes. Ah! madam, how you charm me with this goodness! Could I receive an order more pleasing? a favour more agreeable?

SCENE XII.

MR. JORDAIN, MRS. JORDAIN, CLEONTES,
LUCILIA, COVIEL, NICOLA.

CLEONTES.

SIR, I was unwilling to employ any other person
to make a certain demand of you, which I have
long meditated. The confequence is a fufficient motive for me to undertake it in my own perfon; and,
without further circumlocution, I fhall inform you,
that the honour of being your fon-in-law is an illuftrious favour which I intreat you to grant me.

Mr. Jordain. Before I give you an anfwer, Sir,
pray tell me whether you are a gentleman.

Cleontes. Sir, few people would hefitate to reply to
fuch a queftion. Every one affumes this title, and cu-
ftom now-a-days feems to authorize the theft. For my
part, I confefs to you, my fentiments in this matter
are fomewhat more delicate. I look upon all impofture as unworthy an honeft man; and that it is a bafe-
nefs to difguife the condition in which heaven has placed us; in tricking ourfelves out to the eyes of the
world, in a ftolen title; in defiring to put ourfelves off
for what we are not. I am undoubtedly born of parents who have held honourable pofts in the ftate. I have
had the honour of fix years' fervice in the army; and
have fortune enough to maintain a tolerable rank in the
world; but for all this I will not give myfelf a name,
which others in my place would think they had fufficient pretenfions to, and I will tell you frankly that I
am no gentleman.

Mr. Jordain. Your hand, Sir, my daughter is not
for you.

Cleontes. How?

Mr. Jordain. You are no gentleman, you shall not have my daughter.

Mrs. Jordain. What would you be at then with your gentleman? Are we gentle folks pray?

Mr. Jordain. Hold your tongue, wife.

Mrs. Jordain. Are we either of us otherwise descended than of plain citizens?

Mr. Jordain. There is a scandalous reflection for you!

Mrs. Jordain. And was not your father a tradesman as well as mine?

Mr. Jordain. Plague take the woman, she is constantly harping on this string. If your father was a tradesman, so much the worse for him; but as for mine, they are ignorant fools that say he was. All that I have to say to you, is that I will have a gentleman for my son-in-law.

Mrs. Jordain. Your daughter should have a husband that is suitable to her; and an honest man, who is rich and agreeable, would be much better for her than a gentleman who is a beggar.

Nicola. That is very true. We have a young squire in our town who is the greatest blockhead that I ever set my eyes on.

Mr. Jordain. Hold your prate, Mrs. Impertinence. Must you always be meddling? I have means sufficient for my daughter, and want nothing but honour, and I will have her a marchioness.

Mrs. Jordain. A marchioness!

Mr. Jordain. Yes, a marchioness.

Mrs. Jordain. Marry, heavens preserve me from it!

Mr. Jordain. I am resolved upon it.

Mrs. Jordain. It is what I shall never consent to. Matches with superiors always occasion unhappiness.

I do not like that a fon-in-law fhould have it in his
power to reproach my daughter with her parents, or
that fhe fhould have children who fhould be afhamed
to call me grand-mother. Should fhe come and vifit
me with the equipage of a grand lady, and through
inadvertency mifs faluting any of the neighbourhood,
they would not fail prefently faying an hundred idle
things. Do but fee, would they fay, this lady marchionefs, what haughty airs fhe gives herfelf! She is
the daughter of Mr. Jordain, who was glad when fhe
was a little one, to play with us. She was not always
fo lofty as fhe is now; and her two grand-fathers acquired their riches by felling cloth, which perhaps
they may have to anfwer for in the other world: people do not generally grow fo rich by being honeft. I
will not have all thefe tittle-tattle ftories; in one word,
I will have a man who will thank me for his wife, and
to whom I can fay, fit you down there, fon-in-law, and
dine with me.

Mr. Jordain. Thefe are only the fentiments of mean
fouls, who defire always to continue in a mean condition. Let me have no more replies; my daughter fhall
be a marchionefs in fpite of the world; and if you vex
me, I will make her a duchefs.

S C E N E XIII.

MRS. JORDAIN, LUCILIA, CLEON-
TES, NICOLA, COVIEL.

MRS. JORDAIN.

LET not this difcourage you, Cleontes, [to Lucilia.] Follow me, daughter, and come tell your
father refolutely, that if you have not him, you will
not have any body.

SCENE XIV.

CLEONTES, COVIEL.

COVIEL.

YOU have made a pretty piece of work of it with your delicate fentiments.

Cleontes. What could I do? they are fuch as I cannot fubdue.

Coviel. You are in the wrong to be ferious with fuch a man as that. Do not you fee that he is a fool? And would it coft you any thing to have humoured his whims?

Cleontes. You are in the right; but I did not think there was any neceffity to prove my being of a noble race to be fon-in-law to Mr. Jordain.

Coviel laughing.] Ha, ha, ha!

Cleontes. What do you laugh at?

Coviel. At a thought that is come into my head to put a trick upon our fpark, and help you to obtain what you defire.

Cleontes. What is it?

Coviel. The thought is abfoluely droll.

Cleontes. What is it?

Coviel. There was a certain mafquerade performed not long fince, which comes in here the beft in the world; and which I intend to infert into a piece of roguery I defign to make for our coxcomb. This whole affair looks a little like making a joke of him; but with him we may hazard every thing, there is no need here to ftudy fineffe fo much, he is a man who will play his part to a wonder; and will eafily give in to all the fham tales we fhall take in our heads to tell him. I have actors, I have habits all ready, only let me alone.

Cleontes. But inform me of it.

Coviel. You fhall know all, but let us begone, for I fee him coming.

S C E N E XV.

M R. J O R D A I N alone.

I Cannot underftand what thefe people would be at; they have nothing but great lords to reproach me with; and I, for my part, fee nothing fo fine as keep-ing company with people of quality; there is nothing but honour and civility among them; and I would wil-lingly give two fingers of a hand to have been born a count or a marquis.

S C E N E XVI.

M R. J O R D A I N, F O O T M A N.

F O O T M A N.

SIR, here is the count, and a lady, whom he is han-ding in.

Mr. Jordain. Good lack a-day! I have fome orders to give. Tell them that I will wait on them imme-diately.

S C E N E XVII.

D O R I M E N E, D O R A N T E S, F O O T M A N.

F O O T M A N.

MY mafter fays he will be with you immediate-ly.

Dorantes. Very well.

SCENE XVIII.

DORIMENE, DORANTES.

DORIMENE.

I HAVE taken a strange step, Dorantes, in suffering you to bring me to a house where I know no-body.

Dorantes. What place then, madam, would you have a lover choose to entertain you in, since, to avoid clamour, you neither allow of your own house nor mine?

Dorimene. You do not consider that I am every day insensibly engaged to receive too great proofs of your passion. In vain do I refuse things, you weary me out of resistance, and you have a civil kind of obstinacy, which makes me come gently into whatsoever you please. Frequent visits have commenced, declarations came next, which drew after them serenades and entertainments, which were followed by presents. I opposed all these things, but you are not disheartned, and you become master of my resolutions step by step. For my part, I can answer for nothing hereafter, and I believe in the end you will bring me to matrimony, notwithstanding I am so averse to it.

Dorantes. Faith, madam, you ought to have been in that state before now. You are a widow, and depend upon no body but yourself. I am my own master, and love you more than my life. What does it stick at then, that you should not, from this day forward, compleat my happiness?

Dorimene. Alas! Dorantes, there must go a great many qualities on both sides, to make the marriage state happy; and two of the most reasonable persons in the world have often much ado to compofe an union to both their fatisfactions.

Dorantes. You are in the wrong, madam, to reprefent to yourfelf fo many difficulties in this affair; and the experience you have had is no rule for others.

Dorimene. In fhort, I always abide by this. The expences you put yourfelf to for me, gives me uneafinefs for two reafons; one is, they engage me more than I could wifh; and the other is, I am fure, no offence to you, that you cannot do this, but you muft incommode yourfelf, and I would not have you do that.

Dorantes. Thefe are trifles, madam, and it is not by that——

Dorimene. I know what I fay; and, amongft other things, the diamond you forced me to take, is of a value——

Dorantes. Pray, madam, fet not fuch a value upon a thing my love thinks unworthy of you: and permit ——But here comes the mafter of the houfe.

S C E N E XIX.

MR. JORDAIN, DORIMENE, DORANTES.

MR. JORDAIN, after having made two bows, finding himfelf too near Dorimene.

A LITTLE farther, madam.
    Dorimene. How?
Mr. Jordain. One ftep, if you pleafe.
Dorimene. What then?
Mr. Jordain. Fall back a little for the third.
Dorantes. Mr. Jordain, madam, knows the world.
Mr. Jordain. Madam, I efteem it the greateft ho-

nour to be so fortunate, to be so happy, to have the felicity that you should have the goodness, to grant me the favour, to do me the honour, to honour me with the favour of your presence; and had I also the merit to merit a merit like yours, and that heaven—envious of my good—had granted me—the advantage of being worthy—of—

Dorantes. Enough, Mr. Jordain, my lady hates too many compliments, and she is very well acquainted with your understanding. [aside to Dorimene.] This is a foolish cit, as you may see by his whole behaviour.

Dorimene aside to Dorantes.] It is not very difficult to perceive that.

Dorantes. Madam, this gentleman is one of my sincere friends.

Mr. Jordain. You do me too much honour.

Dorantes. A very polite man.

Dorimene. I greatly esteem him.

Mr. Jordain. I have done nothing yet, madam, to merit this favour.

Dorantes aside to Mr. Jordain.] Take good care you do not mention the diamond ring you gave her.

Mr. Jordain aside to Dorantes.] May not I ask her only how she likes it?

Dorantes aside to Mr. Jordain.] How! take special care you do not. It would be very low and ill-bred of you; and to act like a man of gallantry, you should make as if it were not you who made the present. [aloud.] Mr. Jordain, madam, says that he is in raptures to see you at his house.

Dorimene. He does me a great deal of honour.

Mr. Jordain aside to Dorantes.] I am very much obliged to you, Sir, for speaking to her in that manner on my account.

Dorantes afide to Mr. Jordain.] I have had much a-do to prevail on her to come hither.

Mr. Jordain afide to Dorantes.] I do not know how to thank you enough for it.

Dorantes. He fays, madam, that he thinks you the moft charming perfon in the world.

Dorimene. I am very much obliged to him.

Mr. Jordain. Madam, it is I who am fo to you, and——

Dorantes. Let us think of fitting down to table.

SCENE XX.

MRS. JORDAIN, DORIMENE, DO-RANTES, FOOTMAN.

FOOTMAN to Mr. Jordain.

SIR, every thing is ready.
    Dorantes. Come then, let us fit down to table; and order the muficians to come in.

❖✳❖✳❖✳❖✳❖✳❖✳❖✳❖✳❖✳❖✳❖

ACT IV.   SCENE I.

DORIMENE, MR. JORDAIN, DORANTES, THREE MUSICIANS, FOOTMEN.

DORIMENE.

THIS is a fumptuous entertainment indeed, Do-rantes.

Mr. Jordain. You are pleafed to banter, madam, I wifh it were more worthy of your acceptance. [Dorimene, Mr. Jordain, Dorantes, and three muficians fit down at the table.]

Dorantes. Mr. Jordain, madam, is perfectly right in what he fays, and he obliges me in paying you, after fo genteel a manner, the honours of his houfe. I agree with him that the entertainment is not worthy of you. As it was myfelf that ordered it, and I am not fo clear-fighted in thefe affairs, as certain of our friends, you have here no very artful feaft; and you will find incongruities of good cheer in it, fome barbarifms of good tafte. Had our friend Damis lent his affiftance, every thing had been done by rule; elegance and erudition would have run through the whole, and he would not have failed exaggerating all the parts of the entertainment he gave you, and force you to own his great genius in the fcience of good eating; he would have told you of bread de Rive, with the golden kiffing-cruft, raifed too all round with a cruft that crumples tenderly in your teeth; of wine with a velvet fap, armed with a tartnefs not too poignant; of a breaft of mutton ftuffed with parfley; of a loin of veal thus long, white, delicate, and taftes like almond-pafte; partridges of a fuper-excellent flavour; and then by way of farce or entertainment, of a foup with gelly broth, fortified with a young plump turkey-pout, garnifhed with pigeons, and fmothered with onions and fuccory. But for my part, I confefs to you my ignorance; and as Mr. Jordain has juftly obferved, I wifh the repaft were more worthy of your acceptance.

Dorimene. I make no other anfwer to this compliment than eating as I do.

Mr. Jordain. Ah! what pretty hands are there!

Dorimene. The hands are fo fo, Mr. Jordain; but you mean to fpeak of the diamond, which is very fine.

Mr. Jordain. I, madam? I would not mention it

'for the world, it would be quite ill-bred. The diamond
is a mere trifle.

Dorimene. You eat very little, Mr. Jordain.

Mr. Jordain. You have too much goodnefs——

Dorantes having made figns to Mr. Jordain.] Come,
give fome wine to Mr. Jordain, and to thofe gentlemen,
who will favour us with a fong.

Dorimene. Mufic is an excellent feafoner to good
cheer. I muft own I was never more elegantly treated.

Mr. Jordain. Madam it is not——

Dorantes. Mr. Jordain, let us liften to thefe gentlemen, their mufic will be better than any thing we can
poffibly fay.

Firft and Second MUSICIAN together, each having a
glafs in his hand.

Put it round, my dear Phillis, invert the bright glafs;
 Oh what charms to the cryftal thofe fingers impart!
You and Bacchus combin'd, all refiftance furpafs,
 And with paffion redoubled have ravifh'd my heart.
  'Twixt him, you, and me, my charmer, my fair,
   Eternal affection let's fwear.

At the touch of thofe lips how he fparkles more bright!
 And his touch in return, thofe lips does embellifh:
I cou'd quaff 'em all day, and drink bumpers all night.'
 What longing each gives me, what gufto, what relifh!
  'Twixt him, you, and me, my charmer, my fair,
   Eternal affection let's fwear.

Second and Third MUSICIAN together.

Since time flies so nimbly away,
  Come drink, my dear boys, drink about;
  Let's husband him well while we may,
For life may be gone before the mug's out.
  When Charon has got us aboard,
  Our drinking and wooing are past;
  We ne'er to lose time can afford,
For drinking's a trade not always to last.
  Let your puzzling rogues in the schools,
  Dispute of the Bonum of man;
  Philosophers dry are but fools,
The secret is this, drink, drink off your can.
  When Charon has got us aboard,
  Our drinking and wooing are past,
  We ne'er to lose time can afford,
For drinking's a trade not always to last.

All three together.

Why hoh there! some wine, boys! come fill the glass,
    fill,
Round and round let it go, till we bid it stand still.

Dorimene. Vastly well sung, and the words are excellent.

Mr. Jordain. I see something here though, madam,
more excellent.

Dorimene. Hey! Mr. Jordain is more gallant than
I thought he was.

Dorantes. How, madam! who do you take Mr. Jordain for?

Mr. Jordain. I wifh fhe would take me for what I could wifh to ftile myfelf.

Dorimene. Again?

Dorantes to Dorimene.] You do not know him.

Mr. Jordain. She fhall know me whenever fhe pleafes.

Dorimene. Oh! Too much.

Dorantes. He is one who has a repartee always ready. But you do not fee, madam, that Mr. Jordain eats all the pieces you have touched.

Dorimene. I am really very much charmed with Mr. Jordain.

Mr. Jordain. If I could charm your heart I fhould be——

SCENE II.

MRS. JORDAIN, MR. JORDAIN, DORIMENE, DORANTES, MUSICIANS, FOOTMEN.

MRS. JORDAIN.

HEY-DAY! why here is a jolly company of you, and I plainly fee mine was not expected. It was for this pretty affair then, Mr. Hufband of mine, that you were in fuch a violent hurry to fend me to dine with my fifter; I juft now found open houfe below, and here I find a dinner fit for a wedding. This is the way you fpend your money, and thus it is you feaft the ladies when I am from home, with your balls and your concerts; very fine doings, truly!

Dorantes. What do you mean, Madam Jordain? I dare fay you are not in your right fenfes, to fay that your hufband fpends his money, and that it is he who entertains my lady? Know, pray, that it is I do it, that

he only lends me his houfe, and that you ought to confider a little better what you fay.

Mr. Jordain. Yes, Mrs. Impertinence, his lordfhip
gives this entertainment to her ladyfhip, who is a perfon of quality. He does me the honour to borrow
my houfe, and is pleafed to admit me as one of his
guefts.

Mrs. Jordain. It is all ftuff this. I know what I
know.

Dorantes. Mrs. Jordain, pray make ufe of your fpectacles.

Mrs. Jordain. I have no need of fpectacles, Sir, I
am clear-fighted enough; I have fmelt things out a
great while ago, I am no afs. It is bafe in you, who
are a great lord, to make fuch an ideot, as you do, of
my hufband. And you, madam, who are a great lady, it is neither handfome, nor honeft in you, to fow
diffenfion in a family, and to encourage my hufband
to make love to you.

Dorimene. What can be the meaning of all this?
Did you mean to make a jeft of me, Dorantes, by
bringing me here to be expofed to the filly vifions of
this raving woman?

Dorantes following Dorimene who goes out.] Madam, why, madam, where are you running?

Mr. Jordain. Madam———My lord, make my excufes to her, and perfuade her to return, if poffible.

SCENE III.

MRS. JORDAIN AND MR. JORDAIN, FOOT-
MEN

MR. JORDAIN.

YOU see what a fine piece of work you have made, Mrs. Impertinence; you come and affront me in the face of the world, and drive people of quality away from my houfe.

Mrs. Jordain. I value not their quality.

Mr. Jordain. I do not know what hinders me, you gipfey, from breaking your head with the fragments of the feaft you came to difturb.

[Footmen take away the table.

Mrs. Jordain going.] I laugh at all this. I defend my own rights, and I am fure of having all the married women on my fide.

Mr. Jordain. You do well to leave me, elfe I——

SCENE IV.

MR. JORDAIN alone.

WHAT a pity it is that fhe came here at this moft unlucky time! I was in the humour of faying the prettieft things in the world, and never did I find myfelf fo witty   But who the devil is this coming?

SCENE V.

MR. JORDAIN, COVIEL difguifed.

COVIEL.

GOod-morrow, Sir; I do not know whether I have
the honour to be known to you.

Mr. Jordain. Indeed, Sir, I cannot fay that I do
know you.

Coviel. Very probable; but I remember you fince
you were not thus tall.

Mr. Jordain. Me?

Coviel. Yes, you: you were one of the fweeteft
children in the world; and all the ladies ufed to take
you in their arms to kifs you.

Mr. Jordain. To kifs me?

Coviel. Yes, I was an intimate friend of the worthy gentleman your father.

Mr. Jordain. Of the worthy gentleman my father?

Coviel. Yes. He was a worthy gentleman.

Mr. Jordain. What do you fay?

Coviel. I fay that he was a worthy gentleman.

Mr. Jordain. My father?

Coviel. Yes.

Mr. Jordain. And you knew him then?

Coviel. Indeed I did.

Mr. Jordain. And did you know him for a gentleman?

Coviel. Moft certainly.

Mr. Jordain. Well, this is an odd world, and it is
not to be wondered at.

Coviel. How?

Mr. Jordain. Why, there are fome ridiculous people, who would infift that he was a tradefman.

Coviel. He a tradefman! It is a mere fcandal, he never was one. All the affair was, that being a very obliging, officious, worthy gentleman, and being a great connoiffeur in ftuffs, he ufed to pick them up every where, have them carried to his houfe, and gave them to his friends for money. A tradefman indeed!

Mr. Jordain. I am very glad of your acquaintance, that you may bear witnefs that my father was a gentleman.

Coviel. I will fwear that he was a gentleman.

Mr. Jordain. You will very much oblige me. But what bufinefs brings you to me?

Coviel. Since my acquaintance with the late gentleman your father, honeft gentleman, as I was telling you, I have made a tour round the globe.

Mr. Jordain. Round the globe?

Coviel. Yes.

Mr. Jordain. I fancy it is a huge way off, that fame country.

Coviel. Moft certainly. It is but four days fince I returned from thefe tedious travels of mine: and becaufe I have an intereft in every thing that concerns you, I come to tell you the beft news you can poffibly receive.

Mr. Jordain. And pray, what is that?

Coviel. You know that the fon of the great Turk is juft arrived?

Mr. Jordain. I? No.

Coviel. How? He has a moft magnificent train: all the world goes to fee him; and he has been received will all the honours due to a perfon of his importance.

Mr. Jordain. In troth, I did not know that.

Coviel. But what will give you the greateft pleafure is, that he is in love with your daughter.

Mr. Jordain. Who, the fon of the great Turk?

Coviel. Yes, and wants to be your son-in-law.

Mr. Jordain. My son-in-law? the son of the great Turk my son-in-law?

Coviel. Even so.   As I have been to see him, and perfectly understand his language, we had a long conversation together; and after some other discourse, says he to me, *Acciam croc soler, onch alla moustaph gidelum amanahem varahini oussere carbulath?*   That is to say, Have you not seen a beautiful young creature, who is the daughter of Mr. Jordain, a gentleman of Paris?

Mr. Jordain. Did the son of the great Turk say that of me?

Coviel. Yes.   When I told him, that I knew you perfectly well, and that I had seen your daughter, ah! says he to me, *Marababa sahem;* that is to say, Ah! how am I enamoured with her!

Mr. Jordain. *Maraba basahem* means, Ah! how am I enamoured with her?

Coviel. Yes.

Mr. Jordain. Marry, you did well to tell me so, for I should never have thought that *Mardbaba sahem* had meant, Ah! how am I enamoured with her!   The Turkish is an excellent language!

Coviel. More so than you imagine. Do you know very well what is the meaning of *Cacaramouchen?*

Mr. Jordain. Cacaramouchen? Indeed I do not.

Coviel. It means, my dear soul.

Mr. Jordain. Cacaramouchen means, my dear soul?

Coviel. Yes.

Mr. Jordain. Why, it is very wonderful! *Cacaramouchen,* my dear soul. Who would ever have thought it? I am perfectly confounded at it.

Coviel. In short, to finish my embassy, he comes to demand your daughter in marriage; and to have a father-in-law who should be suitable to him, he designs to make you a *Mamamouchi,* which is a certain great rank in his country.

Mr. Jordain. A *Mamamouchi?*

Coviel. Yes, a *Mamamouchi:* that is to fay, in our language, a Paladine. Now Paladine, with the antients——Paladine, I fay, there is nothing in the world more noble than this; and you will rank with the grandeft lords upon earth.

Mr. Jordain. The fon of the great Turk does me a great deal of honour, and I defire you will bring him here, that I may return him my hearty thanks.

Coviel. How? Why he is juft a coming hither.

Mr. Jordain. Is he a coming hither?

Coviel. Yes. And he brings all things along with him for the ceremony of your dignity.

Mr. Jordain. He does not want to put off any time.

Coviel. His love will fuffer no delay.

Mr. Jordain. All that perplexes me, in this cafe, is that my daughter is an obftinate huffy, who has taken into her head one Cleontes, and fhe has fworn to have him or nobody.

Coviel. She will change her opinion, when fhe fees the fon of the grand Turk; and it happens very luckily, though fomewhat unaccountable, that the fon of the grand Turk very much refembles this Cleontes. I juft now came from him, they fhewed him me; and the love fhe bears for one, may eafily pafs to the other, and——But here comes the prince.

SCENE VI.

CLEONTES like a Turk, three pages bearing up the train of Cleontes, Mr. JORDAIN, COVIEL.

CLEONTES.

AMBOUSAHIM oqui boraf, Iordina, falamalequi.
Coviel to Mr. Jordain.] That is to fay, Mr. Jordain, may your heart be all the year like a rofe-bufh in bloffom. It is a polite way of faluting perfons in his country.

Mr. Jordain. I am his Turkifh highnefs's moft humble fervant.

Coviel. *Carigar camboto ouftin moraf.*

Cleontes. *Ouftin yoc catamalequi bafum bafe alla moran.*

Coviel. He fays, may heaven give you the ftrength of lions, and the prudence of ferpents.

Mr. Jordain. His Turkifh highnefs does me too much honour; and I wifh him all manner of profperity.

Coviel. *Offa binamin fadoc babally oracaf ouram.*

Cleontes. *Bel-men.*

Coviel. He fays that you fhould go with him immediately to prepare yourfelf for the ceremony, in order afterwards to fee your daughter, and to conclude the marriage.

Mr. Jordain. So many things in two words?

Coviel. Yes, it is the nature of the language, to fay a great deal in few words. Follow him quickly.

SCENE VII.

COVIEL alone.

HA, ha, ha! I'faith, this is very comical. What a dupe! Had he ſtudied his part, he could not have played it better. O, hoh!

SCENE VIII.

DORANTES, COVIEL.

COVIEL.

OH, Sir, I beſeech you lend us a helping-hand in an affair which is in agitation.

Dorantes. Ah! ah! Coviel, who could have known thee in this dreſs?

Coviel. You ſee. Ha, ha!

Dorontes. What do you laugh at?

Coviel. At ſomething, Sir, that well deſerves it.

Dorantes. What is it?

Coviel. I could give you a good many times, Sir, to gueſs the ſtratagem we are making uſe of with Mr. Jordain, to get his daughter for my maſter.

Dorantes. I do not at all gueſs the ſtratagem, but I dare ſay it will have the deſired effect, ſince you un‑dertake it.

Coviel. I know, Sir, you are not unacquainted with the fool we have to deal with.

Dorantes. Tell me what it is.

Coviel. Come a little this way, if you pleaſe, to make room for what I ſee a-coming. You may be ſpectator of part of the ſtory, whilſt I inform you of the reſt.

SCENE IX.

The TURKISH CEREMONY.

The MUFTI, DERVISES, TURKS aſſiſting the MUFTI, Singers and Dancers.

SIX Turks enter gravely, two and two, to the found of inſtruments. They bear three carpets, with which they dance in ſeveral figures, and then lift them up very high: the Turks ſinging, paſs under the carpets, and range themſelves on each ſide of the ſtage. The Mufti, accompanied by Derviſes, cloſe the march.

THEN the Turks ſpread the carpets on the ground, and kneel down upon them, the Mufti and the Derviſes ſtanding in the middle of them; while the Mufti invokes Mahomet in dumb contorſions and grimaces, the Turks proſtrate themſelves on the ground, ſinging *Alla*, raiſing their hands to heaven, ſinging *Alla*, and ſo continuing alternately to the end of the invocation: when they all riſe up, ſinging *Alla ekber;* then two Derviſes bring Mr. Jordain.

SCENE X.

The MUFTI, DERVISES, Turkiſh Singers and Dancers, Mr. JORDAIN cloathed like a Turk, his head ſhaved, without a turban or ſabre.

The MUFTI to Mr. Jordain:

IF you can anſwer, ſpeak,
  If not, hold your tongue.
I am Mufti,
  Who art thou?

    If you do not underſtand,
      Hold thy peace, hold thy peace.
       [Two Derviſes retire with Mr Jordain.

SCENE XI.

The MUFTI, DERVISES, TURKS ſinging and dancing.

MUFTI.

TELL me, Turks, who is this,
   An Anabaptiſt, an Anabaptiſt?
The Turks. No.
Mufti. A Zuinglian?
The Turks. No.
Mufti. A Coffite?
The Turks. No.
Mufti. An Uſſite? a Moriſt? a Froneſt?
The Turks. No, no, no.
Mufti. No, no, no. Is he a Pagan?
The Turks. No.
Mufti. A Lutheran?
The Turks. No.
Mufti. A Puritan?
The Turks. No.
Mufti. A Bramin? a Moſhan? a Zurian?
The Turks. No, no, no.
Mufti. No, no, no. A Mahometan, a Mahometan?
The Turks. Ay, there you have it.
Mufti. What do you call him?
The Turks. Jordain, Jordain.
Mufti dancing.] Jordain! Jordain!
The Turks. Jordain, Jordain.
Mufti. To Mahomet for Jordain,
   I pray night and day,
G 5

That he would make a Paladine
Of Jordain, of Jordain.
Give him a turban, and give a fabre,
With a galley and a brigantine,
To defend Paleftine.
To Mahomet for Jordain,
I pray night and day.
            [To the Turks.]
Will Jordain be a good Turk ?
The Turks. Yes, yes.
Mufti finging and dancing.] *Ha la ba, ba la chou, ba.*
The Turks. *Ha la ba, ba la chou, ba la ba ba.*

SCENE XII.

MUFTI, DERVISES, MR. JORDAIN, TURKS
finging and dancing.

THE Mufti returns with the ftate turban, which is
of an immeafurable largenefs, garnifhed with lighted
wax candles, four or five rows deep, accompanied by
two Dervifes bearing the Alcoran with conic caps,
garnifhed alfo with lighted candles.

THE two other Dervifes lead up Mr. Jordain, and
place him on his knees with his hands to the ground,
fo that his back, on which the Alcoran is placed, may
ferve for a defk to the Mufti, who makes a fecond
burlefque invocation, knitting his eyes-brows, ftriking
his hands fometimes upon the Alcoran, and toffing
over the leaves with precipitation; after which, lift-
ing up his hands, and crying with a loud voice, *Hou.*

DURING this fecond invocation, the affiftant Turks
bowing down and raifing themfelves alternately, fing
likewife, *hou, hou, hou.*

Mr. JORDAIN aside after they have taken the Alcoran off his back.

OH! I am tired and bruised almost to death.
Mufti to Mr. Jordain.] Thou wilt not be a
rogue?

The Turks. No, no, no.

Mufti. Not be a thief?

The Turks. No, no, no.

Mufti to the Turks.] Give the turban.

The Turks. Thou wilt not be a knave?

No, no, no.

Not be a thief?

No, no, no.

Give the turban.

The Turks dancing put the turban on Mr. Jordain's
head at the sound of the instruments.

Mufti giving the sabre to Mr. Jordain.] Be brave,
and be no coward,

Take the sabre.

The Turks drawing their sabres.] Be brave, be no
coward,

Take the sabre.

The Turks dancing strike Mr. Jordain several times
with their sabres, to music.

Mufti. Give, give
The bastonade.

The Turks. Give, give
The bastonade.

The Turks dancing give Mr. Jordain several strokes as
before.

Mufti. Be not ashamed,
This is the last affront.

The Turks. Be not ashamed,
This is the last affront.

THE Mufti begins a third invocation. The Der-

G 6

vifes fupport him with great refpect, after which the Turks finging and dancing round the Mufti, retire with him, and lead off Mr. Jordain.

ACT V. SCENE I.

MRS. JORDAIN, MR. JORDAIN.

MRS. JORDAIN,

WHAT is the matter now? Mercy upon us! What have we got here! What a figure! What! are you turned mountebank? Speak therefore, what does this mean? Who has bundled you up thus?

Mr. Jordain. What impertinence, to fpeak thus to a *Mamamouchi!*

Mrs. Jordain. A what?

Mr. Jordain. Yes, you muft fhew me refpect now, I am juft made a *Mamamouchi.*

Mrs. Jordain. What do you mean by a *Mamamouchi?*

Mr. Jordain. *Mamamouchi* I tell you. I am a *Mamamouchi.*

Mrs. Jordain. What a beaft is that?

Mr. Jordain. *Mamamouchi,* in our language, fignifies a *Paladine.*

Mrs. Jordain. A *Baladin?* Are you of an age to be a morrice-dancer?

Mr. Jordain. What a blockhead! I fay *Paladine;* it is a dignity, which has lately been conferred on me with great ceremony.

Mrs. Jordain. What ceremony pray?

Mr. Jordain. *Mahameta per Jordina.*

Mrs. Jordain. What does that mean?

Mr. Jordain. *Jordina,* that is to fay, Jordain.

Mrs. Jordain. Well, and what of Jordain?

Mr. Jordain. *Voler far un Paladina de Jordina.*

Mrs. Jordain. What?

Mr. Jordian. *Dar turbanta con galera.*

Mrs. Jordain. What is the meaning of that?

Mr. Jordain. *Per deffender Paleſtina.*

Mrs. Jordain. What would you be at?

Mr. Jordain. *Dara, dara, baſtonnara.*

Mrs. Jordain. What is this fame jargon?

Mr. Jordain. *Non tener honta, queſta ſtar l'ultima affronta.*

Mrs. Jordain. What in the name of wonder, can all this be?

Mr. Jordain finging and dancing.] *Hou la ba, ba li chou, ba la ba, ba la da.* [Falls down to the ground.

Mrs. Jordain. Mercy defend us! My hufband is turned fool.

Mr. Jordain getting up and walking off.] Peace, infolence, and learn the refpect due to Mr. *Mamamouchi.*

Mrs. Jordain alone.] How could he lofe his fenfes? I muft run and prevent his going out to expofe myfelf. [Seeing Dorimene and Dorantes.] So, fo, here come the reft of our gang. I dare fwear I fhall never fee an end of my vexation.

SCENE II.

DORANTES, DORIMENE.

DORANTES.

YES, madam, I will divert you with the merrieft thing that can be feen; and I do not believe it is poffible, in the whole world, to find fuch another mafter-piece of folly as our cit here. And befides,

madam, we muſt endeavour to aſſiſt Cleontes in his a-
mour, by helping him to carry on his farce.   He is a
very pretty gentleman, and deſerves every thing we
can do for him.

Dorimene. I have a very great value for him, and
really think he deſerves a good fortune.

Dorantes. Beſides, we have here, madam, an entertainment that will ſuit us, and which we ought not
to loſe; and I muſt, by al! means, ſee whether my fancy will ſucceed.

Dorimene. I ſaw there magnificent preparations,
and theſe are things, Dorantes, I can no longer ſuffer.
Yes, I am reſolved to put a ſtop, at laſt, to your pro-
fuſions; and to cut ſhort the enormous expences you
are at on my account, I have determined to marry you
out of hand.   This is the real ſecret of the affair, and
all theſe things end, as you know, with marriage.

Dorantes. Ah! madam, is it poſſible you ſhould form
ſo delightful and generous a reſolution in my behalf?

Dorimene. I only do it to prevent you from ruin-
ing yourſelf; and without this, I ſee plainly, that before it is long you will not be worth a farthing.

Dorantes. How am I obliged to you, madam, for
the care you take to preſerve my eſtate!   Both it and
my heart are wholly at your diſpoſal.

Dorimene. I ſhall make a proper uſe of them both.
But here comes your man; he makes an admirable appearance, truly!

SCENE III.

MR. JORDAIN, DORIMENE, DORANTES.

DORANTES.

SIR, this lady and I are come to pay our homage to your new dignity, and heartily to congratulate you on the marriage you are concluding betwixt your daughter and the fon of the grand Turk.

Mr. Jordain bowing firſt in the Turkiſh manner.] Sir, I wiſh you the ſtrength of ſerpents, and the prudence of lions.

Dorimene. I was exceeding glad to be one of the firſt, Sir, who ſhould come to rejoice with you upon the high degree of glory to which you are raiſed.

Mr. Jordain. Madam, may your roſe-tree flower all the year round; I am very much obliged to you for intereſting yourſelves in the honour which have been conferred on me; and I am greatly rejoiced to ſee you returned hither, that I may make my moſt humble excuſes for the ridiculous behaviour of my wife.

Dorimene. That is nothing at all, I readily excuſe ſuch little ſtarts of paſſion; your heart ought to be precious to her, and it is not at all ſtrange the poſſeſſion of ſuch a man as you are, ſhould give her ſome alarms.

Mr. Jordain. The poſſeſſion of my heart, madam, is wholly yours.

Dorantes. You ſee, madam, that Mr. Jordain is none of thoſe people whom proſperity blinds; he ſtill remembers his friends, even in the midſt of his greatneſs.

Dorimene. It is the mark of a noble ſoul.

Dorantes. Where is his Turkiſh highneſs?   We

should be glad, as your friends, to pay our dutiful respects to him.

Mr. Jordain. There he comes, and I have sent to bring my daughter to give her hand to him.

SCENE IV.

MR. JORDAIN, DORIMENE, DORANTES, CLEONTES in a Turkish dress.

DORANTES to Cleontes.

MOST noble prince, we come to compliment your highness, as friends of the gentleman your father-in-law, and to assure you, with respect, of our most humble services.

Mr. Jordain. Where is the interpreter, to tell him who you are, and make him understand what you say; you shall see that he will answer you, and he speaks Turkish admirably. Hola there; where the duce is he gone? [to Cleontes.] *Stref, strif, strof, straf.* The gentleman is a *grande segnore, grande segnore, grande segnore;* and madam is a *granda dama, granda dama.* [seeing he cannot make himself understood.] Lack-a-day! [to Cleontes.] Sir, he be a French *Mamamouchi,* and madam a French *Mamamouchess.* I cannot speak plainer. Oh! but here comes the interpreter.

SCENE V.

MR. JORDAIN, DORIMENE, DORAN-
TES, CLEONTES in a Turkiſh
habit, COVIEL diſguiſed.

MR. JORDAIN.

WHERE do you run? We can have no converſation without you. [pointing to Cleontes.]
Inform him that the gentleman and lady are perſons
of great quality, who come to pay their compliments
to him, as friends of mine, and to aſſure him of their
ſervices. [to Dorimene and Dorantes.] Now you ſhall
hear how finely he anſwers.

Coviel. *Alabala creciam, acci boram alabamen.*

Cleontes. *Catalequi tubal ourin ſotor amalouchan.*

Mr. Jordain to Dorimene and Dorantes.] Do ye ſee?

Coviel. He ſays, he wiſhes that the rain of proſperity may at all ſeaſons water the garden of your family.

Mr. Jordain. I told you how excellently he ſpeaks
Turkiſh.

Dorantes. This is admirable.

SCENE VI.

CLEONTES, MR. JORDAIN, LUCILIA, DO-
RIMENE, DORANTES, COVIEL.

MR. JORDAIN.

COME, daughter, come near, and give his Turkiſh highneſs your hand, who does you the honour of demanding you in marriage.

Lucilia. Dear father, what means this fooliſh dreſs?
Are you going to play a part in the farce?

Mr. Jordain. No, no, it is no farce, it is a very serious affair; and the most honourable for you that possibly can be wished. [pointing to Cleontes.] This is the husband I give you.

Lucilia. Give me, father?

Mr. Jordain. Yes, you. Come, give your hand, and thank heaven for your good fortune.

Lucilia. I will not marry.

Mr. Jordain. I will make you, am I not your father?

Lucilia. I cannot consent.

Mr. Jordain. Here is a noise indeed! Come, I tell you. Your hand here.

Lucilia. No, father, I have told you before that no power on earth can oblige me to marry any other person than Cleontes; and I am determined upon all extremities rather than—— [discovering Cleontes.] It is true that you are my father; I owe you absolute obedience; and you have an undoubted right to dispose of me according to your pleasure.

Mr. Jordain. Hah! I am charmed to see you return so readily to your duty; and it is a pleasure to me to have so obedient a daughter.

SCENE THE LAST.

CLEONTES, MRS. JORDAIN, MR. JORDAIN, LUCILIA, DORIMENE, DORANTES, COVIEL.

MRS. JORDAIN.

WHAT is the matter now, husband? They tell me you design to marry your daughter to a mountebank.

Mr. Jordain. Peace, impertinence, you are always

coming to mix your extravagances with every thing; there is no poffibility of teaching you reafon.

Mrs. Jordain. It is you whom there is no teaching to be wife, who are perpetually running from folly to folly. What is your defign? What would you do with this croud of people?

Mr. Jordain. I am going to marry my daughter to the fon of the grand Turk.

Mrs. Jordain. To the fon of the grand Turk?

Mr. Jordain. Yes, [pointing to Coviel.] Make your compliments to him by the interpreter there.

Mrs. Jordain. I have nothing to do with the interpreter; and I fhall tell him plainly to his face, that he fhall have none of my daughter.

Mr Jordain. I beg you would hold that foolifh tongue of yours.

Dorantes. What, Mrs. Jordain, do you oppofe fuch an honour as this? Do you refufe his Turkifh highnefs for a fon-in-law?

Mrs. Jordain. Pray, good Sir, meddle you with your own affairs.

Dorimene. It is a great honour, it is by no means to be rejected.

Mrs. Jordain. Madam, I beg you would not trouble yourfelf about what no ways concerns you.

Dorantes. It is our friendfhip that makes us intereft ourfelves in what is of advantage to you.

Mrs. Jordain. I fhall eafily excufe your friendfhip.

Dorantes. Your daughter is all obedience to her father's pleafure.

Mrs. Jordain. My daughter confent to marry a Turk?

Dorantes. Certainly.

Mrs. Jordain. Can fhe forget Cleontes?

Dorantes. What would one not do to be a princefs?

Mrs. Jordain. I would ſtrangle her with my own hands, had ſhe done ſuch a thing as this.

Mr. Jordain. What a babbling is here! I tell you this marriage ſhall be conſummated.

Mrs. Jordain. And I ſay it ſhall not.

Mr. Jordain. What a noiſe is here!

Lucilia. Mother!

Mrs. Jordain. Go, you are a pitiful huſſy.

Mr. Jordain to Mrs. Jordain.] What! are you angry with her for being obedient to me?

Mrs. Jordain. Yes, ſhe ought to obey me as well as you.

Coviel to Mrs. Jordain.] Madam.

Mrs. Jordain. What would you ſay to me, you?

Coviel. One word.

Mrs. Jordain. I have nothing to do with you nor your word.

Coviel to Mr. Jordain.] Sir, would ſhe hear me but one word in private, I will promiſe you to make her conſent to your pleaſure.

Mrs. Jordain. I will not conſent to it.

Coviel. Only hear me.

Mrs. Jordain. No.

Mr. Jordain to Mrs. Jordain.] Give him the hearing.

Mrs. Jordain. No, I will not hear him.

Mr. Jordain. He will tell you——

Mrs. Jordain. He ſhall tell me nothing.

Mr. Jordain. Do but ſee the great obſtinacy of the woman! Can it do you any harm to hear him?

Coviel. Only hear me; you may do your pleaſure afterwards.

Mrs. Jordain. Well, what?

Coviel aſide to Mrs. Jordain.] We have made ſigns to you, madam, this hour. Do not you ſee plainly that all this is done purely to humour your huſband's ftly whom we have impofed upon under this difguife? and that it is Cleontes himfelf who is the fon of the great Turk?

Mrs. Jordain afide to Coviel.] Oh, hoh!

Coviel afide to Mrs. Jordain.] And that it is me, Coviel, who am the interpreter?

Mrs. Jordain afide to Coviel.] Hoh! in that cafe, I give my confent.

Coviel afide to Mrs. Jordain.] Do not feem to know any thing of the matter.

Mrs. Jordain aloud.] Yes, it is all done, I confent to the marriage.

Mr. Jordain. Ay, all the world fubmits to reafon. [to Mrs. Jordain.] You would not hear him! I knew he would explain to you what the fon of the great Turk is.

Mrs. Jordain. Yes, yes, he has explained it to me fufficiently, and I am fatisfied with it.   Send for a notary.

Dorantes. That is well faid. And, Mrs. Jordain, that you may be perfectly contented, and that you fhould this day quit all jealoufy which you may have entertained of the gentleman your hufband, my lady and I fhall make ufe of the fame notary for our marriage.

Mrs. Jordain. With all my heart.

Mr. Jordain afide to Dorantes.] It is to make her believe.

Dorantes afide to Mr. Jordain.] We muft by all means amufe her a little with this pretenfe.

Mr. Jordain. Good, good. [aloud.] Let fomebody go immediately for the notary.

Dorantes. While he is forming the contract, let us divert his highnefs with the entertainment we have made for him.

Mr. Jordain. Well thought on: come, let us take our places.

Mrs. Jordain. But can we not find a match for poor Nicola too?

Mr. Jordain. I will give her to the interpreter; and my wife to any body that chuses her.

Coviel. I am very much obliged to you, Sir. [aside.] Were there a greater fool upon earth than this, I should certainly go to Rome and inform the Pope of it.

T H E   E N D.

THE

MPERTINENTS.

A

COMEDY.

The IMPERTINENTS, *a Comedy of Three Acts, performed at Vaux in August* 1661, *and at Paris at
the Theatre of the Palace-Royal the* 4th *of Novem-
ber the same Year.*

THE theatre as yet refounded with the just applause
which was given to the SCHOOL for HUS-
BANDS, when the IMPERTINENTS was performed at
Vaux, in the house of M. Fouquet, Superintendant
of the Finances, before the king and court.   Paul Pe-
lisson, famous for the delicacy of his wit, but much
more so for his inviolable attachment to the person of
M. Fouquet, even in his misfortunes composed the
Prologue to it in praise of the king: the scene of the
Hunter, the hint of which the king gave Moliere, was
afterwards added when it was acted at St. Germains.
This species of comedy is almost void of all plot; the
scenes having no necessary connection with one another, you may change the order of them, leave out
some, and substitute others without injuring the work;
but the main point was to keep up the attention of the
spectator by the variety of characters, the justness of
the portraits, and the continued elegance of the style;
it was the assemblage of these exquisite beauties, together with this image, or rather reality itself of the
embarrassments and importunities of a court, which
made the Impertinents meet with so much success.

VOL. V.   H

ACTORS.

DAMIS, guardian of Orphifa.
ORPHISA.
ERASTUS, in love with Orphifa.

ALCIDORUS.
LYSANDER.
ALCANDER.
ALCIPPUS.
ORANTE.
CLIMENE.
DORANTES.
CARITIDES.
ORMIN.
PHILINTES.

} Impertinents.

MONTAIGN, fervant of Eraftus.
L'ESPINE, fervant of Damis.
LA RIVIERE, and two other fervants of Eraftus.

SCENE, PARIS.

THE

IMPERTINENTS.

ACT I. SCENE I.

ERASTUS, MONTAIGN.

ERASTUS.

KIND heaven, under what planet am I born, that I muſt be continually plagued with impertinents? Wherever I go, fortune throws them in my way, and every day I ſee ſome new ſpecies of them; but nothing can come up to this day's impertinent. In ſhort, I deſpaired of being free from him, and a thouſand times I curſed the innocent fancy, which I took at dinner, of going to a play to amuſe myſelf; I was ſeverely puniſhed for my ſins; I will give thee an account of it, for my paſſion riſes whenever it comes into my head. I went upon the ſtage with an intention to attend to the piece, which I had heard a great deal in praiſe of: the actors began, and all the people were ſilent, when a man with a bluſtering air, full of extravagance, with huge pantaloons, bruſhes in, crying, Soho there! a chair immediately; and with his intolerable noiſe diſturbed the company in one of the moſt beautiful paſſages of the piece. Heaven defend us! ſays I, will our Frenchmen, who are corrected so often, never learn to behave like sensible men? Must we expose our folly in a public theatre, and by the noise of fools confirm what is said every where? While this reflection made me shrug up my shoulders, the actors seemed desirous to go on with their parts, but the fellow made a new disturbance in seating himself, and though he might have sat a-greeably on either side, he made large strides across the stage, placed his chair in the middle of the front, where with his brawny back he intercepted the actors from three fourths of the pit. They set up a noise which would have made any other person ashamed, but he did not mind it in the least, and would have re-mained in the same position, had he not discovered me. Ha! marquis, cried he, placing himself near me, how dost thou do? give me leave to embrace thee. It put me to the blush, that people should see I was acquainted with such a hair-brained fellow; though I know very little of him: but it will be seen in those people who will be very great with you from nothing, whose kisses you must bear as you tender your happi-ness, and who treat you with so much familiarity, as e-ven to *thee* and *thou* you. He directly asked a hun-dred trifling questions, raising his voice above the actors. Every body present was cursing him, and I, by way of putting an end to his conversation, told him I would be glad to hear the play. Thou hast not seen this before, marquis, heh! Rat me, if I do not think it very droll, and I am no fool in these things; I know by what rules a work is to be finished, and Corneille reads every thing that he does to me. Upon this he gave me a short account of the whole piece, telling me scene by scene, what was to be be done next, and e-ven the verses he could say by heart he repeated a-loud to me in the presence of the actors. It was to no purpofe for me to refift, he pufhed his point, and towards the end got up long before the time; for thefe fine fellows, to act genteelly, take great care above all things not to hear the conclufion. I thanked heaven, and reafonably thought that with the play my mifery was ended: but, as if I had come off too cheap, my gentleman joined me again; rehearfed his exploits to me, his great virtue, and talked of his good fortune and his horfes, the favour he had at court, fincerely offering me his fervice there. I returned him thanks with a genteel nod, confidering all the time attentively how I fhould retreat: he obferving me upon the move, fays, Come, let us walk, every body is gone. When we got into the ftreet, he fays, Marquis, come, let us go to the ring, you fhall fee my chariot how well contrived it is; dukes and lords have took pattern by it. I returned him thanks, and to get rid of him, faid, I had a certain entertainment to make. Hah! egad, I will make one at it, being in the number of thy friends, and difappoint the man of quality I was engaged to. I dare not invite a perfon of your condition to fuch poor cheer faid I; but he replied, I am a man of no ceremony, and go only to have a little talk with thee; I declare I am quite tired of great entertainments. I told him it would be wrong to difappoint the company. Thou art miftaken, marquis, we all underftand each other, and I prefer an entertainment with thee. I ftruggled within myfelf, was confufed and melancholy at the unhappy fuccefs my excufes had, and was at a lofs where to betake myfelf to get free of a trouble that tormented me; when an elegant chariot, loaded before and behind with footmen, ftopped before us, from whence fprings a young fellow dreffed moft genteelly; he and my impertinent meeting to embrace, amazed the paffengers by their violent encounters, in the midft of which I flipped a-way without faying a word. I had long groaned under the torture, and cu'rfed the impertinent, whofe obftinate fondnefs prevented me from making my appointment good here.

Montaign. Ah, Sir, men would be too happy here below, if the pleafures of this life were not mixed with vexations; we cannot have every thing as we would wifh it; it is the will of heaven that we fhould have our impertinents here.

Eraftus. But the worft of all my impertinents is. Damis, the guardian of the lady I adore, who difappoints all the hopes fhe favours me with in my addreffes, and notwithftanding her kindnefs, prevents me from feeing her. It was in this walk Orphifa was to be, I am afraid it is paft the hour appointed.

Montaign. An appointed hour is not always confined to the limits of an inftant, it has generally fome latitude.

Eraftus. That is true; but I tremble, and the excefs of my paffion makes a crime even of nothing towards her I love.

Montaign. If this perfect love, which you fo well teftify, makes a fault of nothing, towards her you love; in return, the juft paffion fhe entertains for you, makes nothing of all your faults.

Eraftus. But doft thou really believe fhe loves me?

Montaign. What! do you ftill doubt of a confirmed love?

Eraftus. How can a heart enflamed with love be fatisfied in fuch a cafe? It is afraid of flattering itfelf, and in the midft of its various cares, it leaft believes what it wifhes moft for. But let us go in fearch of the dear creature.

Montaign. Sir, your band gapes before.

Eraftus. It is no matter.

Montaign. Pray, let me put it right.

Eraftus. Pho! you ftrangle me; fool, let it be as it is.

Montaign. Let me comb you a little——

Eraftus. Thou haft almoft took off one of my ears with a tooth of the comb. Was ever any body fo ftupid!

Montaign. Your pantaloons——

Eraftus. Let me alone, you are too exact.

Montaign. They are all rumpled.

Eraftus. They fhall be fo.

Montaign. For goodnefs fake, allow me to brufh your hat, it is all dufty.

Eraftus. Brufh it then, fince I muft bear all this.

Montaign. Do you chufe to wear it cocked, as it is?

Eraftus. S'death! be quick.

Montaign. It would be fhameful——

Eraftus having waited fome time.] It is enough.

Montaign. Have a little patience.

Eraftus. Do you intend to keep the hat for ever?

Montaign. It is done.

Eraftus. Then give it me.

Montaign letting the hat fall.]   Hey!

Eraftus. There, it is down! A plague take thee, I am finely affifted.

Montaign. Let me with a rub or two take off——

Eraftus. I will not have it done. A duce take all troublefome fervants who fatigue their mafters, and do nothing but difpleafe by mere affectation of being ufeful.

H. 4

SCENE II.

ORPHISA, ALCIDORE, ERASTUS,
MONTAIGN.

ERASTUS.

IS not this Orphisa who comes? Yes, it is she. Where is she gone so quick, and who is he that hands her? [He salutes her as she passes by, and she turns her head from him.

SCENE III.

ERASTUS, MONTAIGN.

ERASTUS.

HEAVENS! am I awake? Did she really pass me, pretending not to know me? What can I think? What say you? Speak, if you will.

Montaign. Sir, I say nothing, for fear of being thought impertinent.

Eraſtus. And to say nothing to me, in the extremity of this cruel torture, is really being so. Make some answer to my oppreſſed mind. What am I to imagine? Speak, give me your opinion of it.

Montaign. Sir, I shall be silent, and do not desire to affect being useful.

Eraſtus. Plague on the impertinent puppy! Go follow them; and do not quit them, till you see what becomes of them.

Montaign coming back.] Muſt I follow them at a distance?

Eraſtus. Certainly.

Montaign coming back.] Without being perceived by them, or appearing as if I were sent after them?

Eraſtus. No, you will do better to tell them, that you follow them by my deſire.

Montaign coming back.] Shall I find you here, when I return?

Eraſtus. Heaven confound thee! I dare ſay there never was ſuch an impertinent blockhead.

SCENE IV.

ERASTUS alone.

OH! what miſery am I in! it had been happy for me, had I been diſappointed of this fatal appointment. Inſtead of finding every thing propitious to me, according to my expectation, I have ſeen what ſtabs me to the heart.

SCENE V.

LYSANDER, ERASTUS.

LYSANDER.

MY dear marquis, I knew it was thee, even at this diſtance, under theſe trees, and made up to thee directly. I muſt ſing to thee, as one of my friends, a certain air of a little courant that I have made, which all the people at court, who have any ſkill, are very fond of; and to which more than twenty have already made verſes. I have fortune, birth, and a tolerable good employment, and make a figure in France, conſiderable enough; but I would not, for all I am worth, but have made that air, which I am go-

ing to shew thee: fal, lal, hem, hem; pr'ythee mind
it.   [He sings his courant.] Is it not very pretty?

Erastus. Oh!

Lysander. This close is pretty. [He sings the close
over again four or five times successively.] Now what
is your opinion of it?

Erastus. Very pretty, indeed.

Lysander. The steps I have made to it are not less
agreeable; and above all, the figure has a surprising
grace. [He sings, talks, and dances all together.] Stay,
the man crosses thus: then the woman crosses again:
together, then they quit, and the woman comes there:
dost thou see this pretty touch of a feint here? this
fleuret? these coupees running after the fair one? back
to back; face to face pressing up close to her? What
dost thou think of it, marquis?

Erastus. These steps are certainly very fine.

Lysander. For my part, I despise the dancing-masters.

Erastus. I see so.

Lysander. Then the steps?

Erastus. Have nothing but what is marvellous.

Lysander. Wouldst thou have me teach them thee
out of friendship?

Erastus. Indeed, at present, I am a little perplexed
about——

Lysander. Well then, it shall be at your own time;
if I had these new words about me, we would read them
together, and see which were prettiest.

Erastus. Another time.

Lysander. Adieu.   My dearest Baptist has not seen
my courant, and I am going in quest of him.   We
have a mighty sympathy in our taste for tunes, and I
will desire him to add the parts to it.

[Exit, singing as he goes.

SCENE VI.

ERASTUS alone.

HEAVENS! muſt quality, which covers every fault, oblige us daily to endure the impertinence of a hundred fools! and make us demean ourſelves often even to the complaiſance of applauding their folly!

SCENE VII.

ERASTUS, MONTAIGN.

MONTAIGN.

SIR, Orphiſa is alone, and will be here preſently.

Eraſtus. Oh! what hurry and confuſion am I in! I have ſtill a fondneſs for this cruel beauty, and my reaſon bids me abhor her.

Montaign. Your reaſon, Sir, neither knows what it would have, nor what power a miſtreſs has over a man's mind. Though one has ever ſo juſt cauſe to be out of temper, one word from a fine woman can ſet every thing right.

Eraſtus. Alas! I own it, and the ſight of her has already ſet aſide all my reſentment.

SCENE VIII.

ORPHISA, ERASTUS, MONTAIGN.

ORPHISA.

ERASTUS, there is a ſadneſs in your countenance, can it be my preſence which occaſions

H 6

it? What does this mean? What is it that affects you, and makes you sigh at the sight of me?

Eraſtus. Cruel creature! Can you aſk me what cauſes this ſorrow? Is it not ill-natured to pretend ignorance of what you have done? He whoſe converſation induced you to paſs me in full view——

Oriphiſa laughing.] Is it that which diſturbs you?

Eraſtus. Inhuman creature, will you ſtill inſult my miſery? It ill becomes you to rally my grief, ungrateful as you are; to abuſe my paſſion, on account of the foible of which you are the cauſe.

Orphiſa. One muſt certainly laugh at you, and own that you are very fooliſh to give yourſelf ſo much uneaſineſs. I am ſo far from being pleaſed with the man you ſpeak of, that I think him an impertinent fellow, whom I was endeavouring to ſhake off; one of thoſe troubleſome fools who will not allow one to be alone any where, but come immediately with fawning compliments, to offer their hand, when it is very diſagreeable. To conceal my intention, I pretended to be going away; and he would even hand me to my coach. By this means I got rid of him, and came in again by the other gate to find you.

Eraſtus. Is your heart ſincere to me, Orphiſa? Muſt I believe this ſtory?

Orphiſa. You are a pretty gentleman indeed, to talk thus; when I juſtify myſelf againſt your trifling complaints. I am very weak too, and my fooliſh kindneſs——

Eraſtus. Ah! too ſevere beauty, be not angry, I will not complain. Being abſolutely under your command, I will implicitly believe every thing you are ſo obliging as to tell me. Deceive, if you pleaſe, an unhappy lover: I ſhall reſpect you, even to the grave. Abuſe my love, and refuſe me yours; expoſe to my ſight the triumph of my rival; yes, I will bear with every thing from thofe celeftial charms; I will die for it, but, in fhort, never will complain.

Orphifa. While fuch fentiments reign in your breaft, I fhall on my part——

SCENE IX.

ALCANDER, ORPHISA, ERASTUS, MONTAIGN.

ALCANDER.

A Word with thee, Marquis. [to Orphifa.] Madam, be fo good as forgive the indifcretion of prefuming to whifper before you.   [Orphifa goes out.

SCENE X.

ALCANDER, ERASTUS, MONTAIGN.

ALCANDER.

MARQUIS, it is with reluctance I requeft this of you; but there is a man has juft now groffly affronted me, and I fincerely wifh, not to be behindhand with him, that thou wouldeft directly carry him a challenge from me.   Thou knoweft that I would gladly ferve thee in the like cafe.

Eraftus having remained filent fome time.] I will not now act the *bravo;* yet I have been a foldier before I was a courtier; I ferved fourteen years, and think I may fairly withdraw myfelf from fuch a fcrape, with a good grace, and not be afraid that the refufal of my fword will be looked upon as cowardice. Duelling puts people in a wretched pofture; and our king is no mere painted monarch, he will be obeyed by the people of firft rank in his kingdom; and I think he acts

in this like a worthy prince. When his ſervice calls.
me I will do it chearfully: but I am not willing to.
diſpleaſe him.   I regard his order as a ſupreme law;
ſeek ſomebody elſe, and not me, to diſobey him.   I.
talk very freely to thee, marquis, and am, in any other.
affair, thy moſt obedient.   Farewel.

S C E N E XI.

E R A S T U S, M O N T A I G N.

E R A S T U S.

THE devil take all impertinents, ſay I. Where is
this dear object of my vows retired to? ·
Montaign. Really, Sir, I do not know.
Eraſtus. Go ſearch every where to find her out. You.
will ſee me in this walk..

A C T II. S C E N E I.

E R A S T U S.

LORD be thanked, I am once more freed from
theſe impertinents. I think it rains impertinents
from every quarter.   I fly from them, and meet them;
and for an additional torment, I cannot find her of
whom I am in purſuit.   The thunder and rain are
quickly over, and have not chaced away the *beau monde*.
Would heaven, among the favours it beſtows here ſo
profuſely, they had but chaced away the people that
perplex me! The ſun is now almoſt ſet, and I am ſurpriſed that my man is not yet returned.

SCENE II.

ALCIPPUS, ERASTUS.

ALCIPPUS.

GOOD-morrow, Sir.

[*Eraftus afide.*] Will my love always be diverted?

Alcippus. Marquis, comfort me for the ftrange hand I yefterday loft at piquet, with one St. Bovain, to whom I could have given fifteen, and the eldeft hand. It is a blow would make one mad, it difturbs me ever fince yefterday, and would make one wifh all gamefters at the devil; a blow moft certainly to make one hang one's felf at the market-crofs. I want but two, and the other wants a pique: I deal, he takes fix, and demands to deal over again: I feeing myfelf almoft up, would not confent to it. I go out ace of clubs, (do but admire my misfortune) the ace, king, knave, ten, and eight of hearts; and throw out, as my policy was to go for point, queen and ten of diamonds; ten and queen of fpades. To my five hearts that I went out, I took in alfo the queen, which made me exactly a quint major: but my gentleman with the ace, not without my great amazement, fpreads upon the table a fixiéme of low diamonds. I had thrown out the queen of the fame with the king, but he miffing of his pique, I recovered my fright, and reafonably thought I fhould make at leaft two poor tricks. With the feven diamonds he had four fpades; and playing the laft of them, it puzzled me cruelly, as not knowing which of my two aces to keep. I threw away the ace of hearts, as I think, with good reafon, but he had difcarded four clubs, And there was I capoted with a fix of hearts, without being able, through vexation, to speak one syllable. S'heart, do me justice for this terrible stroke: one could not have believed it had they not seen it.

Erastus. The greatest strokes of fortune are observed to be in play.

Alcippus. S'death, you shall judge whether I am wrong; and whether I complain without a cause, for here are our two games, which I have directly about me; stay, this is the hand I went out as I told you; and her——

Erastus. I understand it all by the description you give of it, and see the justice of the passion which ruffles you; but I must leave you, upon a particular affair. Farewel, comfort yourself however under your misfortune.

Alcippus. Who, I? I shall always have it next my heart: it is worse than a thunderbolt to my mind: I am resolved to shew it to all the world. [He goes a little way, and ready to turn back, calls out.] A six of hearts! Two tricks!

Erastus alone.] Turn which way one will, one sees nothing but fools! What place are we got into?

SCENE III.

ERASTUS, MONTAIGN.

ERASTUS.

HAH! How impatient have I been for your coming!

Montaign. Sir, I could not come sooner.

Erastus. But dost thou bring me any news at last?

Montaign. Indeed I do, and from the object on whom your fate depends. I have by her express commands something to tell you.

Eraftus. Speak: I am impatient to hear it.

Montaign. Do you wifh to know what it is?

Eraftus. Yes, fpeak immediately.

Montaign. Stop a little, Sir, if you pleafe; I have almoft loft my breath with running.

Eraftus. Doft thou delight in keeping me in fufpence?

Montaign. Since you are fo defirous of knowing the order I received from this charming object, I will tell you——Believe me, without bragging to you of my diligence, I went a great way to find the lady; and if——

Eraftus. Have done with thy digreffions.

Montaign. Fy! you fhould moderate a little your paffions; and Seneca——

Eraftus. Seneca's a fool, in thy mouth, fince he tells me not a word that concerns me. Give me the order immediately.

Montaign. To fatisfy your longing, your Orphifa—there is an infect got into your hair.

Eraftus. Let it ftay there.

Montaign. This fair one bids me acquaint you on her part——

Eraftus. What?

Montaign. Guefs.

Eraftus. Pr'ythee tell me, I am not in a laughing humour at prefent.

Montaign. Her order is, that you are to ftay here, affuring yourfelf, that in a little while fhe will come to you, when fhe has got rid of fome country ladies, who are a troublefome fort of animals to courtiers.

Eraftus. Let us then remain in the place that fhe was pleafed to fix upon: but as this appointment gives me here fome time, leave me to think a little. [Montaign goes out.] I have an intention of making her some verses to a tune which I know she is very fond of.

[Musing.

SCENE IV.

ORANTE, CLIMENE, ERASTUS
at a corner of the stage without being seen.

ORONTE.

EVERY body will be of the same opinion with me.

Climene. Do you think to carry it by obstinacy?

Orante. I approve of my own reasons.

Climene. I wish somebody would hear us both.

Orante seeing Erastus.] I see a man here who is no blockhead; he may be judge in our difference. [to Erastus.] Marquis, a word with you, if you please; allow us to appeal to you, to be judge in a quarrel betwixt us two, in a debate arising from our different sentiments, about what is the sign of the most perfect lover.

Erastus. It is a difficult question to decide, and you had best look for a more skilful judge.

Orante. No, these stories you tell us will have no effect: we know you very well; you are a noted wit, every body gives you that character very justly, and—

Erastus. Oh! I intreat you——

Orante. In one word, you must bestow a minute or two upon us, and be our arbitrator.

Climene to Orante.] You retain here a person who will condemn you: for in short, if what I venture to believe of him be true, the gentleman will honour my reasons with victory.

Eraftus afide.] I wifh my rafcal would invent fomething to get me off.

Orante to Climene.] For my part, I have too good
proof of his wit, to fear he fhould pronounce any thing
to my difadvantage. [to Eraftus.] In fhort, this grand
debate which is kindled betwixt us, is whether a lover
fhould be jealous or not.

Climene. Or, to explain our thoughts better,. who
fhould pleafe moft, one that is jealous, or one that is
not fo.

Orante. For my part, undoubtedly, I am for the
laft.

Climene. And I am for the former.

Orante. I think we fhould give our vote on the fide
of him who fhews moft refpect.

Climene.   And I, that if our inclinations muft appear, it fhould be in favour of him who difcovers moft
love.

Orante. Yes, but one difcovers the warmth of a lover's paffion much better by refpect, than jealoufy.

Climene. And my opinion is, that whoever has an
attachment to us, is by fo much the more loving, as he
is the more jealous.

Orante. Fy, Climene, talk not to me of thofe people for lovers, whofe love refembles hatred, and who,.
inftead of refpect and gentle addreffes, are ever troublefome; whofe minds, being always prompted by a gloomy paffion, bufy themfelves in converting our leaft actions into a crime; fubject our innocence to their blindnefs, and want an explanation from us upon the leaft
glance of an eye; who perceiving in us any fadnefs,.
immediately complain that their prefence is the caufe of
it; and when the leaft joy brightens in our eyes, fu-
fpect their rivals is the occafion of it: in fhort, who
taking privilege from the fury of their love, never fpeak

to us but with an intention to quarrel with us; they presume to forbid every body approaching us, and set themselves up for tyrants over their very conquerors. Give me the lovers who are inspired by respect, I think their submission the greatest mark of our power.

Climene. Tell me not that those persons are true lovers who feel no transports; those luke-warm gallants, whose quiet hearts reckon already upon every thing as secure in their favour; are not afraid of losing us, and through too great a confidence, suffer their love to fall asleep at every turn; have a good intelligence with their rivals, and leave them a clear stage to push their point. This sedate love raises my resentment. Love without jealousy, is loving with indifference; I would have a lover continually suspicious, to convince me of his passion; one who, by hasty transports, gives a glaring token of the esteem he has for me. One then applauds one's self for his disquiet; and if he chances to treat us rudely, the pleasure of seeing him on his knees to excuse the violence of his passion, his tears and vexation are a sufficient revenge for our anger.

Orante. If so much raving is necessary to please you, I can tell you one who will satisfy you; and I am acquainted with five or six people in Paris, who love so excessively as to go to cuffs about it.

Climene. I know some people who would suit you exactly, if you do not like jealousy: men so patient in their love, that they could see you in the arms of thirty, and be quite unconcerned.

Orante. Indeed you must declare which person's love you would prefer.

[Orphisa appears at the farther end of the stage, and sees Erastus between Orante and Climene.]

Erastus. As I must give my opinion, I will please you both, and not give sentence against what is agree-

able to either of you: I think the jealous loves moft,
and the other loves beft.

Climene. Certainly the fentence is a very judicious
one; but——

Eraftus. Allow me to leave you. After what I have
faid, I will have no more to do with it.

S C E N E V.

ORPHISA, ERASTUS.

ERASTUS perceiving Orphifa, and going up to her.

WHAT a ftay you have made, madam; I fee
plainly——
Orphifa. I beg you may not quit fuch agreeable converfation. I dare fay you could difpenfe with my abfence very well; it is wrong to blame me for ftaying.

Eraftus. And will you be angry with me without
reafon, and blame me for the trouble they have given
me? I intreat you to ftay——

Orphifa. Pray go join your company again, and let
me alone.

S C E N E VI.

ERASTUS alone.

LET me follow her, in fpite of her oppofition; I
muft clear up my innocence. Heavens! muft
impertinents of both fexes confpire to fruftrate my deareft wifhes this day?

SCENE VII.

DORANTES, ERASTUS.

DORANTES.

AH! Marquis, what a multitude of impertinents does one meet with every day, to interrupt one's pleasures! I am so angry at a very fine chace which a booby——I must tell thee the story.

Erastus. I cannot stay, for I am in quest of a particular person.

Dorantes. I'gad, I will tell it thee as we walk along. We were an agreeable select company of us, who made a party yesterday to hunt a stag; and we went on purpose into the country to lie upon the spot, that is to say, my dear, into the thickest part of the forest. As this exercise is a very great delight to me, I had a mind, that the thing might be well done, to go into the wood myself; and we all determined to bend all our efforts upon a stag, which every body told us was a full-made stag; but for my part, my judgment was, without standing to observe the marks, that he was only a stag of the second head.   We had separated our relays properly, and were breakfasting hastily, upon some new-laid eggs, when a peasant, with a long rapier, vainly mounting his breeding-mare, came to make us an aukward compliment, presenting us also, to compleat the vexation, with a great booby of a son, as great a fool as his father.   He called himself a great hunter, and desired that he might have the favour of the chace along with us. Heaven preserve every skilful person, when hunting, from a fellow that blows his horn unseasonably, from people, who, having half a score scabby beagles at their heels, cry, *my pack*, and are marvellous hunt-

ers! His requeſt being granted, and his virtues eſteemed, we were all purſuing our blinks. Within the diſtance of three bow-ſhots, all of a ſudden was cried;
Ilho! Ilho! The dogs were laid on the ſtag: I ſecond
it, and blow aloud; my ſtag unharbours, and paſſes a
pretty long plain, and my dogs after him, but ſo well
in breath that you might have covered them all with a
cloak. He made to the foreſt. We then ſlip the old
pack upon him, and I, in great haſte, take my horſe
Allezan. Pray have you ſeen him?

Eraſtus. I think not.

Dorantes. How! it is a horſe as good as he is handſome, and which I bought a few days ago of Gaveau.
I leave you to judge whether he would deceive me in
ſuch an affair as this, he that conſiders who I am; ſo
that I am quite eaſy about him; and in reality he never ſold a better horſe, nor a better made one. The
head of a barb, with a fair ſtar, the neck of a ſwan,
ſlender, and very ſtraight; no more ſhoulders than a
hare, ſhort-jointed, and that ſhews his vivacity by his
carriage; feet, i'gad, ſuch feet! double-rein'd; to ſpeak
the truth, I was the only perſon could find the way to
maſter him, and young Jack Gaveau never mounted
him without fear, though he ſet the beſt face he could
on it. His buttocks are not to be equalled for large-
neſs, and legs, mercy on me! In ſhort he is a miracle;
if you will believe me, I refuſed a hundred pieces for
him, and one of the king's horſes to boot. I mount,
therefore, and was in high pleaſure to ſee the vintagers
in rows at a great diſtance on the plain; I ſpur on, and
find myſelf in a by-thicket at the heels of the dogs, only
I and Drecar: within that our ſtag ſtood at bay for an
hour; upon this I cheer the dogs, and played the duce
and all among them. In ſhort, never was hunter in
higher glee; I imprimed him myſelf, and all things

went fwimmingly; ours joined company with a young hind; one part of my dogs divided from the other, then, marquis, as you may imagine, they all hunted timorous, and Jowler was at a lofs; he turned all of a fudden, which made my heart leap for joy; he ftruck in afrefh upon the track, and I found my horn, and cry, hark to Jowler, hark to Jowler; I traced him again with pleafure upon a mole-hill, and founded again a long while. Some of the dogs came back to me, when, as ill-luck would have it, the young hind, marquis, paffes my country bumpkin. My hair-brains, as was likely, falls a blowing his horn, and bellowing aloud, *Ilho, Ilho, Ilhoy*. My dogs all left me, and make directly to my booby; I puts on thither, and difcovered the track again in the high-road; but no fooner had I caft my eyes on the ground, than I found out the change, and was greatly mortified. In vain did I fhew him all the differences between the edge of my ftag's hoofs, and his marks; he ftill maintains to me like a blockhead of a fportfman, that it is the pack-ftag, and by this difpute he gave time to the dogs to get a great way off. I ftormed at it, and curfing the mortal heartily, I fpurs my horfe full fpeed over hill and dale, who brufhed through boughs as thick as my arm: I recovered the dogs to my firft fcent, who, to my great joy, run upon the queft of our ftag, as if they had been in full view. They imprime him afrefh; but was ever fuch a trick feen before? To tell thee the truth, marquis, it vexes me to death; our ftag being imprimed, runs by our fpark, who thinking to do the exploit of a moft laudable huntfman, with a holfter-piftol, that he had brought along with him, fhoots him directly thro' the head, and cries out to me, a great way off, I have fetched the beaft down. Good heaven! Did ever any body hear of piftols in ftag-hunting? For my part,

when I reached the ſpot, I thought it was ſo out-of-
the-way an action, that I claps both ſpurs to my horſe
in a fury, and never ſtopped gallop until I got home,
without ſpeaking ſo much as one word to the ignorant
fool.

Eraſtus. I admire your prudence, you could not
have done better; in this manner we ſhould ſhake off
all impertinents.   Farewel.

Dorantes. When you pleaſe, we will go to ſome
place where we ſhall avoid your country hunters.

Eraſtus. Very well. [alone.] I think at laſt I ſhall
loſe all patience.   Let me make all poſſible haſte to excuſe myſelf.

ACT III. SCENE I.

ERASTUS, MONTAIGN.

ERASTUS.

INDEED my diligence hath at laſt ſucceeded on
one hand: I at laſt got the dear object appeaſed:
but on the other hand, they quite tire me; my cruel
ſtars have perſecuted me in my amour with double fury.   Yes, Damis, her tutor, one of my moſt ſhocking
impertinents, oppoſes my moſt tender addreſſes afreſh;
he even has forbid me the ſight of his lovely niece, and
intends to provide her another huſband to-morrow.
But notwithſtanding this, Orphiſa deigns to grant one
favour to my love this evening; and I have prevailed
upon the fair one to allow me to wait upon her at her
own houſe privately.   Love delights in ſecret favours
above every thing; it finds a pleaſure in breaking
through oppoſition, and when forbid, the ſhorteſt con-

verfation with the dear object is an immenfe favour. It is near the hour of my appointment, I muft go; I would not chufe to be later, but rather before the time.

Montaign. Muft I follow you?

Eraftus. No, I am afraid you would difcover me to fome fufpicious perfon or other.

Montaign. But————

Eraftus I will not bave you.

Montaign. I muft obey your orders: but at a diftance, at leaft————

Eraftus. Muft I bid thee hold thy tongue twenty times over? Wilt thou never leave off this way of making thyfelf troublefome, at every turn, for an impertinent varlet?

SCENE II.

CARITIDES, ERASTUS.

CARITIDES.

SIR, it is an improper time to do myfelf the honour of waiting upon you, the morning being more feafonable for the performance of that duty: but it is not very eafy to meet with you; for you are always either afleep, or abroad; at leaft your fervants always tell me fo; and I took this opportunity to find you; it is a great happinefs too that fortune favours me with, for I had miffed of you again, if I had been two moments later.

Eraftus. Do you want any thing with me, Sir?

Caritides. Sir, I acquit myfelf of the duty I owe you: and come————excufe the boldnefs that infpires me, if————

Eraftus. Set ceremony afide, and tell me plainly what you have to fay to me.

Caritides. As the rank, the wit, the generofity, which every body extols in you————

Eraftus. Yes, I am very much extolled; go on, Sir.

Caritides. Sir, it is a very great difficulty upon a man, when he is obliged to introduce himfelf to any perfon: and one fhould always be introduced to great men, by people who fet us forth a little; whofe difcourfe being liftened to, difplays, with fome weight, what our little merit can fhew: for my part, I fhould have been glad that fomebody, who are well apprized of it, could have told you, Sir, who I am.

Eraftus. Sir, your manner of accofting me lets me know what you are.

Caritides. Yes, Sir, I am a learned man, who am delighted with your virtues; none of thofe learned men whofe name ends only in *us*; there is nothing fo common as a name after the Latin termination; they who are habited after the Greek manner, have a much better mien; and that I might have one which fhould terminate in *es*, I call myfelf Mr. Caritides.

Eraftus. Mr. Caritides be it. What have you to fay?

Caritides. Sir, I have a petition, which I will read to you, and I prefume to defire you will prefent it to the king.

Eraftus. Alas, Sir, you can prefent it better yourfelf.

Caritides. Sir, the king grants this extreme favour, it is true, but through this very excefs of his unparalleled goodnefs, fo many villainous petitions are prefented, that they ftifle the good ones; and what my hope refts upon, is, that fomebody would give mine when the king is by himfelf.

Eraſtus. Well, take your time to do it.

Caritides. Ah! Sir, the door-keepers are ſad fel-lows, they treat men of learning with a filip on the noſe, as if they were ſcoundrels; and I can get no farther than the guard-room. The ill treatment I muſt en-dure would make me retire from court for ever, had I not conceived great hope that you will be my patron with his Majeſty. Yes, your credit is a certain means——

Eraſtus. Well, I will preſent it. ·Give me it me.

Caritides. Here it is; but pleaſe to hear it read how-ever firſt.

Eraſtus. No——

Caritides. I intreat you will, Sir, that you may be acquainted with it.

A

PETITION

TO THE

KING.

May it pleaſe your Majeſty,

" YOUR moſt humble, moſt obedient, moſt faith-
" ful, and moſt learned ſubjeСt and ſervant,
" Caritides, a Frenchman by nation, a Grecian by pro-
" feſſion, having ſtudied the great and notable abuſes
" committed in the inſcriptions upon ſigns of houſes,
" ſhops, taverns, ninepin-alleys, and other places of
" Your good city of Paris; in that certain ignorant
" compoſers of the ſaid inſcriptions, do ſubvert by a
" barbarous, pernicious, and deteſtable orthography,

" all manner of fenfe and reafon, without regard to a-
" ny etymology, analogy, energy, or allegory whatfo-
" ever, to the great fhame of the republic of letters,
" and of the French nation, which is difcredited and
" difhonoured by the faid abufes and grofs faults, in
" regard to ftrangers, and notorioufly, in refpeċt to the
" Germans, curious readers and infpeċtors of the faid
" infcriptions————

Eraftus. This petition being fo long may poffibly
tire————

Caritides. Oh! Sir, every word of it is abfolutely
neceffary.
[He continues.]

" Humbly fupplicates Your Majefty, for the good-
" of Your kingdom, and honour of Your government,
" to inftitute an office of comptroller, intendant, cor-
" reċtor, revifer, and reftorer-general of the faid in-
" fcriptions; and to honour Your fupplicant with this,
" as well in confideration of his rare and eminent e-
" rudition, as of the great and fignal fervices he has
" done to the ftate, and to Your Majefty in compof-
" ing an anagram on Your faid Majefty in French, La-
" tin, Greek, Hebrew, Chaldee, Arabic————

Eraftus interrupting him.] Very well: give it me
immediately, and retire; the king fhall fee it; the thing
is as good as done.

Caritides. Oh! Sir, if you but fhew my petition, it
is enough. If the king but fees it, I am fure of my
point: for as his juftice is fo great in every thing, he
cannot refufe my demand. And now, to exalt your
name to the fkies, give me your name and firname in
writing, and I will make a poem that fhall have the

I 3

form of an acroſtic at both ends of the verſe, and in
each hemiſtich.

Eraſtus. Yes, Mr. Caritides, I will give it you to-
morrow. [Alone.] Really, ſuch learned fellows are
moſt admirable aſſes. I ſhould have laughed heartily
at his folly at another time.

SCENE III.

ORMIN, ERASTUS.

ORMIN.

I CHOSE to let that man have done with you before I ſpoke, though an affair of great conſequence
brings me here.

Eraſtus. Very well, but I muſt be gone, ſo diſpatch.

Ormin. Sir, I make no doubt but you are quite tired of the fellow who has juſt left you, he is a troubleſome mortal, a little crack-brained; I have always ſome
invention ready to get rid of him. In the Mall, at
Luxemburgh, and in the Tuilleries, he tires all the
world with his fooliſh fancies; and ſuch people as you
ſhould avoid the converſation of theſe pedantic ſcho-
lars. For my part, I am not afraid of being troubleſome, as I come to make your fortune.

Eraſtus aſide.] This is ſome whiſling alcbymiſt, one
of thoſe fellows who are not worth a ſixpence; and are
always promiſing you great riches. [Loud.] You have
hit upon that bleſſed ſtone, Sir, which of itſelf can en-
rich all the kings of the earth?

Ormin. A pretty fancy! Oh! you are quite miſta-
ken, Sir; heaven preſerve me from being one of thoſe
ſort of fools! I do not feed upon trifling viſions, I
bring you here ſolid words of a propoſal which I would
communicate by you to the king, and which I always

carry about me safe under seal. None of thofe filly pro-
jeƈts, thofe vain fancies which the fuper-intendants
have dinned in their ears; none of thofe beggarly pro-
pofals, whofe pretenfions go no farther than to talk of
twenty or thirty millions of livres; but one which, at a
moderate computation, will bring in to the king yearly
four hundred millions clear money, with eafe, without
hazard or fufpicion, and without the leaft hardfhip upon the fubjeƈt. In fhort, it is a hint of inconceivable
gain, and which at the firft word you will find to be
feafible. Yes, if I can but be encouraged by you—

Eraftus. Well, I am a little in hafte at prefent, we
fhall talk of it afterwards.

Ormin. I will difcover this important projeƈt to you,
if you will promife to keep it a profound fecret.

Eraftus. No, no, I will not be let into your fecret.

Ormin. Sir, I will freely inform you of the fecret, I
believe you too prudent to betray it——let us take care
no body overhears us— [Whifpers Eraftus] This furprifing projeƈt of which I am the inventor, is that—

Eraftus. At a greater diftance, Sir, for a particular
reafon.

Ormin. I do not need to tell you of the great profits
which the king receives annually from his fea-ports.
Now, the projeƈt, which no body has hit upon as yet,
and is an eafy matter, is that you fhould turn all the
coafts of France into famous fea-ports. This would
amount to immenfe fums; and if——

Eraftus. The projeƈt is good, and will pleafe the king
extremely. Farewel. We fhall fee you.

Ormin. At leaft ftand by me for having difcovered
the firft hint of it.

Eraftus. I will, I will.

Ormin. If you would lend me a brace of pieces,

which you might repay yourfelf, Sir, out of the profits of the invention——

Eraſtus gives two pieces of gold to Ormin.] Yes, with all my heart. [Alone.] Would to heaven I could get rid of all the impertinents in this manner! To ſee the unſeaſonableneſs of their viſits! I hope at laſt to get clear. Will not ſomebody elſe come and divert me?

SCENE IV.

PHILINTES, ERASTUS.

PHILINTES.

I HAVE heard ſtrange news juſt now, marquis.

Eraſtus. What is it?

Philintes. That a man has quarrelled with thee lately.

Eraſtus. With me?

Philintes. To diſſemble the matter ſignifies nothing; I am well informed, that you have had a challenge ſent you; and as your friend, I come to offer my ſervice to you againſt all the world.

Eraſtus. I am obliged to you; but believe me, you—

Philintes. You will not own it; but you come a-broad without ſervants: ſtay you in town, or go into the country, you ſhall go no where but I will accompany you.

Eraſtus aſide.] Plague! I ſhall go diſtracted.

Philintes. To what purpoſe can you hide it from me?

Eraſtus. I declare, marquis, they have impoſed upon you.

Philintes. It is in vain for you to deny it.

Eraftus. May I be thunder-ftruck, if I have had any quarrel——

Philintes. Do you think that I believe you?

Eraftus. Blefs me! I tell you ferioufly, that——

Philintes. Do not fuppofe me either a dupe or credulous upon this point.

Eraftus. Will you oblige me?

Philintes. No.

Eraftus. Pray leave me.

Philintes. By no means, marquis.

Eraftus. A little affair of galantry calls me this evening to a particular place——

Philintes. I will not leave you: I fhall follow you, be it to what place it will.

Eraftus. S'death! fince you will have me have a quarrel, I confent to it, to fatisfy your zeal; it fhall be with you who plague me to diftraction, and from whom I cannot by fair means difengage myfelf.

Philintes. This is not accepting a piece of fervice in a friendly manner: but as I do you fo ill an office, farewel. Determine all your affairs without me.

Eraftus. When you leave me, you will be my friend. [alone.] But what misfortunes perfecute me! They will have made me flip the appointed hour.

SCENE V.

DAMIS, L'ESPINE, ERASTUS, LA RIVIERE and his Comrades.

DAMIS to L'Efpine.

IS the villain fo impudent as to expect to gain her in fpite of me? My juft vengeance fhall prevent him.

Eraftus afide.] I have a glance of fomebody there,

I 5

before Orphifa's door.   What! muft I always have
fome obftacle or other in the way of a paffion fhe is
pleafed to authorize?

Damis to L'Efpine.] Yes, I am informed, that in
fpite of all my care, my niece is to have a private interview this evening with Eraftus, in her chamber,
without witneffes.

La Riviere to his comrades.] What! do I hear thofe
people there talking of our mafter? let us draw nearer
foftly, without difcovering ourfelves.

Damis to L'Efpine.] But I muft ftab the traitor's
heart in a hundred places, before he gets time to ac-
complifh his defign.   Go and bring thofe people I
was juft now fpeaking of, place them in ambufh where
I would have them, that at hearing the name of Eraftus, you may be ready to revenge my honour, which
his paffion has the impudence to injure; break the af-
fignation which brings him here, and fmother his paffion in his own blood.

La Riviere with his comrades attacking Damis.]
Thou muft fay fomething to us, traitor, before they
can facrifice him to thy rage.

Eraftus. Honour urges me to affift my miftrefs's
uncle, though he would have taken my life. [to Damis.] I am your man, Sir. [draws his fword againft
Riviere and his companions, whom he drives off.]

Damis. Heavens! who am I obliged to for fo great
a fervice? by whofe affiftance is my life preferved?

Eraftus returning.] In faving you, I have only done
an act of juftice.

Damis. O heaven! can I believe my ears? Is it
Eraftus's hand——

Eraftus. Yes, yes, Sir, it is I; too happy in that my
hand hath faved you; too unhappy, in having deferv-
ed your difpleafure.

Damis. Is he whofe death I had determined upon, the perfon who has done me this favour? Indeed it is too much; my heart is obliged to furrender, and whatever might be the intention of your love, this night, this amazing generofity fhould ftifle all animofity. I am afhamed of my caprice. You have been too much injured by my hatred; and to make amends, you fhall be joined to the object of your wifhes this night.

SCENE VI.

ORPHISA, DAMIS, ERASTUS.

ORPHISA, coming out of her houfe with a candle.

PRAY, Sir, what is the reafon of this terrible noife?

Damis. Nothing but what is agreeable, fince, after my blaming your paffion fo long, it is what gives you Eraftus for a hufband. His arm has faved me from a death I moft narrowly efcaped; and I defire you may requite him for me by giving him your hand.

Orphifa. I agree to it, Sir, if it is to difcharge the debt you owe, and particularly as he has faved your life.

Eraftus. Am I awake? I am fo amazed at this wonder.

Damis. We will celebrate the happy ftate you are going to enjoy, and be regaled by our violins.

[A knocking at Damis's door.

Eraftus. Who is that knocks fo hard there?

SCENE THE LAST.

DAMIS, ORPHISA, ERASTUS, L'ESPINE.

L'ESPINE.

I HAVE brought the masks, Sir, with their kits and tabors.

      [Enter masques, who cover the whole stage.

Erastus. Shall I never be free of these impertinents? Come hither, Swiss, and turn them about their business.

THE END.

THE
SICILIAN:

OR,

LOVE makes a PAINTER.

A

COMEDY.

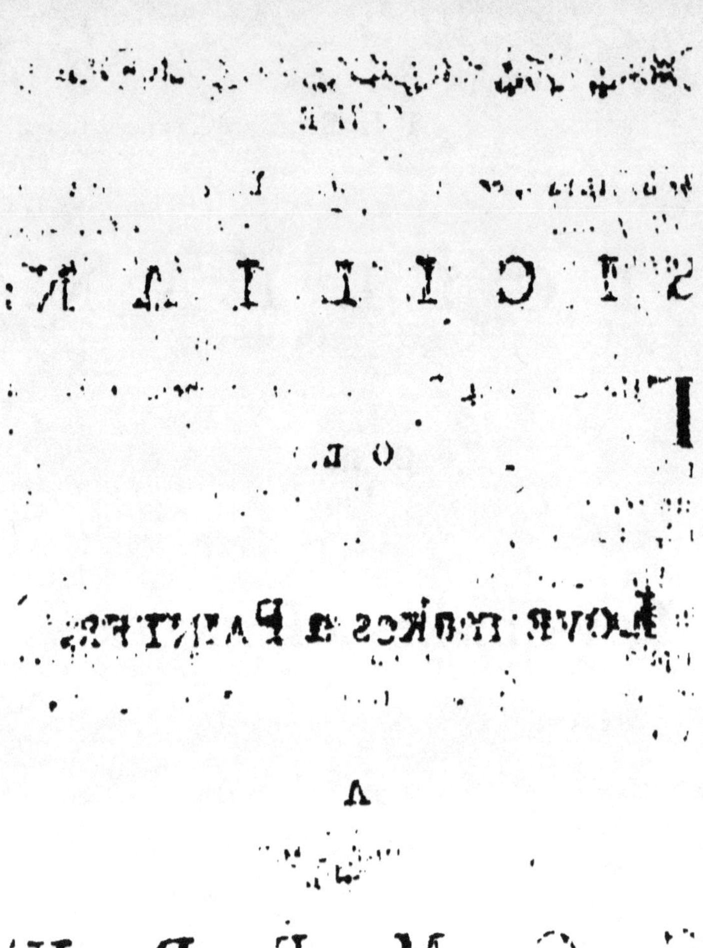

The SICILIAN, *or* LOVE *makes a* PAINTER, *a Comedy of One Act, performed at St. Germain in January,
1667, and at Paris at the Theatre of the Palace-
Royal the 10th of June the same Year.*

THE following Comedy is one of thofe of the in-
triguing kind, the unravelling of which is fimi-
lar to that of the SCHOOL for HUSBANDS, efpecially
with regard to the veil by which Don Pedro is deceived in the SICILIAN, as Sganarel is in the SCHOOL
for HUSBANDS. The chief merit of this comedy confifts in the delicacy of the dialogue, and the lively de-
fcription of love in an Italian lover and a French lover: but it was greatly ornamented with dancing and
mufic.

A C T O R S.

DON PEDRO, a Sicilian gentleman.

ADRASTUS, a French gentleman, in love with Iſiodor

ISIODORA, a Grecian, ſlave to Don Pedro.

ZAIDE, a young ſlave.

A SENATOR.

HALI, a Turk, ſlave to Adraſtus.

TWO FOOTMEN.

SCENE at Meſſina, in a public place.

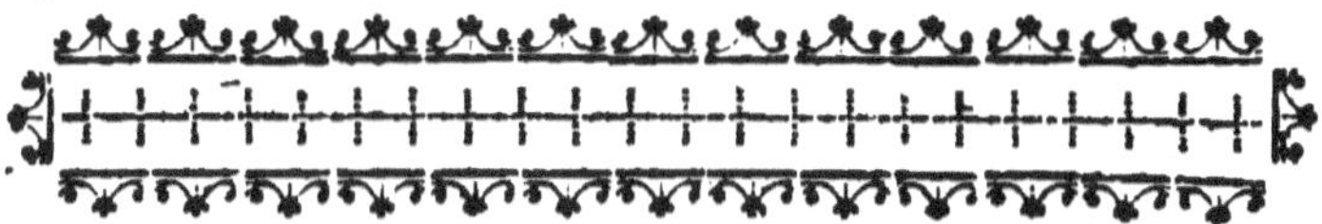

THE

S I C I L I A N:

O R,

LOVE makes a PAINTER.

S C E N E I.

H A L I, M U S I C I A N S.

HALI to the Muficians.

STOP where you are, and come no farther; but be careful not to make a noife.

S C E N E II.

H A L I alone.

THE fky is dreffed like Scaramouche to-night, not a ftar to be feen to fhew one the end of one's nofe; a man may as well be in an oven. What a forry condition is that of a flave, to be entirely engroffed by the paffions of a mafter, and never to live for one's felf! To be governed by his humours alone, and obliged to make all his views one's own bufinefs! My master makes me espouse all his anxieties, and forsooth, because he is in love, I must have no rest day or night. But here come the flambeaux, and undoubtedly it must be him.

SCENE III.

ADRASTUS, and two Footmen, carrying each a Flambeau, HALI.

ADRASTUS.

HALI, is it thee?

Hali. Who else could you expect to see at this hour but me? Besides you, and myself, Sir, I do not believe any body takes it into his head to wander about the streets at such hours.

Adrastus. Nor can I imagine there is a man who suffers the pain I feel. I think it trifling to have the cruelty or indifference of the object one loves to combat with, if one has the liberty of complaining and sighing to her; but to be debarred of the pleasure of an opportunity of telling her so, and not to be able to learn from her whether the love she inspires one with is pleasing or displeasing to her, is in my opinion the greatest of all perplexities; and to this unhappy state am I reduced by the jealous fellow who watches my lovely Grecian with so much care, and never goes any where without dragging her with him.

Hali. But there are many ways for people who are in love to speak to each other; I think your eyes and her's have said a great many things within these two months.

Adrastus. Indeed our eyes have often spoke: but how shall I know if each of us have mutually explained this language as we should do? Perhaps she may

not underſtand all my looks tell her, nor her looks tell
me what I ſometimes imagine.

Hali. We muſt find out ſome means of talking together after another manner.

Adraſtus. Are your muſicians there?

Hali. Yes.

Adraſtus. Order them to come nearer. [alone.] I
will have them ſing here till day-light, and ſee whether their muſic will not draw the fair one to ſome
window.

SCENE IV.

ADRASTUS, HALI, MUSICIANS.

HALI.

HERE they are.   Pray what ſhall they ſing?
     Adraſtus. What they moſt approve of.

Hali. They ſhall ſing a three-part ſong, which they
ſung me the other day.

Adraſtus. No, that does not pleaſe me.

Hali. Oh! Sir, indeed it is a fine Beccare.

Adraſtus. What the devil doſt thou mean with thy
fine Beccare?

Hali. Sir, I am for the Beccare.   You know that I
am a Connoiſſeur in that.   The Beccare delights me:
ſetting aſide the Beccare, no ſoundneſs in harmony.
Liſten to this three-part ſong a little.

Adraſtus. No.   I will have ſomething tender and
paſſionate, that will entertain me with a ſoothing pen-
ſiveneſs.

Hali. Then the Bemol will ſuit you; but we may
both be pleaſed. They muſt even ſing a particular ſcene
of a ſhort play, which I ſaw them practiſe. There are
two amorous ſhepherds, all full of languiſhment, who,

in the Bemol, come feparately to make their complain
in the grove; afterwards they difcover to each otl
the cruelty of their miftreffes, upon which comes
jolly fwain, with an admirable Beccare, who laughs
their folly.

Adraftus. Well, let us fee what it is.

Hali. Here is a very proper place to ferve for
fcene; and there are flambeaux to light the play.

Adraftus. Place yourfelf oppofite to this houfe; tl
I may order the lights to be ftruck at the leaft no
within.

A FRAGMENT OF A COMEDY,

Sung and accompanied by the Muficians whi
H A L I had brought.

SCENE I.

PHYLENA, THYRSIS.

1. MUSICIAN reprefenting PHYLENA.

IF to recite my amorous care,
  Difturb your folitary reft,
    Forgive, ye rocks, and hear my pray'r;
Let me but tell what anguifh racks my breaft,
    Rocks though you are, my moving ditty
    Shall melt your flinty hearts to pity.
    2. Mufician reprefenting Thyrfis.
Through thefe vaft groves the feather'd throng,
Salute each dawn with fprightly fong;
Whilft I, with each returning day,
My forrows vent in doleful lay.
        My dear Phylena.

Phylena. My Thyfis dear.
Thyrfis. Great is my pain.
Phylena. As great my care.
Thyrfis. Climene's deaf to all my vows.
Phylena. Cloris nor love, nor pity knows.

Both together.

O love, inhuman are thy laws!
Their breafts with ardent paffion warm,
Or leave 'em not the power to charm.

S C E N E II.

P H Y L E N A, T H Y R S I S, A S H E P H E R D.

3. MUSICIAN reprefenting a fhepherd.

YE captivated youths, no more
   The cruel and the fierce adore:
Upon himfelf no wifer fwain
Will e'er revenge the nymph's difdain.
Give me the maid that's foft and kind,
'Tis fhe alone my heart can bind.

   Thefe plains are throng'd by numerous fair;
Whom I addrefs with ftudious care;
To each I vow, to each complain,
In humbleft guife, in fofteft ftrain:
But if a tigrefs I muft woo,
I court her as a tiger too.

Phylena and Thyrfis both together.

Happy the fwains who thus the fair purfue!

Hali. Hark, Sir, do you not hear fomebody ftirring.
Adraftus. Put out the flambeaux immediately, and
retire.

SCENE IV.

DON PEDRO, ADRASTUS, HALI.

Don Pedro coming out of his house in his night-cap and night-gown, with a sword under his arm.

I HAVE heard, for fome time, a finging at my door; and it muft undoubtedly be for fome rea-fon. I muft endeavour, in the dark, to difcover who thefe people are.

Adraftus. Hali?

Hali. What?

Adraftus. Do you hear nothing more?

Hali. No.

[*Don Pedro is behind them, and overhears them.*

Adraftus. What! cannot all our efforts procure one minute's converfation with this lovely Greek? And this curfed jealous-pate, this traitor of a Sicilian, will he always prevent me from having accefs to her?

Hali. I wifh fincerely that the devil had him, for the trouble he gives us, peftering cur, a hang-dog as he is. Oh! if we had him here, with what pleafure fhould I revenge myfelf upon his fhoulders, all the fruitlefs fteps his jealoufy has made me take.

Adraftus. We muft invent fome means, fome cun-ning trick to catch our bear; I am too far engaged here, to bear a difappointment; and though I fhould employ——

Hali. Sir, I do not know what is the meaning of this; but the door is open; if you pleafe I will go in foftly, to difcover whence this happens.

[*Don Pedro retires within his door.*

Adraftus. Yes, do fo, but foftly, I fhall not be

far behind thee.   Would to heaven it were the lovely
Isiodora!

Don Pedro giving Hali a blow.] Who is this?

Hali striking Don Pedro again.] A friend.

Don Pedro. Why, hoh! Francis, Dominic, Simon,
Martin, Peter, Thomas, George, Charles, Bartholomew;
here, quickly, my sword, my target, my halbert, my
pistols, my blunderbusses, my carbines; quick, dispatch;
here, kill and slay, no quarter.

SCENE V.

ADRASTUS, HALI.

ADRASTUS.

I DO not hear any body stirring.   Hali! Hali!
Hali hid in a corner.] Sir.

Adrastus. Where art thou hidden?

Hali. Are all these fellows come out?

Adrastus. No, nobody stirs.

Hali coming out of the place where he had hid himself.] If they do come, I will drub them heartily.

Adrastus. What! must all the trouble we have taken then be to no purpose? Must this old jealous fellow always prevent our intensions?

Hali. No, the rage of honour seizes me; it shall
never be said that they triumph over my dexterity. My
quality of sharper despises all those obstacles, and I shall
take upon me fully to display the talents which heaven
has bestowed upon me.

Adrastus. Were she but informed of the sentiments
I entertain for her, and I informed of her's, upon this
head one might find out some method——

Hali. Leave it to me, I will try many experiments
till some succeed.   But the day breaks; I will go

bring my people, and come wait here till that jealous fellow comes abroad.

SCENE VI.

DON PEDRO, ISIODORA.

ISIODORA.

WHAT can be your meaning for awaking me so early in the morning; I should think it not suitable to your design of having my picture drawn to-day; and it is by no means the way to have a blooming colour and sparkling eyes, to rise by break of day.

Don Pedro. I have business which obliges me to go abroad at this time.

Isiodora. But, I think, you might, without any inconvenience to yourself, allow me to taste the sweets of a morning nap. Your business might have dispensed with my absence.

Don Pedro. Yes, but it gives me pleasure to have you always in my sight. There is no harm in being guarded against the designs of spies; and this night again, people came and sung under our windows.

Isiodora. It is true. The music was delightful.

Don Pedro. That was all done on your account.

Isiodora. You tell me so, I will believe it.

Don Pedro. Pray, do you know who it was that gave this serenade?

Isiodora. No; but whoever it was, I am much obliged to him.

Don Pedro. Obliged?

Isiodora. Undoubtedly, as he endeavours to divert me.

Don Pedro. Then you like to be admired?

Isiodora. Mightily, that must always be agreeable.

Don Pedro. And do you wish all those well who take this trouble?

Isiodora. Indeed I do.

Don-Pedro. That is speaking your thoughts sin--cerely.

Isiodora. Why should I dissemble? Whatever looks one may put on, one always likes to be beloved; this homage to our charms is never displeasing to us. Whatever they may say, believe me, the great ambition of women is to inspire love. All the pains they take are for nothing else but that: and one does not see a woman so disdainful, but in her heart applauds herself for the conquests her eyes make.

Don Pedro. But if you, for your part, take pleasure in being admired; do you know that I who love you, take no manner of pleasure in it?

Isiodora. Why do you not? If I were in love with any body, I should have no greater pleasure than in seeing him beloved by all the world. Is there any thing can more shew the goodness of our choice? And is it not what we should applaud ourselves for, that what we love all the world thinks lovely?

Don Pedro. That is not my way of thinking; I should be very glad that you were not so much admired. You will oblige me if you will not endeavour to appear so in the eyes of other people.

Isiodora. What! jealous of these matters?

Don Pedro. Yes, jealous of these matters; but jealous as a tiger, and, if you please, as a devil. My love would have you intirely to myself: its delicacy takes offence at a smile, at a glance that any person forces from you, and all the care you see me take, is to debar all access of galants, and secure to myself the possession of a heart, which I cannot bear any body should share with me.

Isiodora. Indeed I think you take a very wrong method; when people expect to keep a heart by force, it must be very ill secured. For my part, I declare to you, were I a galant to a lady, who is in the power of another, I should bend all my study to make that other person jealous, and oblige him to watch the fair one I had a mind to win day and night. It is the best way to advance our affairs; and persons will not fail taking advantage of the uneasiness and resentments, which constraint and servitude create in the mind of a woman.

Don Pedro. Then, should any man make love to you, he would find you disposed to receive his addresses.

Isiodora. I say nothing of that. But in short, women do not like to be restrained, and it is running a great hazard, only to discover a suspicion of them, and keep them locked up.

Don Pedro. This is a very poor reward for what you owe me; and, methinks, a slave whom I have set at liberty, and intend to make my wife——

Isiodora. What am I obliged to you, if you change my slavery into one much more severe; if you let me enjoy no manner of liberty, and teize me, as you do, with a constant guard?

Don Pedro. But all this proceeds only from my great love for you.

Isiodora. If this is your manner of loving, your hate will be more agreeable.

Don Pedro. You are in a very ill humour to-day; but I forgive these speeches, on account of the uneasiness you may be under from getting up so early.

SCENE VII.

Don Pedro, Isiodora, Hali dreſſed like
a Turk, making ſeveral bows to Don Pedro.

DON PEDRO.

YOU are too ceremonious. What is your buſineſs?

Hali ſtands between Don Pedro and Iſiodora. He
turns to Iſiodora at every word he ſpeaks to Don Pedro,
and makes ſigns to her to let her underſtand the deſign
of his maſter.] Sir, (with the lady's permiſſion) I ſhall
inform you (with the lady's permiſſion) that I come to
ſee you (with the lady's permiſſion) to deſire of you
(with the lady's permiſſion) that you would be ſo good
(with the lady's permiſſion)————

Don Pedro. With the lady's permiſſion, come a little this way.

[Don Pedro goes between Hali and Iſiodora.

Hali. Sir, I am a virtuoſo.

Don Pedro. I have nothing to give.

Hali. I do not aſk that. But as I practiſe a little
in muſic and dancing, I have inſtructed ſome ſlaves
who would be glad to find a maſter who has a taſte in
theſe things, and as I know you are a perſon of note, I
would deſire you to ſee and hear them, to buy them,
if you chuſe it, or to recommend them to ſome of your
friends, whom they would ſuit.

Iſiodora. It is a thing worth ſeeing, and will divert
us. Bring them hither.

Hali. Chala bala————This is a new ſong, and very
much in vogue. Be attentive. Chala bala.

S C E N E　VIII.

DON PEDRO, ISIODORA, HALI, TUR-
KISH SLAVES.

A Slave finging to ISIODORA.

A SWAIN purfues his lovely fair,
　　With eager heart from place to place,
But an old churl, with jealous care,
For ever interrupts the chace,
And leaves no commerce, or accefs,
But by the language of the eyes;
Say then, what greater pain than this,
Can lover fear, or heart devife?

To Don Pedro.

Chiribirida ouch alla,
Star bon Turca
Non avar danara
Ti voler comprara,
Me fervir à ti,
Si pagar per mi,
Far bona coucina,
Mi levar matina,
Far boller caldara,
Parlara, parlara,
Ti voler comprara.

Slave fings to Ifiodora.

'Tis more than death at every ftroke,
Th' expiring tortur'd lover feels;
But if his faint, with one kind look,
His fuff'ring martyr cheers and heals,
And grants him but his farther boon,
In public to confefs his love,
His rival's jealous arts would foon
The fubject of his mockery prove.

To Don Pedro.

Chiribirida ouch alla,
Star bon Turca,
Mon aver danara·
Ti voler comprara,
Mi fervir à ti,
Se pagar per mi,
Far bona coucina,
Mi levar matina,
Far boller caldara,
Parlara, parlara,
Ti voler comprara.

Don Pedro fings.

D'ye know, ye arch wags,
That either I judge ill;
Or this pretty fong
Smells ftrong of a cudgel?

Chiribirida ouch alla,
Mi ti non comprara,
Ma ti baftonnara,
Si, fi, non andara,
Andara, andara,
O ti baftonnara.

Oh, oh! the wanton rogues! [to Ifiodora.] Come, let us go in again, I have altered my mind, fince the weather is a little overcaft. [To Hali, who ftill continues there.] Ay, fcoundrel, let me find you there.

Hali. Well, it is certain my mafter adores her; there is nothing he is more defirous of than to difcover his paffion to her; and he will marry her, if one confents to it.

Don Pedro. Yes, yes, I keep her for him.

Hali. We fhall have her in fpite of you.

Don Pedro. How, rafcal?

Hali. I tell you, we will have her in spite of your teeth.

Don Pedro. If I lay hold————

Hali. Your guard is to no purpose, she shall be ours, I have sworn it.

Don Pedro. Let me come; scamper, or I shall catch thee.

Hali. We shall catch you; she shall be our wife, that is resolved; [alone.] I will bring it about or I will hang for it.

SCENE IX.

ADRASTUS, HALI, TWO FOOTMEN.

ADRASTUS.

WELL, Hali, how goes our affairs?

Hali, Sir, I have made a little sort of a push already, but I————

Adrastus. Do not give yourself any more trouble, I have, by accident, met with all I could wish, and am going to enjoy the happiness of an interview with this fair one at her own house. I was at my friend Damon's the painter, who told me, that to-day he was to draw the picture of this charming creature; and as he has been, this long time, one of my most intimate friends, he was pleased to favour my passion, and sends me in his place, with a short letter to gain me admittance. You know, I always took delight in painting, and that I sometimes handle the pencil, contrary to the custom of France, which will not allow that a gentleman should know how to do any thing: thus I shall have the liberty of seeing my adorable at my leisure. But I make no doubt but our impertinent jealous mortal will always be present, and prevent all the

converfation we might have together; and to tell thee
the truth, I have a ftratagem in readinefs, by the means
of a young flave, to get this fair Greek out of her jealous pate's hands, if I can obtain her coufent.

Hali. Let me alone, I will fhew you the way
to entertain him a little. [Whifpers Adraftus.] It
fhall never be faid that I am of no fervice in the affair. When do you go?

Adraftus. Directly; and every thing is already
prepared.

Hali. I am going to prepare myfelf too, on my part.

Adraftus alone.] I will not lofe time. Ho! there,
I am impatient to fee her.

S C E N E X.

DON PEDRO, ADRASTUS, TWO FOOTMEN.

DON PEDRO.

WHO do you want here?
  Adraftus. I want fignior Don Pedro.
Don Pedro. I am he.

Adraftus. Pray take the trouble of reading this
letter.

Don Pedro. " I fend you, in my room, this French
" gentleman, to draw the picture you know of, who,
" being a perfon ambitious of obliging people of worth,
" was very ready to undertake this trouble, upon my
" propofing it to him. He is, without doubt, the
" firft man in the world for thefe fort of perform-
" ances; and I thought I could not do you a more a-
" greeable piece of fervice, than to fend him to you,
" as your defign is to have a finifhed picture of her
" you love. Have a care, above all things, how you
" mention a word of recompence; for he is a man

" who would be affronted at it, and who does things
" only for his glory and reputation."

Signior François, it is a great favour you intend
me; and I am extremely obliged to you.

Adraſtus. All my ambition is to ſerve people of
merit and character.

Don Pedro. I will bring the perſon whoſe picture
you are to draw.

SCENE XI.

ISIODORA, DON PEDRO, ADRASTUS, AND
TWO FOOTMEN.

Don Pedro to Iſiodora.

DAMON has ſent this gentleman to us, who is
ſo kind as to give himſelf the trouble of taking
your picture. [to Adraſtus who embraces Iſiodora by
way of ſalutation.] Hold, ſignior François, this way of
ſaluting is not cuſtomary in this country.

Adraſtus. It is the French way.

Don Pedro. The French way is well enough for
your women, but it is a little too familiar for ours.

Iſiodora. I accept this honour with a great deal of
pleaſure; I am ſurpriſed at the adventure; and, to
ſpeak freely, I did not expect ſo illuſtrious a painter.

Adraſtus. Any body would think it a glory to touch
upon ſuch a piece of work. I have no great judgment; but here, the ſubject furniſhes but too much
of itſelf; and there is room to make ſomething beautiful upon ſuch an original as this is.

Iſiodora. The original is trifling, but the painter's
ſkill can hide its defects.

Adraſtus. The painter can diſcover none in it; and
only wiſhes to be able to repreſent thoſe graces to the
eyes of all the world, as great as they appear to him.

Isiodora. If your pencil flatters as much as your tongue, you will draw a picture which will not resemble me at all.

Adrastus. Heaven, which formed the original, deprives us of the power of doing a picture which can flatter.

Isiodora. Heaven, say what you will, did not——

Don Pedro. Have done with this, and set about the picture.

Adrastus to the Footmen.] Come, bring every thing.

[They bring every thing necessary to paint Isiodora.

Isiodora to Adrastus.] Where shall I place myself?

Adrastus. Here. This is the most advantageous place, and best admits of those favourable degrees of light which are necessary.

Isiodora sitting down.] Is this right?

Adrastus sitting.] Yes. A little more erect, if you please; a little more on that side; your body turned so; the head lifted up a little that the beauty of the neck may be seen. This a little more uncovered. [Uncovering her neck a little more.] Good. A little more; the least more imaginable.

Don Pedro to Isiodora.] There is a great deal of trouble in placing you properly; cannot you keep yourself as you should do.

Isiodora. I am quite unacquainted with these things; and it is the gentleman's part to place me as he would have me.

Adrastus. It is very well now, and you behave surprisingly. [Turning her a little towards him.] So, if you please. All depends on the attitudes we give the persons we paint.

Don Pedro. Very well.

Adrastus. A little more on this side: your eyes

turned always towards me, pray; your looks fixed upon mine.

Isiodora. I should love a picture really like myself, that people may not be obliged to ask who it is. I am not like those women who would have a portrait that is none of their own, and are displeased with the painter, if he does not make them handsomer than they are. One picture may do for all, for all require the same things: a complexion of lillies and roses, a fine nose, small mouth, fine large lively eyes, well divided, a small face, not larger than one's hand, though it were a foot square.

Adrastus. Should they ask that of yours, it would be very hard indeed; for your features very few resemble. What charms and sweetness they have! one runs a great hazard in painting them.

Don Pedro. The nose appears to me a little too large.

Adrastus. I have read, I do not know where, that Apelles formerly painted a mistress of Alexander, of amazing beauty, and that in painting her, he fell so desperately in love with her, that he had like to have lost his life; insomuch that Alexander, in generosity, gave him up the object of his wishes. [to Don Pedro.] I might do now, what Apelles did formerly; but, perhaps, you would not do what Alexander did.

[Don Pedro looks ill-natured.

Isiodora to Don Pedro.] All this shews the nation; the gentlemen of France have always a fund of galantry which displays itself on all occasions.

Adrastus. One is not easily deceived in these sort of things, and you have too discerning a judgment, not to perceive the source from whence these things I have said, proceed. Yes, though Alexander were here, and he were your lover, I could not forbear telling you, that I never faw any thing fo beautiful as what I now fee, and that——

Don Pedro. Signior François, methinks you fhould not talk fo much, it takes your attention from your work.

Adraftus. Oh! not in the leaft; I always accuftom myfelf to talk when I paint; and a little converfation is neceffary in thefe affairs, to revive the fancy, and keep the face in fuch a gaiety as is neceffary in perfons we are painting.

SCENE XII.

HALI dreffed like a Spaniard, DON PEDRO, ADRASTUS, ISIODORA.

DON PEDRO.

WHAT can this man want here? And who allows people to come up ftairs, without coming to inform us of it?

Hali to Don Pedro.] I enter here with freedom; but fuch liberties are allowed amongft gentlemen. Do you not know me, Sir?

Don Pedro. No, Sir.

Hali. I am Don Gilles d' Avalos; and the hiftory of Spain muft have informed you of my merit.

Don Pedro. Is there any thing I can ferve you in?

Hali. Yes, advice upon a point of honour. I know that in thefe fort of matters, there is not a more confummate gentleman than yourfelf; but I beg the favour of you, that we may ftep afide a little.

Don Pedro. We are at a great enough diftance.

Adraftus to Don Pedro, who furprifes him as he is whifpering Ifiodora.] I was obferving the colour of her eyes a little nearer.

Hali taking Don Pedro aside.] Sir, I received a flap on the face. You know what a flap on the face is, when it is given with the open hand, full on the middle of the cheek. This flap on the face sticks grievously in my stomach; and I am uncertain whether to revenge the affront, I should fight my man, or rather have him affassinated.

Don Pedro. Affassinating is the surest and shortest way. Pray who is your enemy?

Hali. Pray, let us speak softly.

Adrastus kneels to Isiodora, during the time that Don Pedro and Hali whisper.] Yes, charming Isiodora, my looks have told it you this two months past; and you must have understood them. I love you above every thing that man can love, and I have no other thought, no other end, no other passion, but to be intirely yours for my whole life.

Isiodora. I do not know whether you speak truth, but you persuade.

Adrastus. But do I so persuade you, as to inspire you with ever so small a degree of kindness for me?

Isiodora. I only fear I have too much.

Adrastus. Fair Isiodora, have you enough to consent to the intention I have told you of?

Isiodora. I cannot tell you as yet.

Adrastus. What do you wait for, as to that?

Isiodora. To form a resolution.

Adrastus. Ah! when one is really in love, one soon forms a resolution.

Isiodora. Well, go; yes, I do consent to it.

Adrastus. But, tell me, do you consent that it shall be this very moment?

Isiodora. When a person is once determined upon a thing, do they stick at the time?

Don Pedro to Hali.] You have my opinion, and I kiſs your hand.

Hali. Sir, when you have received any flap on the face, I am a man alſo to be adviſed with, and I may do the ſame for you.

Don Pedro. I leave you without waiting on you down again; but theſe freedoms are allowed amongſt gentlemen.

Adraſtus to Iſiodora.] No there is nothing can efface from my mind the tender proofs—[Adraſtus perceiving that Don Pedro obſerved him in cloſe converſation with Iſiodora.] I was looking upon this ſmall dimple on her chin; and I thought at firſt that it had been a mole. But we have done enough for to-day, we ſhall finiſh another time. [to Don Pedro, who would look at the picture.] No, pray, do not look at any thing as yet; let it be locked up, pray. [to Iſiodora.] And you, madam, I intreat you not to droop; and to keep yourſelf chearful for the intention I have of finiſhing our work.

Iſiodora. I ſhall preſerve all the gaiety neceſſary for that purpoſe.

SCENE XIII.

DON PEDRO, ISIODORA.

ISIODORA.

WHAT think you of him? This gentleman ſeems to me the moſt obliging that can be; and one muſt confeſs, that the French have ſomething galant and polite in them, that other nations have not.

Don Pedro. Yes, but they have this bad property, that they give themſelves too much liberty, and make love to every woman they meet at random.

Isiodora. That is because they think these things are agreeable to the ladies.

Don Pedro. Yes, but if they are agreeable to the ladies, they are very disagreeable to the gentlemen; and one does not much like to see a man court one's wife, or mistress, under our nose so freely.

Isiodora. It is only for amusement they do it.

SCENE XIV.

ZAIDE, DON PEDRO, ISIODORA.

ZAIDE.

PRAY, good Sir, save me from the hands of an angry husband, by whom I am pursued. His jealousy is incredible, and works him up to an excess beyond imagination. He goes so far as to desire I should be veiled continually, and because he caught me with my face a little uncovered, he snatched up his sword, and forced me to fly to your house to ask your protection against his injustice. But I see him coming. For heaven's sake, good Sir, save me from his anger.

Don Pedro to Zaide, and pointing to Isiodora.] Step in thither with her, and be not afraid.

SCENE XV.

ADRASTUS, DON PEDRO.

DON PEDRO.

FOR shame, Sir! a Frenchman to discover so much jealousy! I thought we alone were capable of it.

Adrastus. The French excel in every thing they do: and when we have reason to be jealous, we are

twenty times more fo than a Sicilian.   The infamous
creature thinks fhe has found a certain refuge in your
houfe, but you are too prudent to blame my refentment.   Pray allow me to treat her as fhe deferves.

Don Pedro. Nay, for goodnefs fake, have patience.
The offence is too fmall for fo much anger.

Adraftus. The greatnefs of an offence of this nature is not fo much in the things people do; it is in
tranfgreffing the orders given them; and in fuch affairs as this, what is but a trifle becomes very criminal, when it is forbidden.

Don Pedro. In the manner fhe told the ftory, all
fhe did was without intention; and, in fhort, I beg
you may be reconciled to each other.

Adraftus. How! do you take her part, you who are
fo delicate in thefe affairs?

Don Pedro. Yes, I take her part; and you will o-
blige me by forgetting your paffion, and by reconcil-
ing yourfelves to each other. I afk it of you as a favour,
and I fhall take it as an inftance of that friendfhip
which I defire may be betwixt us.

Adraftus. I cannot, upon thefe conditions, refufe
you any thing: I fhall do as you defire.

S C E N E   XVI.

ZAIDE, DON PEDRO, ADRASTUS at a corner of
the ftage.

DON PEDRO to Zaide.

HOH there, come; you have nothing to do but
to follow me.   You could never fall into better hands than mine, I have made your peace.

Zaide. I am obliged to you more than can be imagined: but I muſt take my veil, I care not to appear before him without it.

SCENE XVII.

DON PEDRO, ADRASTUS.

DON PEDRO.

HERE ſhe comes; and I aſſure you ſhe appeared all joy, when I told her that I had made up the whole matter.

SCENE XVIII.

IſIODORA in Zaide's veil, ADRASTUS, DON PEDRO.

DON PEDRO to Adraſtus.

SINCE you were ſo kind to give up your reſentment, ſuffer me to join your hands, and to intreat you both out of love to me, to live in perfect union.

Adraſtus. Yes, I promiſe you that out of love to you, I ſhall live with her in the beſt manner imaginable.

Don Pedro. You oblige me very much, and I ſhall not forget it.

Adraſtus. I promiſe you, ſignior Don Pedro, that, out of reſpect to you, I ſhall treat her in the beſt way I poſſibly can.

Don Pedro. You do me too great a favour: [alone.] it is good always to make peace, and to ſoften matters. Hola, Iſiodora, come.

S C E N E XIX.

Z A I D E, D O N P E D R O.

DON PEDRO.

HOW! What do you mean by this?
Zaide unveiled.] The meaning of it is, that a
jealous man is a monster detested by all the world;
and that it would be a pleasure to every one to do him
a mischief, had he no other interest in it; that all the
locks and bars in the world will not secure people, and
that the heart should be secured by gentleness; that I-
siodora is in the hands of a gentleman whom she loves,
and that you are caught for a dupe.

Don Pedro. Shall Don Pedro bear this insuffera-
ble injury! No, no, I have too great a soul, and I
will demand the assistance of law to prosecute the perfidious man to the utmost. I believe a senator lives
here. Hola!   [He knocks.

S C E N E T H E L A S T.

A S E N A T O R, D O N P E D R O.

SENATOR.

YOUR servant, signior Don Pedro. You are
come at a lucky time.

Don Pedro. I come to make a complaint to you of
an affront offered me.

Senator. I have made one of the finest masquerades
imaginable.

Don Pedro. A traitor of a Frenchman has tricked me.

Senator. You never saw any thing in your life so
delightful.

Don Pedro. He has carried off a young woman to whom I had given her freedom.

Senator. They are all dreſſed like Moors, who dance wonderfully.

Don Pedro. Do but ſee whether it is an injury to be endured.

Senator. The habits are ſurpriſing, and made on purpoſe.

Don Pedro. I demand the help of juſtice againſt this action.

Senator. I muſt have you ſee this; they are going to rehearſe it, to entertain the public with it.

Don Pedro. How! What is it you ſpeak of?

Senator. I ſpeak of my maſquerade.

Don Pedro. I talk to you of my buſineſs.

Senator. I will have no other buſineſs to-day but pleaſure. Come, gentlemen, come; let us ſee whether it will take well.

Don Pedro. The devil take you and your maſquerade both, what have I to do with it?

Senator. He is very welcome to take you, for I will not meddle with your affair.

THE END.

THE

LEARNED LADIES.

A

COMEDY.

The LEARNED LADIES, *a Comedy of Five Acts, performed at Paris at the Theatre of the Palace-Royal,
March 11th, 1672.*

THIS comedy was not compofed in fuch a hurry
as the moft part of Moliere's generally were.
He very ingenioufly ridicules the folly of a pedantic
education and falfe wit.   A fubject in appearance very unlikely to furnifh any thing which could be entertaining on the ftage; a prejudice which at firft prevented the fuccefs of the piece, but which did not continue long, for they foon perceived with what art the
author had fpun out into five acts a fubject which was
dry in itfelf, without mixing any thing foreign in it;
and he was greatly praifed for prefenting in a comic
drefs what did not appear fufceptible of it.

SOME confufed and fuperficial notions of fciences,
ill-chofen terms of art, and an ill-placed affectation of
grammatical purity, compofed in different colours the
grounds of the characters of Philaminta, Armanda and
Belifa.   Henrietta alone preferved herfelf from the
contagion, which rendered her more beloved by her
father than the reft, the diftemper making him very
uneafy, without knowing how to cure it.   The infatuation of Philaminta, and the high notion fhe had
conceived of the talents and wit of Triffotin, make the
plot of the piece.   A fonnet and madrigal, which this
pretended wit very emphatically reads in the fecond fcene
of the third act, confirm her in the refolution fhe had
already taken of marrying Henrietta as foon as poffible to

him whom she esteemed above any man. It were to be wished that Philaminta had been undeceived by a more likely and better-concerted incident than that of the two letters which Aristus brings in the fifth act; but the reciprocal generosity of Clitander and Henrietta makes amends in some measure for this fault. It is pretended, that the quarrel between Trissotin and Vadius was copied after one that happened at the palace of Luxembourgh, at the king's sister's, between two authors of that time.

ACTORS.

CHRISALUS, a citizen.
PHILAMINTA, wife to Chrisalus.
ARMANDA, } daughters to Chrisalus and Philaminta.
HENRIETTA, }
ARISTUS, brother to Chrisalus.
BELISA, sister to Chrisalus.
CLITANDER, in love with Henrietta.
TRISSOTIN, a wit.
VADIUS, a pedant.
MARTINA, a cook-maid.
L'EPINE, a lacquey.
JULIAN, Vadius's valet.
A NOTARY.

SCENE, PARIS, in Chrisalus's House.

LEARNED LADIES.

ACT I. SCENE I.

ARMANDA, HENRIETTA.

ARMANDA.

BLESS me! fister, can you entertain that vulgar intention of marrying? Will you quit the lovely name of maid?

Henrietta. Yes.

Armanda. Ah! can one hear that Yes, without being fick at heart?

Henrietta. Pray, fifter, what is there in matrimony which obliges you————

Armanda. Fie! O heavens!

Henrietta. Pray, what afflicts you fo?

Armanda. Ah! fhame, fifter! cannot you fuppofe what a furfeit fuch a word gives to a delicate imagination? What a ftrange image it fhocks one with, and leads the mind to a difagreeable profpect! How can you bring yourfelf to bear the confequence of that word?   Do you not tremble when you think of it?

Henrietta. When I confider the confequences of that word, fifter, it fets before me a hufband, children, and a family; and if I think reafonably of it, there is nothing in all this fo fhocking to an imagination.

Armanda. Heavens! can fuch attachments be agreeable?

Henrietta. I do not fee that one can do better at my age, than to fix one's felf to a man under the name of hufband, who loves and is beloved; has fuch a one, when well matched, no pleafure?   I think one may expect from this tender union to fecure the pleafure of an innocent life.

Armanda. Lard, fifter! what a groveling mind you have! to act fo mean a part in the world, as to immure yourfelf with family affairs!   Can you not difcover more fenfible pleafure than a hufband and children?   Leave thofe low amufements to the vulgar, and raife your defires to more worthy objects; endeavour to treat fenfe and matter with contempt, and get a tafte for noble pleafures like us; give yourfelf up to underftanding.   Our mother, who is always honoured with the name of Learned, may be an example; like me, endeavour to fhew yourfelf her daughter; afpire to that brightnefs natural to the family, and make yourfelf fenfible of the delightful pleafures which a love for ftudy fills the mind with; marry yourfelf to philofophy, fifter, inftead of being in fervile bondage to the will of a man; this will raife you above the reft of the human race, and give the fovereign empire to reafon, fubjecting the animal part to its laws, the grofs appetite of which debafes us to beafts.   Thefe are the foft attachments, the lovely flames which ought to employ the moments of life; thofe cares with which I fee many women taken up, feems to me terrible meannefles.

Henrietta. Sifter, we obferve the order of heaven to be almighty, it forms us from our births for different employments, and every mind is not compofed of materials proper for a philofopher. If your mind, fifter, is proper for thofe heights which the fpeculations of the learned mount to, mine is formed for the trifling cares here below. Do not let us diforder the regulations of heaven, but follow the inftigation of our different inftincts. You may by the flight of a fine genius inhabit the lofty regions of philofophy, whilft my imagination will be fatisfied with tafting the terreftrial charms of matrimony. Thus we both follow our mother's example in our different ways; you with regard to the mind, and noble defires, and I in refpect to fenfe, and grofs pleafures; you in productions of genius, and I in thofe of matter.

Armanda. When we pretend to follow a perfon's example, fifter, we ought to refemble them in the fineft parts.

Henrietta. But, fifter, allow me to tell you, that if my mother had only had thofe fine parts you fpeak of, you would not here been what you boaft yourfelf of; fhe did not always apply her noble genius to philofophy. I beg you will, out of a little goodnefs, leave me to thofe meannefles to which you owe the light, and do not prevent a little fcholar from coming into the world by perfuading me to follow your example.

Armanda. I find there is no curing you of that filly infatuation of taking a hufband: pray who do you intend to have? You certainly do not aim at Clitander?

Henrietta. Why not? Do you think it a low choice? Or do you think he wants merit?

Armanda. No, but it would be a difhoneft intention, to endeavour to take away another perfon's conqueft: it is very well known, that Clitander has long fighed for me.

Henrietta. Yes, but all thofe fighs are in vain, as you do not intend to fall into human meanneffes; as you have in your heart no defign upon Clitander, it need give you no concern, though another pretend to him: your mind has renounced matrimony for ever, and philofophy has all your affections.

Armanda. The empire which reafon holds over the fenfes does not make us give up the pleafures of being praifed; one may chufe to have a man of merit in the train of our admirers, though one do not chufe to marry him.

Henrietta. I did not prevent him from continuing his admiration of your perfections, but only received one, who offered me his paffion, on your refufing it.

Armanda. Can you fuppofe that you are quite fafe in the offer of a difgufted lover's vows? Do you imagine all his paffion for me to be quite dead, and his affection for you very ftrong?

Henrietta. So he tells me, fifter, and I am ready to believe him.

Armanda. Do not let your faith be too ftrong, fifter, you may be deceived; when he tells you, that he loves me and you, he does not really mean it.

Henrietta. Indeed I cannot tell, but I fee him coming, and we may very eafily be informed of the whole matter.

SCENE II.

CLITANDER, ARMANDA, HENRIETTA.

HENRIETTA.

CLitander, you muſt free me from a doubt which my ſiſter has involved me in; open your heart, and diſcover freely which of us has the beſt right to your addreſſes.

Armanda. Excuſe me, I do no chuſe to impoſe the hardſhip of an explanation on your paſſion; I do not love to give people pain, and ſuch a confeſſion to one's face muſt be very perplexing.

Clitander. Madam, my heart ſeldom diſſembles, and feels no conſtraint to make an open acknowledgment; it does not perplex me in the leaſt, and I honeſtly confeſs, that the tender cords I am bound by, my addreſſes and love are on this ſide. [pointing to Henrietta.] Let this confeſſion give you no uneaſineſs, it was your deſire that it ſhould be ſo. I own your attractions caught me, and my tender ſighs proved very plainly the ardour of my deſires; my eyes conſecrated to you an immortal flame, but your eyes did not think their conqueſt ſufficient; I bore a thouſand different ſlights under their yoke; they reigned over my heart, like proud tyrants, till worn out by ſo much torment, I found more humane conquerors, and leſs cruel chains. [pointing to Henrietta.] In thoſe eyes I have found them, and their bonds ſhall ever be dear to me; they dried up my tears with a tender regard, and did not diſdain the refuſe of your charms; ſuch uncommon favours affected me ſo deeply, that nothing can deliver me from my chains, and I intreat you, madam, never to endeavour to recall a heart determined to die in this soft ardour.

Armanda. Alas! pray who told you, Sir, that they cared so much for you? I think you very impertinent in declaring it: you must be a strange creature to imagine so.

Henrietta. Hold, sister, where now is the moral part, which so well regulates the animal, and bridles the sallies of wrath?

Armanda. But how do you practise it, in answering a passion which is discovered to you, without consent from those who gave you being, without whose leave it is criminal to dispose of yourself? You must be sensible that duty subjects you to their laws, and you must love according to their choice, as they have a supreme authority over you.

Henrietta. I return you thanks for teaching me my duty; my heart will regulate its conduct by your instruction; and to shew you that I profit by it, Clitander, take care to support your love by the consent of those who gave me birth; gain a lawful power over my desires, and put me into a method of loving you without a crime.

Clitander. I will go and labour after it with the utmost care, for I have only waited for your kind permission.

Armanda. You triumph, my sister, and look as if you thought that this shagreens me.

Henrietta. Not at all, sister, I am sensible that the laws of reason always prevail over sense, and that by the assistance of wise lessons you are above such weaknesses. I am so far from supposing that you are under any concern, that I make no doubt but you will employ your interest in the affair, and by your approbation haften the happy moment; and I intreat you to do it.

Armanda. You feem very proud of a heart one throws to you; your trifling wit affects raillery.

Henrietta. You would pick up this thrown heart from me if you could, notwithftanding the indifference you affect.

Armanda. Thcfe are filly difcourfes, which one ought not to bear; I fhall not condefcend to anfwer them.

Henrietta. Your command of temper in this affair fhews great moderation; you are certainly quite right in behaving fo.

SCENE III.

CLITANDER, HENRIETTA,

HENRIETTA.

SHE is very much furprifed at your fincere confeffion.

Clitander. Her proud folly deferves my plain dealing; but, madam, I will vifit your father, as I have permiffion to———

Henrietta. The muft effectual method is to procure my mother's confent; my father's good temper will agree to any thing, but pays little regard to what he determines; he is bleffed with a particular meeknefs of temper, which makes him fubmit to every thing that is agreeable to his wife, therefore what fhe fays is a law. I fincerely wifh that you were of a temper to behave with a little flattering complaifance to my mother and aunt, which would procure their efteem for you.

Clitander. My heart is too fincere to be capable of

flattery; I even cannot flatter your sister's character. I do not approve of those female doctors. It is certainly right for a woman to have an insight into every thing; but I would not have her to indulge herself in such a passion, to make herself learned merely for the sake of being so; and I love to have her know sometimes when questions are put to her, how to appear ignorant of what she is asked. In short, I would chuse she should have knowledge without discovering it to the world. I do not approve of women citing authors, using bombast words, and shewing their learning upon all occasions. I revere your mother, but cannot approve of her fancy, or make myself an echo of what she says, to the incense she offers her heroes of genius. I am provoked to see her esteem such a fellow as Mr. Trissotin, to place such a blockhead in the rank of fine geniuses; a pedant, whose writings are damned, and whose pen furnishes the Market-hall with officious papers.

Henrietta. I find you are much of my taste and opinion; I think both his writings and conversation are very tiresome; but as he has great sway with my mother, you ought to appear a little complaisant. A lover, who pays court where his heart is sincerely engaged, would endeavour to gain the favour of the whole world with regard to that; he even endeavours to be in friendship with the very house-dog, that no creature may oppose his flame.

Clitander. I approve of what you say; but Mr. Trissotin inspires my soul with such spleen, that I cannot lessen myself by praising his works for the sake of hearing his approbation. I knew him before I saw him. It was his works which gave me such a despicable opinion of him; that extreme confidence which makes him always so pleased with himself, and in such good humour with every thing he writes. I dare fay he would not change his fame for that of the greateft general.

Henrietta. You muft have great penetration to difcover all this.

Clitander. Nay, further, I know his very figure by his verfes; they difcovered to me the air of the poet; fo well did they make me acquainted with his appearance, that one day meeting a man in the palace, I wagered that it was Triffotin, and won it.

Henrietta. O what a fable!

Clitander. Indeed it is as I tell you: but here comes your aunt. Allow me to declare our fecret to her, and gain her good influence with your mother.

SCENE IV.

BELISA, CLITANDER.

CLITANDER.

PRAY, madam, allow a lover to embrace this lucky opportunity of difcovering to you a fincere paffion.

Belifa. Hold, foftly, pray do not open your heart too freely; if I have placed you amongft the number of my lovers, be contented with making your eyes your only interpreters, and do not by any other language explain your love. Love me, burn and figh for my charms, but keep me ignorant of it. I can wink at your fecret flames, while you confine yourfelf to dumb interpreters; but if you open your mouth, I muft banifh you from my prefence.

Clitander. Pray, madam, do not be alarmed at my intentions; Henrietta is the object which delights me, and I come earnestly to desire that your goodness will assist my love for her charms.

Belisa. Ha? I protest in all the romances I ever read, I never met with any thing more ingenious; this is certainly a very witty turn, such an evasion deserves praise.

Clitander. No wit at all, madam, but a sincere confession of what my heart feels. Heaven has bound my heart to Henrietta by the ties of an immutable ardour; she retains me in her amiable empire, and the greatest happiness I aspire to is to wed Henrietta; you can do much towards it, and I beg the favour of you to assist my addresses.

Belisa. I perceive your aim, and know what I should understand; it is artful enough. I must acquaint you that Henrietta is a rebel to matrimony, and you may burn for her without relief.

Clitander. Alas! madam, why will you perplex me with uncertainties?

Belisa. Alas! no formalities; do not deny what your looks have often told me; it is sufficient that we are satisfied with the turn which you gave to your passion, and that under the figure which respect obliges it to, we willingly determine to suffer its homage; provided its transports are enlightened by honour, and offer only pure vows at my altar.

Clitander. But——

Belisa. Farewel, this is sufficient to satisfy you for this time; I have told you more than I otherwise would.

Clitander. But your mistake——

Belisa. Enough. My modesty has endured an amazing attack, I blush at it.

Clitander. I declare I do not love you, and will——

Belisa. I will hear no more.

SCENE V.

CLITANDER alone.

THE devil take the fool with her visions! did one ever hear any thing equal to these prepossessions? I must commit this business to another, and be assisted by somebody of more experience.

{}*{}*{}*{}*{}*{}*{}*{}*{}*{}*{}*{}*{}

ACT II. SCENE I.

ARISTUS leaving Clitander, but continuing to speak to him.

YES, I will presently bring you an answer; I will press, insist, in short do all that can be done. What a great deal has a lover to say for one word! and with what impatience does he desire any thing! Never————

SCENE II.

CHRISALUS, ARISTUS.

ARISTUS.

GOD bless you, brother.

Chrisalus. I wish you the same, brother.

Aristus. Do you know what brings me here?

Chrisalus. No, but I am ready to learn it.

Aristus. Is it not a long time since you were acquainted with Clitander?

Chrisalus. Yes, and he comes to our house frequently.

Ariftus. And what efteem is he in with you, brother?

Chrifalus. As a man of wit, courage, honour and conduct; there are very few men of more merit.

Ariftus. I am come here by his particular defire, and am extremely glad to find you have a regard for him.

Chrifalus. I got acquainted with his late father in my journey to Rome.

Ariftus. Very well.

Chrifalus. He was a very honeft gentleman, brother.

Ariftus. They fay fo indeed.

Chrifalus. At that time we were but twenty-eight years old, and two brifk fparks, I affure you.

Ariftus. I do not doubt it.

Chrifalus. We vifited the Roman ladies, and every body fpoke of our frolicks; we even created jealoufy in the breaft of fome people.

Ariftus. Very well, but let us talk of what brought me here.

SCENE III.

BELISA entering foftly, and liftening. CHRISALUS, ARISTUS.

ARISTUS.

CLITANDER makes me his interpreter to you, and I am to acquaint you that his heart is fmitten with Henrietta.

Chrifalus. My daughter?

Ariftus. Yes, he is moft paffionately in love with her.

Belifa to Ariftus.] No, no, I underftand it. The thing is not as you imagine; you are not acquainted with the ftory.

Ariſtus. How, ſiſter?

Beliſa. You are deceived by Clitander, his heart is ſmitten with another object.

Ariſtus. You are in jeſt. Is he not in love with Henrietta?

Beliſa. I am certain it is not Henrietta.

Ariſtus. He told me ſo himſelf.

Beliſa. Oh, yes.

Ariſtus. I am commiſſioned by him to aſk her of her father this very day.

Beliſa. Very well.

Ariſtus. And his extreme love made him very deſirous to haſten ſuch an alliance.

Beliſa. Still better. There could not be a more ingenious deception. Henrietta, betwixt us, is a curious veil, a pretence, brother, to conceal another flame, the myſtery of which I am acquainted with, and will undeceive you both.

Ariſtus. But, ſiſter, as you are ſo well acquainted with it, pray let us know who the other object of his love is.

Beliſa. Are you deſirous to know it?

Ariſtus. Yes I am.

Beliſa. It is I.

Ariſtus. You!

Beliſa. Yes indeed.

Ariſtus. Hah, ſiſter!

Beliſa. What do you mean by that Hah? Is there any thing ſurpriſing in it? We are formed of an air, I ſuppoſe, to be able to ſay we have one heart in ſubjection to our empire; Damis, Dorantes, Cleontes, and Licidas, may ſhew plainly that we are not deſtitute of charms.

Ariſtus. Are you beloved by thoſe people?

Beliſa. Yes, extreamly.

Ariftus. Have they told you fo?

Belifa. That is a liberty which their refpect for me has prevented them from mentioning; but the filent interpreters have done all their office in offering their heart and fervice to me.

Ariftus. I think Damis comes very feldom here.

Belifa. That is to fhew me his fubmiffive refpect.

Ariftus. Dorantes is continually affronting you with his fatirical language.

Belifa. The tranfports of a jealous rage.

Ariftus. Cleontes and Licidas are both married.

Belifa. They did that through defpair, which their paffion for me reduced them to.

Ariftus. Indeed, my dear fifter, you take fancies.

Chrifalus to Belifa.] You ought to lay afide thefe fancies.

Belifa. Fancies do you call them? I fancy! very good indeed! I rejoice very much at fancies, brother, and I did not know I had them.

S C E N E IV.

CHRISALUS, ARISTUS.

CHRISALUS.

I REALLY think our fifter is mad.

Ariftus. Indeed it grows upon her every day; but let us return to our converfation. Clitander afks Henrietta of you. What anfwer fhould be made to his paffion?

Chrifalus. Need you afk? I confent with all my heart, and look upon an alliance with him as an honour.

Ariftus. You are fenfible that he is not rich, and——

Chrifalus. That I am not concerned about; he has abundance of virtue, which is true riches; befides, his father and I were one.

Ariftus. Let us talk to your wife about it, and have her approbation.

Chrifalus. It is fufficient that I accept him for a fon-in-law.

Ariftus. Very true, brother, but it is not amifs to have her confent to fupport yours.

Chrifalus. I tell you, it is not at all neceffary: I will anfwer for my wife, and take it upon myfelf.

Ariftus. But——

Chrifalus. There is no need I fay of apprehenfion; I will go and fet things to rights immediately.

Ariftus. Do fo then, and I will found Henrietta upon it, and return to know——

Chrifalus. It is a done thing, and I will go to my wife, and talk to her about it.

S C E N E. V.

C H R I S A L U S, M A R T I N A.

M A R T I N A.

I AM very fortunate indeed! Alas! it is a true faying, He who accufes a dog of madnefs would drown him; another's fervice is no inheritance.

Chrifalus. What ails you, Martina? what is the matter?

Martina. Do you afk what is the matter?

Chrifalus. Yes.

Martina. Why the matter is, that I am difcharged to-day.

Chrisalus. What, discharged?

Martina. Yes, I am turned off by madam.

Chrisalus. How, pray? I do not understand that.

Martina. They threaten to beat me if I do not march off.

Chrisalus. No, stay, I am pleased with you, and that is enough; my wife is often a little hot-headed, and I will not——

SCENE VI.

PHILAMINTA, BELISA, CHRISALUS, MARTINA.

PHILAMINTA perceiving MARTINA.

IS it you I see, hussey? You jade, begone immediately, and never let me see you more.

Chrisalus. Not so fast.

Philaminta. No, it is over.

Chrisalus. Hey!

Philaminta. She shall be gone.

Chrisalus. What has she been guilty of, that you have determined to——

Philaminta. Do you uphold her?

Chrisalus. Not at all.

Philaminta. Do you take her part, and condemn me?

Chrisalus. Alas! not I. I only enquire what her crime is.

Philaminta. Do you imagine that I would turn her away without reason?

Chrisalus. I do not say that you do; but with respect to the servants, I ought——

Philaminta. No, I am determined she shall go out of our house.

Chrisalus. Well, nobody says she shall not go.

Philaminta. I will not be contradicted.

Chrisalus. Be it so.

Philamita. And if you were a reasonable husband, you would join with me against her.

Chrisalus turning to Martina.] So I do. Yes, gipsey, my wife does not put you away without reason; your crime ought not to be forgiven.

Martina. What have I done?

Chrisalus aside.] I cannot tell indeed.

Philaminta. She is still of a temper to make it of no consequence.

Chrisalus. Has she broke some looking-glass, or china, to provoke your anger?

— Philaminta. Do you suppose so small a matter would enrage me so much as to oblige me to turn her away?

Chrisalus to Martina.] What is the meaning of this? [to Philaminta.] It must be something considerable.

Philaminta. To be sure it is. Am I ever unreasonable?

Chrisalus. Is there some ewer or piece of plate stolen through her negligence?

Philaminta. That would be a trifle.

Chrisalus to Martina.] Oho! gipsey! plague! [to Philaminta.] Have you surprised her in some dishonesty?

Philaminta. Worse still.

Chrisalus. What worse?

Philaminta. Yes, worse.

Chrisalus to Martina.] What the devil, you jade? [to Philaminta.] Hey! has she been guilty of——

Philaminta. She has with unequalled impudence, after numerous lectures about it, insulted my ear with the impropriety of a vulgar savage word, which Vaugelas expresly condemns.

Chrisalus. Is that——

Philaminta. What, notwithstanding all our reasoning, continually to shock the foundation of all the sciences, grammar, which even rules over kings, and makes them with an high hand obey its laws!

Chrisalus. I imagined that she had committed some very great offence.

Philaminta. Do not you think this an unpardonable crime?

Chrisalus. Indeed I do.

Philaminta. I should wish you would excuse her.

Chrisalus. I will be careful of that.

Belisa. Indeed it is a pity that all construction should be destroyed by her, when she has been instructed in the laws of language a thousand times.

Martina. I believe all you preach is fine and good, but indeed I cannot talk your jargon.

Philaminta. Such insolence! to call a language jargon, which is founded upon reason and polite custom.

Martina. All your fine terms are not of no use to make ones self understood in speaking well.

Philaminta. Still in the same style, *Are not of no use.*

Belisa. Shall we never be able to teach this indocible animal to talk congruously, notwithstanding all the trouble we are at? *Not* joined with *no* is a recidivation, as we have frequently told you, and is too much of a negative.

Martina. Zooks! I speak, just as they speak in our country; I are not a scollard like you.

Philaminta. Oh! how can this be born?

Belisa. What a shocking solecism!

Philaminta. It is sufficient to kill a sensible ear.

Belisa. I must confess that thy genius is very gross.

I is but fingular, *are* is plural. Wilt thou continually offend grammar in this manner?

Martina. You do not hear me fpeak of offending
either grand-father or grand-mother?

Philaminta. Heavens!

Belifa. You underftand grammar in a wrong fenfe,
I have already told you whence that word comes.

Martina. It is nothing to me, let it come from
Scotland, Ireland, or Wales.

Belifa. O what an aukward creature fhe is! Grammar teaches us the laws of the Nominative cafe, and
the Verb, as well as of the Adjective and Subftantive.

Martina. Madam, I muft tell you, that I do not
know thefe people.

Philaminta. What a creature!

Belifa. They are names of words, not of people,
and you ought to take notice in what it is that they
muft be made to agree together.

Martina. Is it of any confequence whether they a-
gree or quarrel?

Philaminta. Heavens! let us finifh this converfation. [to Chrifalus.] Will you not make her begone
from me?

Chrifalus. Certainly. [afide.] I muft agree to her
humour. Martina, retire, and do not vex her.

Philaminta. You fpeak very obliging, are you a-
fraid of offending the creature?

Chrifalus. Not I indeed. [In a harfh tone.] Be
gone. [In a milder tone.] Go thy ways, poor girl.

SCENE VII.

PHILAMINTA, CHRISALUS, BELISA.

CHRISALUS.

YOU are pleased, and she is gone; but I do not approve of her going in this way; she is a girl proper for her business, and you have turned her out of my house for a trifling cause.

Philaminta. Would you have me to keep her in my service, continually to put my ear to torment? To break all the laws of custom and reason by a barbarous heap of vices in speech, of lame expressions, intermixed between times with proverbs taken from Billingsgate?

Belisa. Indeed it gives one pain to hear her discourses. She pulls Vaugelas to pieces every day, and the least blunders of her gross genius are either Pleonasm, or Cacophony.

Chrisalus. Of what consequence is it if she does fail in the laws of Vaugelas, provided she does not fail in the kitchen? For my part, I had much rather that she joined the Nouns and Verbs falsly, and repeated a servile bad word a hundred times in picking her herbs, than have her overdo my meat, or make my broth over salt. I live by good soup, and not by fine language. Vaugelas does not teach how to make good soup; and Malherbe and Balzac, so learned in fine words, would probably have been blockheads in the kitchen.

Philaminta. How am I shocked at this discourse! and how unworthy it is of one who calls himself a man to be continually bent on material cares instead of raising himself up towards spiritual ones! Is the body, that rag, of importance enough, of a value to merit a single thought? And ought we not to leave that far behind?

Chrisalus. Ay, but my body is myself, and I will be careful of it. A rag, if you please, but my rag is dear to me.

Belisa. The body with the mind, makes a figure, brother; but if you will believe all the learned world in the case, the mind ought to have the precedency over the body; and our greatest care, our first concern, should be to nourish it with the juice of science.

Chrisalus. I'faith, if you think about nourishing your mind, it is with very airy diet, as every one says; and you have no care, no solicitude for——

Philaminta. Ah! Solicitude is coarse to my ear, it smells strangely of antiquity.

Belisa. The word is of high date indeed.

Chrisalus. Allow me to speak. In short I must be plain; pull off the mask, and discharge my spleen; people treat you as if you were mad, and I am very much troubled.

Philaminta. How?

Chrisalus to Belisa.] It is to you that I speak, sister. The least solecism in speech is disagreeable to you; but you make strange ones yourself in conduct. I am not pleased with your eternal folio's; and, except a great Plutarch which I put my bands in, you ought to burn all this useless lumber, and leave learning to your great doctors about town; to do right, you should remove that long telescope, enough to frighten people, out of the garret, and a hundred knick-knacks the sight of which gives people offence: not to look after what is done in the moon, but to observe better what is done at home, where every thing is topsy-turvy. For many reasons it is not profitable for a wife to study so many things: to form the minds of her children to good-manners, to see her family go on well, to look well after her servants, and to regulate with oeconomy what is expended, ought to be her study and philoso-phy. Our forefathers were very wise people in this point, who said that a wife always knew enough when the capacity of her genius raised her to understand a doublet and a pair of breeches. Their wives did not read, but they lived well; their families were all their learned discourse, and their books, a thimble, thread, and needles, with which they worked amidst their knot of maids. But the women of this age are very far from behaving themselves in that way, they must write and turn authors. No science is too profound for them; and in my house, more than in any other place in the world, the most lofty secrets are conceived, and they understand every thing but what they ought to understand. They know the motions of the moon, the polar star, Venus, Saturn, and Mars, whom I have nothing to do with; and with all this vain knowledge, which they go so far to look for, they do not know how my pot goes on, which I have occasion for. My servants too to please you aspire after learning, and they all do nothing less than what they have to do; reasoning is the business of all my house, by which they banish all reason out of it. One burns my roast-meat while she is reading some history, the other raves in verse when I call for drink: in short, I per-ceive your example followed by them, and I have no benefit from my servants. One poor wench alone was left me who was not infected with this villanous air, and here is she turned away with a great clutter, be-cause she did not speak according to Vaugelas. I tell you, sister, for it is to you, as I said, that I address myself, all this proceeding is disagreeable to me. I do not like all your scholars should come to my house, and especially this Mr. Trissotin. It was he who lampooned you in verse; all his discourses are foolish trash; one is at a loss for what he says after he has spoke; and I believe, for my part, that he is crack-brained.

Philaminta. Good heaven, what meanness both of foul and language!

Belisa. Can there be a more stupid assemblage of corpuscula? or a mind composed of more city-like atoms? Is it possible that I am of the same blood? I heartily hate myself for being of your stock, and leave the place in amazement.

SCENE VIII.

PHILAMINTA, CHRISALUS.

PHILAMINTA.

HAVE you still some other arrow to shoot?

Chrisalus. I? No. Let us dispute no longer; it is over. Let us talk of another affair. As for your eldest daughter, she shews a distaste for the marriage-tye: in short, she is a philosopher, I say nothing more of her; she is well managed; and you do very right. But her younger sister is of quite another temper, and I think it is good to provide Henrietta with a proper husband, that——

Philaminta. I have considered it, and will tell you my intention. This Mr. Trissotin whom we are accused about, and who has not the honour to be in your esteem, is the person I chuse for a husband for her, and I know better than you how to judge of his merit. All dispute in this case is to no purpose; and I have determined the affair. However, do not say a word of the choice of this husband, I will speak to your daughter about it before you.   I have reasons to make my conduct approved of, and I shall know very well if you have instructed her.

SCENE IX.

ARISTUS, CHRISALUS.

ARISTUS.

WELL, I see your wife is gone, brother, and that you have just had some conversation together.

Chrisalus. Yes.

Aristus. What is the success of it? Shall we have Henrietta? Has she consented? Is the business ended?

Chrisalus. Not yet.

Aristus. Does she refuse?

Chrisalus. No.

Aristus. Does she take time to consider?

Chrisalus. Not at all.

Aristus. What then?

Chrisalus. She has chose another man for a son-in-law.

Aristus. Another man for a son-in-law!

Chrisalus. Yes.

Aristus. Who is he?

Chrisalus. Mr. Trissotin.

Aristus. What, that Mr. Trissotin——

Chrisalus. Yes, that always talks Latin, and repeats verses.

Aristus. Have you accepted of him?

Chrisalus. I! no, heaven forbid.

Aristus. What answer did you make her?

Chrisalus. None; and I am very glad I did not speak, lest I should have got myself into a scrape.

Ariftus. The reafon is very good, and you have made a grand ftep. Did you propofe Clitander to her?

Chrifalus. No; for finding fhe talked of another fon-in-law, I thought it was better for me not to make any advances at prefent.

Ariftus. Indeed your prudence is extraordinary. Are you not afhamed of your effeminacy? Is is poffible a man can be fo weak as to let his wife have an abfolute power, and not to dare to oppofe what fhe has determined?

Chrifalus. Alas, brother! You talk of it with a great deal of eafe, and do not know how noife weighs me down. I love peace and tranquillity exceedingly, and my wife is of a terrible temper; fhe makes a great a-do about the name of a philofopher, but fhe is not lefs paffionate for that; and her morality, which defpifes wealth, has no effect on the eagernefs of her choler; for the leaft oppofition to what comes in her head we have a terrible tempeft for eight days. She makes me tremble whenever fhe begins her note; fhe is fuch a perfect dragon, that I know not where to hide myfelf; and yet, with all her devilifh temper, I am obliged to call her, My joy, and My life.

Ariftus. Go, it is all a jeft. Between us, your wife is an abfolute miftrefs over you, through your cowardice. Her power is founded upon nothing but your weaknefs. It is from you fhe takes the title of miftrefs. You give up yourfelf to her haughty command, and allow yourfelf to be led by the nofe like an afs. What, cannot you for once determine to be a man, feeing you are called fo? To make a wife condefcend to your wifhes, and have fpirit enough to fay once, I will have it fo? Can you, without fhame, leave your daughter to be facrificed to the foolifh vifions which the family are poffeffed with; and to inveft a blockhead with all your wealth for six words of Latin which he bellows out to them? A pedant, whom your wife compliments every turn with the name of fine wit, and great philosopher, of a man that was never equalled for galant verses, when every body knows he is nothing of all this? Come, come; once more, it is a jest; and your cowardice deserves to be laughed at.

Chrisalus. I find that I am wrong. Brother, I will take your advice, and shew a stouter heart.

Aristus. That is well said.

Chrisalus. It is a terrible affair to be subject to the power of a wife.

. Aristus. Indeed it is.

Chrisalus. My mildness gives her too much advantage over me.

Aristus. It does.

Chrisalus. She has played upon my easiness too much.

Aristus. Indeed it is so.

Chrisalus. This day I will let her see that I am master, and that I will chuse a husband to my daughter according to my own mind.

Aristus. Now you are as I would have you, a reasonable man.

Chrisalus. You are Clitander's friend, brother, bring him to me, you know where he lives.

Aristus. I will go and do it directly.

Chrisalus. I will be a man in the face of the world, for I have born it too long.

ACT III.   SCENE I.

PHILAMINTA, ARMANDA, BELISA,
TRISSOTIN, L'EPINE.

PHILAMINTA.

OH! let us fit down here, peaceably to hear thefe verfes, which fhould be weighed word by word.

Armanda. I am impatient to fee them.

Belifa. So are we.

Philaminta to Triffotin.] Whatever comes from you is delightful to me.

Armanda. It gives me inexpreffible pleafure.

Belifa. It affords a moft delicious repaft to my ear.

Philaminta. Pray do not let us languifh under fuch preffing defires.

Armanda. Be quick.

Belifa. Haften our pleafure.

Philaminta. Offer your epigram to our impatience.

Triffotin to Philaminta.] Alas, madam, it is a quite new-born babe. You certainly ought be affected with its fate, for I brought it forth in your court-yard.

Philaminta. It will be dear to me on its father's account.

Triffotin. Your approbation may ferve for a mother to it.

Belifa. How much wit he has!

SCENE II.

HENRIETTA, PHILAMINTA, ARMANDA,
BELISA, TRISSOTIN, L'EPINE.

PHILAMINTA to Henrietta who is going away.
HOW now, why do you run away again?
    Henrietta. For fear of interrupting such an agreeable conversation.

Philaminta. Come hither, with both your ears to share the pleasure of hearing wonders.

Henrietta. Things of genius are not my province; I know very little of the beauties of writing.

Philaminta. It does not signify, I have another secret to tell you afterwards, which it is necessary that you should know.

Trissotin to Henrietta.] The sciences have nothing in them to inflame you, you do not pique yourself upon any thing but to charm.

Henrietta. One as little as the other, and I have no desire——

Belisa. Ah, pray let us think of the new-born babe.

Philaminta to L'Epine.] Come, boy, quickly, something to sit on. [L'Epine falls down.] Do you see the impertinent thing! ought people to fall after having learnt the equilibrium of things?

Belisa. Do you not perceive the cause of your fall, ignorance? and that it proceeded from thy deviating from the fixed point, which we call the center of gravity?

L'Epine. When I was on the ground, madam, I perceived it.

Philaminta to L'Epine, who goes out.] Booby!

Triſſotin. It was happy for him he was not made of glaſs.

Armanda. Ah! Wit continually!

Belifa. That never fails.

Philaminta. [All fit down.] Serve up your amiable repaſt to us immediately.

Triſſotin. A plate of only eight verſes is a ſmall matter, I think, for ſuch a great hunger as you diſco-ver to me, and I believe I ſhould not do amiſs in this caſe if I joined to the epigram, or rather madrigal, the ragoo of a ſonnet which has been eſteemed by a certain princeſs to have ſomething of delicacy in it. It is ſea-ſoned with Attic ſalt throughout, and you will think it, I believe, of pretty good taſte.

Armanda. Oh, I make no doubt of it.

Philaminta. Let us attend immediately.

Belifa interrupting Triſſotin as often as he begins to read.] I feel my heart leap for joy before-hand. I love poetry to madneſs, and eſpecially when the verſes are gallantly turned.

Philaminta. If we talk perpetually, he can ſay no-thing.

Triſſotin. So——

Belifa to Henrietta.] Hold your tongue, niece.

Armanda. Ah! let him read then.

T R I S S O T I N.

A SONNET to the princeſs URANIA upon her fever

A Sleep your prudence ſure muſt be,
        Magnificently thus to treat,
And ſumptuouſly lodge in ſtate,
        Your moſt pernicious enemy.

M 2

Belisa. Ah, what a lovely beginning!

Armanda. What a gallant turn it has!

Philaminta. He alone possesses the talent of making easy verses.

Armanda. We must give up the day to " prudence asleep."

Belisa. " Lodge her enemy," is full of charms to me.

Philaminta. I like " sumptuously and magnificent-ly:" Those two adverbs joined do admirably.

Belisa. Let us listen to the rest.

TRISSOTIN.

Asleep your prudence sure must be,
Magnificently thus to treat,
And sumptuously lodge in state,
Your most pernicious enemy.

Armanda. " Prudence asleep!"

Belisa. " Sumptuously lodge her enemy!"

Philaminta. " Sumptuously! magnificently!"

TRISSOTIN.

Whate'er is said, the serpent send
From your apartment rich and great;
Where insolently the ingrate
Your precious life attempts to end.

Belisa. Ah! softly, pray allow me breath.

Armanda. Pray give us time to admire.

Philaminta. At hearing these verses one feels some-thing run at the very bottom of one's heart, I do not know what that makes one faint.

ARMANDA.

Whate'er is said the serpent send,
From your apartment rich and great.

How finely said is, " apartment rich and great!" And with what wit is the metaphor introduced!

PHILAMINTA.

Whate'er is said the serpent send.

Ah! that "whate'er is said" is admirable for taste! it is a valuable passage in my opinion.

Armanda. I am likewise in love with "whate'er is said."

Belisa. I am of the same opinion, "whate'er is said" is a happy expression.

Armanda. I wish I had written it.

Belisa. It is worth a whole piece.

Philaminta. But do you really comprehend the *Finesse* of it as I do?.

Armanda and Belisa.] Oh! oh!

PHILAMINTA.

. Whate'er is said the serpent send.
Though they should take the fever's part, do not regard it, laugh at their babbling..

Whate'er is said the serpent send.
" Whate'er is said, whate'er is said." This " whate'er is said," says a great deal more than one thinks. I do not know, for my part, if every one be like me, but I understand a million of words under it.

Belisa. It is true, it says more things than it appears to do.

Philaminta to Trissotin.] But when you wrote this charming " whate'er is said," did you yourself understand all its energy? Did you really conceive yourself all that it says to us; and did you then think you were writing such a witty affair?

Trissotin. Ha, ha!

Armanda. I have likewise " the ingrate" in my head: that " ingrate" of a fever, unjust, uncivil, to treat people who entertained it ill.

. Philaminta. In short, both the stanzas of four lines

are excellent. Let us come quickly to the triplets, pray.

Armanda. Ah, pray now, once more " whate'er is said."

TRISSOTIN.

Whate'er is said the serpent send.

PHILAMINTA, ARMANDA and BELISA.
Whate'er is said!

TRISSOTIN.

From your apartment rich and great.

PHILAMINTA, ARMANDA, and BELISA.
Apartment rich and great.

TRISSOTIN.

Where infolently the ingrate

PHILAMINTA, ARMANDA, and BELISA.
That ingrate of a fever!

TRISSOTIN.

Your precious life attempts to end.

PHILAMINTA.
Your precious life!

ARMANDA and BELISA. Ah!

TRISSOTIN.

Who not refpecting your high rank,
Your noble blood has bafely drank,

PHILAMINTA, ARMANDA, and BELISA. Ah!

TRISSOTIN.

And hourly plays fome cruel prank.
The next time to the bath you go,
There take it without more ado,
And in the cruel mifchief throw.

Philaminta. I can hold no longer.

Belifa. I faint!

Armanda. I die with rapture.

Philaminta. One finds one's felf feized with numberlefs gentle thrillings.

ARMANDA.
The next time to the bath you go,
BELISA.
There take it without more ado,
PHILAMINTA.
And in the cruel mischief throw.
Take and drown it in the bath.

Armanda. Every ftep in your verfe one meets with fome delightful beauty.

Belifa. One goes through it with pleafure.

Philaminta. One cannot tread but upon fine things.

Armanda. They are paths ftrewed with rofes.

Triffotin. The fonnet then you think——

Philaminta. Admirable, new, and no body ever made any thing more excellent.

Belifa to Henrietta.] You make a ftrange figure there, niece, not the leaft moved with what has been read.

Henrietta. One cannot be a wit at will, aunt; every one makes fuch a figure as they can.

Triffotin. Perhaps my verfes are troublefome to the lady.

Henrietta. No, I do not attend to them.

Philaminta. Ah! let us fee the epigram.

Triffotin. " Upon a coach of an amarant colour, given to a lady of his acquaintance."

Philaminta. His titles have always fomething in them uncommon.

Armanda. The novelty of them prepares one for a thoufand witty ftrokes.

TRISSOTIN.
Love has fo dearly fold to me his band,
BELISA, ARMANDA, and PHILAMINTA. Ah!
TRISSOTIN.
Already it has coft me half my land,
M 4

And when this beauteous coach you do behold,
Wherein there lies imbossed so much gold,
That all the country round it does amaze,
And yields a pompous triumph to my lays.
Philaminta. Ah, " my lays. There is erudition!
Belisa. The cover is pretty, and worth a million.

TRISSOTIN.

And when this beauteous coach you do behold,
Wherein there lies imbossed so much gold,
That all the country round it does amaze,
And yields a pompous triumph to my lays;
No longer say that it is amarant,
But much, much rather say that 'tis my rent.

Armanda. Oh, oh, oh! she there does not attend
to it in the least.

Philaminta. No body but he, can write in this taste.

BELLSA.

No longer say that it is amarant,
But much, much rather say that 'tis my rent.
This may be declined, " My rent, of my rent, to my
rent."

Philaminta. I do not know but my mind might be
prepossessed in your favour from the minute I was acquainted with you, but I admire your verse and prose
throughout.

Trissotin to Philaminta.] If you would shew us
something of yours, we might admire it also in our
turns.

Philaminta. I have done nothing in verse, but I have
room to hope that I may in a little time be able to shew
you as a friend eight chapters of the plan of our academy.   Plato foolishly forbore the subject when he writ
the treatise of his Republic; but I will carry the idea,
which I have upon paper formed in prose, to the full
effect: For in short I am very much vexed at the wrong

they do us with regard to wit; and I will revenge e-
very one of us of the unworthy clafs men rank us in,
by bounding our talents to trifling things, and fhutting
the door of fublime lights againft us.

Armanda. It is offending our fex extremely, to
make the force of our underftanding extend no farther
than to judge of a petticoat, and the air of a mantua,
or the beauties of a point, or a new brocade.

Belifa. We muft get above this fhameful condition,
and bravely fet our genius at liberty.

Triffotin. Every body is fenfible of my refpect for
the ladies, and if I pay homage to the brilliancy of their
eyes, I likewife honour the brightnefs of their wit.

Philaminta. Our fex alfo do you juftice in thofe things;
but we would fhew certain wits whofe pride makes
them ufe us with contempt, that women are alfo furnifhed with learning; that, like them, they can hold
learned affemblies, regulated in that cafe by better
rules; that they will unite there what is feparated elfewhere, join fine language with fublime fciences, difcover nature in a thoufand experiments; and upon a-
ny queftions that may be propofed, bring in each fect
and efpoufe none.

Triffotin. For order, I am fond of Peripateticifm.

Philaminta. For abftractions, I love Platonifm.

Armanda. Epicurus pleafes me, for his Dogma's are
ftrong.

Belifa. For my part, I agree mightily to the Ato-
mical philofophy; but I think the Vacuum difficult to
be endured, and relifh the fubtle matter much better.

Triffotin. Defcartes for the Magnetifm, gives much
into my opinion.

Armanda. I love his vortexes.

Philaminta. And I admire his falling worlds.

M 5

Armanda. I long to see our assembly opened, and to signalize ourselves by some discovery.

Trissotin. We expect it much from your lively lights, there is little of obscurity in nature to you.

Philaminta. For my part, without flattering myself, I have made one already, and have plainly seen men in the moon.

Belisa. I think I have not yet seen men; but I have perceived steeples as plain as I see you.

Armanda. We will likewise dive into the profundity of grammar, history, poetry, morality and politics, as well as of physics.

Philaminta. My heart is smitten with the charms of morality, and it was formerly the admiration of great genius's; but I give the superiority to the Stoics, and I think nothing so fine as their wise man.

Armanda. As for language, they shall soon see our regulations in that, and we intend to make great changes in it. By either a just or natural antipathy, we have each of us taken a mortal hatred to a number of words, either Verbs or Nouns, which we shall mutually abandon; we are preparing deadly sentences against them, and intend to open our learned conferences by proscription of all those diverse words from which we would purge both verse and prose.

Philaminta. But the finest project of our academy, with which I am delighted, is a glorious intention, and which will be extolled amongst all the great genius's of posterity, is the retrenching those filthy syllables, which in the finest words produce scandal; those eternal jests of fools of all times; those nauseous commonplace things of our wretched buffoons; those sources of a heap of infamous equivocations with which they insult the modesty of women.

Trissotin. These are certainly admirable projects.

Belifa. When our ftatutes are all made, you fhal¹ fee them.

Triffotin. They muft be all beautiful and wife.

Armanda. We fhall by our laws be the judges of performances: By our laws profe and verfe will be both fubject to us; none fhall have wit but we and our friends; we will fearch every where to find fome-thing to blame, and will think no body but ourfelves knows how to write well.

SCENE III.

TRISSOTIN, PHILAMINTA, BELISA, ARMANDA, HENRIETTA, L'EPINE.

L'EPINE to Triffotin:

SIR, here is a man defires to fpeak with you; he is dreffed in black, and fpeaks in a foft tone.

[They rife up.

Triffotin. It is that learned friend who has preffed me fo much to procure him the honour of your ac-quaintance.

Philaminta. Sir, you are extremely welcome to in-troduce him.

SCENE IV.

PHILAMINTA, BELISA, ARMANDA, HENRIETTA.

PHILAMINTA to Armanda and Belifa.

LET us at leaft do him the honour of our wit. Harkye. [to Henrietta, who is going out.] I told you as plain as I could, that I wanted you.

Henrietta. For what?

Philaminta. Come hither, you shall soon know.

SCENE V.

PHILAMINTA, BELISA, ARMANDA, HENRIETTA, VADIUS, TRISSOTIN.

TRISSOTIN presenting Vadius.

MADAM, this is the man who dies with desire to see you. When I introduce him to you, I do not fear being blamed, for having admitted a profane person to you, madam; he may be ranked amongst the greatest wits.

Philaminta. The person who presents him speaks his value sufficiently.

Trissotin. He has a perfect knowledge of the antient authors, madam, and understands Greek as well as any man.

Philaminta to Belisa.] Greek! O heavens! Greek! He understands Greek, sister.

Belisa to Armanda.] Ah! Niece, Greek!

Armanda. Greek! What sweetness!

Philaminta. What, does the gentleman understand Greek? Ah! pray, Sir, let me embrace you, for Greek's sake.

[Vadius embraces both Belisa and Armanda.

Henrietta to Vadius, who would embrace her likewise] Excuse me, Sir, I do not understand Greek.

[They sit down.

Philaminta. I have a great regard for Greek books.

Vadius. I am afraid of being troublesome thro' the great desire which engaged me to pay you my homage to-day, madam, and I have disturbed some learned discourse.

Philaminta. Sir, you can spoil nothing with your Greek.

Trissotin. He might shew you something if he would, he does wonders in verse as well as prose.

Vadius. The fault of authors in their productions is to tyrannize over conversation with them; to be at the palace, in courts, streets, or at table, indefatigable readers of their tiresome verses. For my part, I see nothing more ridiculous, than an author who goes e-very where mumping for praise; who seizing the ears of the very first comers, makes them often martyrs to his lucubrations. They never saw me such a conceit-ed fool; and in this I am of the opinion of a certain Greek, who, by an express dogma, forbids all his wise men the unbecoming forwardness of reading their works. Here are some little verses for young lovers, upon which I would gladly have your opinion.

Trissotin. Your verses have beauties which no others have.

Vadius. Venus and the Graces reign in all yours.

Trissotin. You have the free turn, and a fine choice of words.

Vadius. We see every where the Ethos and Pathos with you.

Trissotin. We have seen eclogues from you in a style which outshines Virgil and Theocritus for sweet-ness.

Vadius. Your odes have a noble, gallant, and tender air, far before your own Horace.

Trissotin. Is there any thing so amorous as your lays?

Vadius. Can one find any thing equal to the sonnets you write?

Trissotin. Any thing more delightful that your little Rondeaus?

Vadius. Any thing so full of wit as your madri-gals?

Trissotin. At ballads especially, you are admirable.

Vadius. And I think you adorable in your Crambo's.

Trissotin. If France could but know your value,

Vadius. If the age did but render justice to men of wit,

Trissotin. You would ride through the streets in a gilded chariot.

Vadius. We should see the public erect statues to you. Hum. [To Trissotin.] Here is a ballad, and I desire you will freely——

Trissotin to Vadius.] Have you seen a certain little sonnet upon the princess Urania's fever.

Vadius. Yes, it was read to me yesterday in company.

Trissotin. Are you acquainted with the author of it?

Vadius. No; but I am very sensible, without flattery, his sonnet is good for nothing.

Trissotin. It is admired by a great many people, however.

Vadius. That does not prevent it from being miserable; and you would be of my opinion, if you saw it.

Trissotin. I know I should not be at all so in that; and that few people are capable of such a sonnet.

Vadius. Heaven preserve me from making such.

Trissotin. I maintain that a better cannot be made; and my grand reason is, because I am the author of it.

Vadius. You?

Trissotin. I.

Vadius. I do not know then how the thing was.

Triſſotin. It was that I was ſo unhappy as not to be able to pleaſe you.

Vadius. My mind has been wandering when I heard it read, or elſe the reader ſpoilt the ſonnet. But let us drop this converſation, and ſee my ballad.

Triſſotin. In my opinion a ballad is an inſipid thing; it is no longer in faſhion, it ſmells of antiquity.

Vadius. Many people are delighted with a ballad.

Triſſotin. That does not hinder but it may diſpleaſe me.

Vadius. It may be never the worſe on that account.

Triſſotin. It has wonderful charms for pedants.

Vadius. And yet we ſee it does not pleaſe you.

Triſſotin. You very fooliſhly give your qualities to others.   [They all riſe.

Vadius. You very impertinently caſt yours upon me.

Triſſotin. Go, ſchoolboy, paper-blotter.

Vadius. Go, pitiful rhimer; ſhame to thy profeſſion!

Triſſotin. Go, verſe-ſtealer, impudent plagiary.

Vadius. Go, pedant——

Philaminta. Oh, gentlemen, what is your intention?

Triſſotin to Vadius.] Go, go, reſtore the ſhameful thefts which the Greeks and Latins challenge from you.

Vadius. Go, go, and do penance on Parnaſſus for having lamed Horace in your verſes.

Triſſotin. Remember your book made little noiſe.

Vadius. Remember your bookſeller reduced to an hoſpital.

Triſſotin. My glory is eſtabliſhed, your endeavours to mangle it is to no purpoſe.

Vadius. Yes, yes, I send you to the author of the satires again.

Trissotin. I send you thither again likewise.

Vadius. I have the pleasure of knowing that people see he has treated me more honourably. He cursorily gives me a slight touch amongst many other authors that are esteemed at court, but he never leaves you at peace in his verses, and we see you throughout the but of his lashes.

Trissotin. I hold the more honourable rank there for that. He puts you in the croud for a miserable wretch, thinks it sufficient to crush you with one blow, and never does you the honour to redouble it; but he attacks me apart as a noble adversary, against whom he thinks all his efforts necessary; and his redoubling his blows against me in all places, shews that he never thinks himself victorious.

Vadius. My pen shall shew you what kind of a man I am.

Trissotin. And mine shall oblige you to know your master.

Vadius. I defy you in verse, prose, Greek, and Latin.

Trissotin. Well, we shall see one another alone at Barbin's.

SCENE VI.

TRISSOTIN, PHILAMINTA, ARMANDA, BELISA, HENRIETTA.

TRISSOTIN.

BE not angry at my passion; it is your judgment that I defend, madam, in the sonnet which he had the impudence to attack.

Philaminta. I will endeavour to reconcile you. But let us talk of another matter. Come hither, Henrietta, it has long given me uneasiness, that I could never discover any genius in you; but I have discovered a method of imparting some to you.

Henrietta. Mother, you take more care of me than is needful; I do not trouble my head about learned discourses; I love to live at ease, and one must be at too much pains in every thing one says to have wit; it is an ambition that I do not aspire to. I am very well satisfied, mother, in being a blockhead; and had rather have only a common way of talking than torment myself to speak fine words.

Philaminta. Yes, but it gives me offence, and it is not my intention to suffer such a stain in my blood. The beauty of the face is a frail ornament, a fading flower, a moment's lustre, and which only cleaves to the Epidermis; but that of the mind is inherent and firm: I have therefore long endeavoured to give you the beauty which time cannot mow down, to inspire you with the love of learning, to insinuate into you fine knowledge; and the resolution my wishes have at last fixed on, is to join you to a man that is full of wit; [pointing to Triffotin.] and that man is this gentleman, whom I determine to have you look on as the husband destined you by my choice.

Henrietta. I, mother?

Philaminta. Yes, you. Behave like a fool, pray do.

Belifa to Triffotin.] I understand you. Your eyes ask my consent to engage elsewhere a heart which I am in possession of. Come, I will so. I give you up to this union. It is a match which will be the making of you.

Triffotin to Henrietta.] I am at a loss what to say

to you in my tranfport, madam; and this match which
I fee myfelf honoured with, puts me——

Henrietta. Softly, Sir, it is not yet done; do not be
in fuch a hurry.

Philaminta. How you anfwer! Do you know that
if—— It is enough, you underftand me. [To Triffotin.] Come, let us leave her; fhe will grow wifer.

SCENE VII.

HENRIETTA, ARMANDA.

ARMANDA.

YOU may eafily perceive how your mother's care
appears; and fhe could not have chofen a more
illuftrious fpoufe——

Henrietta. If the choice is fo agreeable, why do you
not take him?

Armanda. It is to you, not to me, that his hand
is given.

Henrietta. I yield him up to you entirely, as my
eldeft fifter.

Armanda. If matrimony appeared as pleafant to me
as it does to you, I would accept of your offer with
pleafure.

Henrietta. If I had pedants in my head as you have,
I fhould think it a very good match.

Armanda. However different our taftes may be, fifter, we ought to obey our parents. A mother has
an abfolute power over us, and it is to no purpofe
to——.

SCENE VIII.

CHRISALUS, ARISTUS, CLITANDER,
HENRIETTA, ARMANDA.

CHRISALUS to Henrietta, presenting Clitander.

COME, Henrietta, I will have my intention approved of. Pull off this glove. Give the gentleman your hand, and look upon him in your heart,
from this time, as the man whom I intend for your
husband.

Armanda. On this side, sister, your inclinations are
strong enough.

Henrietta. We ought to be obedient to our parents,
sister; a father has an absolute power over our desires.

Armanda. A mother has her share in our obedience.

Chrisalus. What do you mean by that?

Armanda. I say that I very much apprehend my mother and you will not agree in this, and that there is
another husband——

Chrisalus. Hold your peace, Mrs. Pedantress; go,
philosopher, whom she is so fond of, and do not concern yourself with my actions. Tell her my mind,
and advise her not to come and set my ears on fire;
go immediately.

SCENE IX.

CHRISALUS, ARISTUS, HENRIETTA, CLITANDER.

ARISTUS.

WELL done; you do wonders.

Clitander. What transport! What joy! How am I delighted!

Chrisalus to Clitander.] Come, take her hand, and go before us; lead her into her chamber. What soft caresses! [To Aristus.] Hold, my heart is moved with all these tendernesses; this cheers up my old age wonderfully, and brings my youthful amours to my remembrance.

ACT IV. SCENE I.

PHILAMINTA, ARMANDE.

ARMANDA.

INDEED she seemed to make a vanity of her obedience, did not in the least hesitate, and her heart scarce gave itself time to receive the order of surrendering, and seemed less to follow the will of a father than to affect to outbrave the orders of a mother.

Philaminta. I will let her see to whose commands the laws of reason subject all her desires; and who ought to rule, her father or her mother, spirit or body, form or matter.

Armanda. They owed you a compliment upon it, at least; and this little gentleman uses you very strange-y, to determine to be your son-in-law whether you will or not.

Philaminta. He is not so now in the way his heart might have had pretensions to it. I thought him hand-some, and approved of your loves; but I was always displeased with his proceedings; he knew that, thank heaven, I undertook to write; and yet never desired me to read any thing to him.

SCENE II.

CLITANDER entering softly, and listening without being perceived, ARMANDA, PHILAMINTA.

ARMANDA.

WERE I in your place, I would not suffer him to marry Henrietta. They would wrong me very much to imagine that I speak interestedly in this case, and that his unworthy behaviour has occasi-oned any secret indignation in my heart. The assist-ance of philosophy has fortified my soul against such blows; it is sufficient to raise one above every thing; but to treat you so is putting you to a nonplus. You are obliged in honour to oppose his inclinations, and indeed he is a man you ought not to be pleased with. I never found he had any sincere regard for you.

Philaminta. Blockhead!

Armanda. Notwithstanding the noise your fame makes, he always appeared cold in your praises.

Philaminta. Beast!

Armanda. And I have twenty times read some of your verses as new things, which he did not admire.

Philaminta. Impertinence!

Armanda. We frequently quarrelled about it, and you would not think how many follies——

Clitander to Armanda.] Oh, foftly, pray. A little charity, madam, or at leaft a little honefty. What injury have I done you? Or in what have I offended you, that you fhould arm all your eloquence againft me thus? That you fhould endeavour to deftroy me, and take fo much pains to render me odious to thofe I ftand in need of? Speak. Say whence this terrible wrath proceeds? I beg that this lady may be an impartial judge in the cafe.

Armanda. If I had the wrath you would accufe me of, I could find enough to authorize it. You would be too deferving of it; for firft flames fix themfelves by fuch facred rights on the heart, that one ought to lofe fortune, and renounce the light, rather than burn with the fires of another love; no horror is equal to the changing one's vows, and every faithlefs heart is a monfter in morality.

Clitander. Do you call that infidelity, madam, which the fiercenefs of your foul enjoined me; I only obey the laws it impofes on me, and if I offend you, that is entirely the caufe of it. Your charms had at firft got entire poffeffion of my heart; it burnt for two years with a conftant ardour; there is no affiduous care, duty, refpect, fervice, which it did not make amorous facrifices of to you. But all my fires, all my care, could do nothing with you, I found you ftill averfe to my fofteft addreffes. That which you refufe, I offer to the choice of another. See, is it my fault, madam, or yours? Did my heart run to a change, or did you drive it? Is it I that leave you, or you that turn me away?

Armanda. Do you call it, being averfe to your addreffes, Sir, to deprive them of what they had of vulgar in them; and to endeavour reducing them to that purity in which the beauty of perfect love confifts?

You cannot for me keep your thought clear and difentangled from the commerce of fenfe; and you do not
tafte in the greateft of its charms that union of hearts,
where the bodies are not concerned. You cannot love
but with a grofs paffion, but with all the train of material ties; and to nourifh the fires which are produ-
ced in you, there muft be marriage, with all that follows it. Foh! What ftrange love! How far are great
fouls from burning with thefe terreftrial flames! The
fenfes have no fhare in all their ardors; this amiable
paffion would marry nothing but the heart, and leaves
the reft behind as unworthy; it is a fire pure and clear,
like the celeftial fires; with this they breathe only virtuous fighs, and never incline to bafe defires. Nothing impure has to do with the end they propofe.
They love for the fake of loving, and for nothing elfe;
their tranfports are only to the mind; and none can
perceive that they have a body.

Clitander. For my part, madam, with your leave,
I fee that I have unluckily a body as well as a foul,
and find that it fticks too clofe to it to leave it behind;
I do not underftand the art of thefe feparations; heaven has denied me that philofophy, and my body and
foul go together. There is nothing finer, as you have
obferved, than thefe purified defires which regard the
mind only, that union of hearts, and thofe tender
thoughts, fo thoroughly difentangled from the commerce of fenfe: But thefe amours are too refined for
me; I am a little groffer, as you accufe me; I love
entire, myfelf, and I am defirous, I muft confefs, that
the love which any body has for me, fhould be to my
whole perfon. This is not a matter worthy of fuch
great punifhments, and, without doing any wrong to
your fine fentiments, I fee that my method is very much
practifed in the world, and that marriage is quite in

faſhion, paſſes for a tie virtuous and tender enough to warrant the deſire I had of becoming your huſband, without giving you reaſon to take offence at the liberty of ſuch a thought.

Armanda. Mighty well, Sir, extremely well, ſince your brutiſh ſentiments will be ſatisfied without liſtening to me; ſince there muſt be carnal ties and corporeal chains to reduce you to a faithful ardor, if my mother conſents to it, I will bring my mind to agree with you in what we are ſpeaking of.

Clitander. It is now too late, madam, another has taken place; and by ſuch a return I ſhould baſely abuſe my aſylum, and wrong the goodneſs to which I fled from your haughtineſs.

Philaminta. And do you, Sir, aſſure yourſelf of my conſent, when you promiſe yourſelf this other match? Allow me to inform you, that I have another huſband in readineſs for Henrietta.

Clitander. But, pray, madam, think well of your choice, and do not expoſe me to ſo much diſgrace. I beg you will not doom me to the ſhameful fate of finding myſelf a rival of Mr. Triſſotin. The love of wits, which makes you ſo averſe to me, could not oppoſe to me a leſs noble adverſary. There are many whom the ill taſte of the age has reputed wits; but Mr. Triſſotin has not been able to deceive any body, and every one does juſtice to his writings. They take him every where, but here, for what he is, and I have been a hundred times ſurprized to ſee you raiſe to the ſkies ſilly verſes which you would have diſowned had they been of your own making.

Philaminta. If you judge of him quite otherwiſe than we, it is becauſe we ſee him with other eyes than you.

SCENE III.

TRISSOTIN, PHILAMINTA, ARMAN-
DA, CLITANDER.

TRISSOTIN to Philaminta.

MADAM, I am come to tell you a great piece of news. We have escaped finely while we slept. A world has passed along just by us, is fallen acrofs our Vortex, and if it had met our earth in the way, it had been dashed in pieces like glafs.

Philaminta. Let us give up this converfation till another time, this gentleman finds neither rhime nor reafon in it; he profeffes to cherifh ignorance, and to hate wit and learning more than any thing.

Clitander. This truth wants fome foftening, madam. I muft explain myfelf: I only hate that wit and learning which fpoil people. Thefe are things which in themfelves are fine and good; but I would rather chufe to be in the rank of the ignorant, than fee myfelf learned as fome people are.

Triffotin. For my part, I do not hold, whatever effect may be fuppofed, that learning can do any hurt.

Clitander. And it is my opinion that learning often makes very great fools both in word and deed.

Triffotin. That is a great paradox.

Clitander. The proof of it would be very eafy, I believe, without being very wife. If reafons should fail, I am certain examples will not fail me.

Triffotin. You may cite, that will conclude nothing.

Clitander. I will not go very far to find one which will fuit my purpofe.

Triffotin. I do not fee thefe famous examples, for my part.

VOL. V.   N

Clitander. I see them so plainly, that they almost strike me blind.

Trissotin. I imagined that it was ignorance which made great fools, not learning.

Clitander. You have thought very wrong; and I assure you, that a learned fool is more intolerable than an ignorant one.

Trissotin. Common opinion is against your maxims, since ignorant and foolish are synonimous terms.

Clitander. If you will take it according to the use of words, the alliance is greater between pedant and fool.

Trissotin. Folly in the one appears quite pure.

Clitander. And study in the other adds to nature.

Trissotin. Learning in itself has great merit.

Clitander. Learning in a blockhead becomes impertinent.

Trissotin. Ignorance must have very great charms for you, since you take up arms so eagerly in her defence.

Clitander. If ignorance has very great charms for me, it is because certain learned people offer themselves to my view.

Trissotin. Those certain learned people might, if we knew them, be as good as certain other people that we see appear.

Clitander. Yes, if it was to be left to those certain learned people; but the certain other people would not agree to it.

Philaminta to Clitander.] I think, Sir——

Clitander. Good now, madam, the gentleman is able enough, without your assisting him: I have but too rough an assailant already, and I can only defend myself by retreating.

Armanda. But the offensive eagerness of each re-partee which you——

Clitander. Another second! I have done then.

Philaminta. One may bear these sort of combats in conversation, provided the person be not attacked.

Clitander. Alas! all this has nothing offensive in it; he understands raillery as well as any man in France; and he can feel himself piqued with many other strokes, and yet his glory does nothing but make a jest of them.

Trissotin. I am not surprised in the combat I have undertaken, to see the gentleman take the thesis he maintains; he is much in at court, that is sufficient; the court, it is well known, does not stand up for wit; it has an interest in supporting ignorance, and it is as being a courtier that he undertakes its defence.

Clitander. You wish very ill to the poor court, and its unhappiness is very great, to see you wits declaim against it every day; that when any thing chagrins you, you quarrel with it; and arraigning its bad taste, accuse it alone for your bad success. Allow me, Mr. Trissotin, to tell you with all the respect your name inspires me with, that you and your brethren would do very well to speak of the court in a more tender manner; that, take it at the bottom, it is not so ignorant as you gentlemen suppose; that it has common sense to judge of every thing; that something of good taste may be formed there; and that without flattery, the natural wit there is worth all the obscure learning of pedantry.

Trissotin. We see the effects of its good taste, Sir.

Clitander. Do you see, Sir, that it has so bad a one?

Trissotin. What I see, Sir, is, that Rasius and Baldus for learning do honour to France; and that all their merit, which is very plain, does not attract either the eyes or gifts of the court.

Clitander. I see your uneasiness, Sir, and that it is through modesty you do not place yourself with them: not to bring you therefore into the discourse, what do your able heroes do for the state? What service do their writings do it, that they accuse the court of terrible injustice, and complain in all places that it fails to pour down the favour of its gifts upon their learned names? Their learning is very necessary to France, and the court has much to do with the books they write. Three beggarly fellows get into their pitiful heads, that if they are but printed, and bound in calf, they are important persons in the state; that the destiny of crowns depends on their pen; that at the least rumour of their productions they should see pensions flying about them; that the eyes of all the world are fixed upon them; that they are famous prodigies in learning for knowing what others have said before them, for having had ears and eyes for thirty years, for having employed nine or ten thousand nights labour to perplex themselves with Greek and Latin, and loaded their mind with an untelligible booty of the old trash that lies scattered in books; men that always appear stupid with their learning; meritoriously rich in importunate babble; unskilful in every thing, void of common sense, and full of ridicule and impertinence to decry true wit and learning every where.

Philaminta. Your wrath is extreme, and this transport shews the movement of nature in you. It is the name of rival that excites in your breast——

SCENE IV.

TRISSOTIN, PHILAMINTA, CLITANDER, ARMANDA, JULIAN.

JULIAN.

MADAM, the learned perſon who paid you a viſit juſt now, and whoſe humble ſervant I have the honour of being, begs that you would read this letter.

Philaminta. However important this may be which I am deſired to read, know, friend, that it is a piece of rudeneſs to come and interrupt converſation; and that a ſervant who knows how to behave ſhould have re-courſe to the people of the houſe to be introduced.

Julian. Madam, I will note down that in my book.

Philaminta. "Madam, Triſſotin boaſts, that he is
" to marry your daughter. By this I inform you,
" that his philoſophy only aims at your wealth, and
" that you would do well not to conclude the match,
" till you have ſeen the poem which I am compoſing
" againſt him. While you wait for this picture, in
" which I intend to ſet him forth to you in all his co-
" lours, I ſend you Horace, Virgil, Terence, and Ca-
" tullus, where you will ſee all the paſſages he has
" pilfered, marked in the margin."

HERE is a merit attacked by a great many enemies, on account of the marriage I had promiſed myſelf; and this railing invites me to do an action directly which may confound envy, which may let him ſee that this endea-vour of his has brought the ſooner to effect what it thought to have broke off. [to Julian.] Relate this to your maſter immediately, and tell him, that in order to let him know what great value I ſet on his noble advice, and how worthy I think it to be followed, [pointing to Trissotin.] I will this night marry my daughter to the gentleman.

SCENE V.

PHILAMINTA, ARMANDA, CLITANDER.

PHILAMINTA to Clitander.

I Invite you, Sir, as a friend to all the family, to assist at the signing of their contract. Armanda, take care to send to a notary, and to go and acquaint your sister with the business.

Armanda. There is no occasion to acquaint my sister, that gentleman there will take care to run and carry her this news directly, and to dispose her heart to be rebellious to you.

Philaminta. We shall see who has most power over her, and if I am able to recall her to her duty.

SCENE VI.

ARMANDA, CLITANDER.

ARMANDA.

SIR, I am very sorry, to see that things are not altogether disposed according to your wishes.

Clitander. I will go, madam, and labour with diligence, that this great sorrow may not long oppress your mind.

Armanda. I am afraid that your labour will not have much effect.

Clitander. Perhaps you may find yourself in the wrong.

Armanda. I hope I shall.

Clitander. I am perfuaded of it; and that I fhall be feconded by your affiftance.

Armanda. Yes, I will ferve you as much as lies in my power.

Clitander. And that fervice is fure of my acknow-ledgment.

SCENE VII.

CHRISALUS, ARISTUS, HENRIETTA, CLITANDER.

CLITANDER.

I Shall be unhappy, Sir, without your affiftance. Your wife has rejected my inclination, and her heart is prepoffeffed in favour of Triffotin for a fon-in-law.

Chrifalus. What maggot has fhe got in her head then? Why the devil would fhe have this Mr. Trif-fotin?

Ariftus. It is by the honour he has of rhyming in Latin, that he gains the advantage over his rival.

Clitander. She will have the wedding this very evening.

Chrifalus. This evening?

Clitander. This evening.

Chrifalus. And this evening I am determined, in order to thwart her, that you two fhall be married.

Clitander. She has fent to the notary to draw up the contract.

Chrifalus. And I will bring him to draw up that which he fhould do.

Clitander pointing to Henrietta.] And the lady is to be informed by her fifter of the match fhe muft prepare her heart for.

Chrifalus. And I command her with full power to prepare her hand for this other alliance. I will let them fee that there is no other mafter to command in my houfe but myfelf. [To Henrietta.] We fhall return foon, be fure to ftay for us. Come, follow me, brother; and you, fon-in-law.

Henrietta to Ariftus.] Oh! keep him but always in this temper.

Ariftus. I will do every thing to ferve your love.

SCENE VIII.

HENRIETTA, CLITANDER.

CLITANDER:

WHATEVER powerful affiftance is promifed my paffion, my moft folid hope is in your heart, madam.

Henrietta. As for my heart, you may affure yourfelf of that.

Clitander. I muft be happy when I have that fupport.

Henrietta. You fee to what ties they intend to conftrain it.

Clitander. I fee nothing to fear while it is for me.

Henrietta. I will go and try every thing in favour of our tender defires; and if all my endeavours cannot give me to you, there is one retreat my heart is determined on, which will prevent me from being any other perfon's.

Clitander. Heaven forbid that you fhould ever put your love to fuch a trial.

A C T V. S C E N E I.

H E N R I E T T A, T R I S S O T I N.

H E N R I E T T A.

SIR, I wished to talk to you in private concerning the marriage my mother is making preparations for, hoping I might get you to listen to reason. I am sensible that you would expect a considerable fortune with me; but the charms of gold are unworthy of a true philosopher: and the contempt of wealth and frivolous greatness ought not to shine in your words alone.

Triſſotin. It is not riches which charmed me; your sparkling eyes and graceful air have attracted me; those are the treasures with which I am enamoured.

Henrietta. Sir, I admire your generous passion. Your obliging affection confounds me, and I am extremely sorry that I cannot return it properly. I have as great an esteem for you, as any person can have; but there is an obstacle which prevents me from loving you. You are sensible that two people cannot possess one heart, and I find Clitander is master of mine. I know that you are possessed of much greater merit, and I have a bad taste to chuse him for a husband, and and that you have a hundred fine talents which ought to please me. I see plainly that I am in the wrong, but cannot help it; and all the effect reason has upon me is to wish myself far enough from being so blind.

Triſſotin. The gift of your hand, which I am encouraged to make pretensions to, will give me that heart which Clitander is at prefent in poffeffion of; and I flatter myfelf, that by a thoufand foft cares I fhall be able to find the art of making myfelf beloved by you.

Henrietta. No, Sir; my foul is fixed to its firft vows, and cannot be affected by your tendernesses. I dare not explain myfelf freely here to you, and my confeffion has nothing in it that ought to fhock you. This amorous ardour which fprings up in hearts is not, you know, the effect of merit; caprice has a fhare in it, and when any one pleafes us, we are often at a lofs to fay why he does. If people loved through choice and wifdom, you would have had my whole heart; but one fees that love directs itfelf otherwife. I beg you will leave me to my blindnefs, and not make ufe of the violence that is put upon my obedience on your account. A man of honour will owe nothing to the power which parents have over us; he refufes to let what he loves be facrificed to him, and will not obtain a heart from any one but itfelf. Do not fpur on my mother to exercife, by her choice, the rigour of her power upon my inclinations. Remove your love from me to fome other more worthy of it.

Triffotin. Tell me, madam, what way can this heart be able to fatisfy you? Impofe on it any commands that may be be executed. Can it ceafe to love you, unlefs you ceafe, madam, to be amiable, and to difplay in your eyes celeftial charms——

Henrietta. Nay, Sir, let us leave this romantic ftuff. You have fo many Iris's, Phillis's, and Amaranthe's, whom you every where paint fo charming in your verfes, and for whom you vow fuch an amorous ardour——

Triffotin. It is my wit that fpeaks, and not my heart,

I am only in love with them as a poet; but I love the adorable Henrietta sincerely.

Henrietta. O, pray, Sir——

Triffotin. If this gives you offence, I cannot help offending you. This ardour hitherto unknown to you, consecrates vows of eternal duration to you; nothing can put a stop to their amiable transports; and notwithstanding your beauty may condemn my endeavours, I cannot refuse the assistance of a mother who intends to crown so dear a flame; and if I can obtain such happiness as the possession of you, it does not signify in what manner.

Henrietta. People who marry women against their inclinations, run great hazards; it is no trifling affair to use violence to a heart which is not very secure. A woman may be hurried to resentments, which ought to be feared by a husband.

Triffotin. This conversation will not make me change my intention. The wise man is prepared for every thing that may happen; cured, by reason, of vulgar weaknesses, he sets himself above these sort of things, and does not take the smallest trouble about any thing which is not to depend on himself.

Henrietta. Really, Sir, I am transported with you; and I did not think that philosophy was so delightful a thing as it is, to teach people to bear such accidents with constancy. This nobleness of soul, so singular in you, deserves to have an illustrious subject given it; is worthy to find one who may take with pleasure continual pains to place it in full light; and as I dare not, to say the truth, think myself very proper to give it the whole lustre of its glory, I leave it to some other person, and swear to you, between ourselves, that I give up the happiness of seeing you my husband.

Triſſotin going.] We ſhall preſently ſee how the affair will go; for the Notary is already come.

SCENE II.

CHRISALUS, CLITANDER, HENRIETTA, MARTINA.

CHRISALUS.

I AM very glad to ſee you, Henrietta. Come and do your duty, and ſubmit your deſires to the will of your father. I will, I will teach your mother how to behave; and to brave her the more, here I bring back Martina, and will fix her in the houſe again in ſpite of all her endeavours to the contrary.

Henrietta. Your determinations are praiſe-worthy. Take care that this humour do not alter, father. Be firm in reſolving on what you wiſh, and do not allow yourſelf to be ſeduced from your good intentions. Do not ſlacken; but act ſo as to prevent my mother from getting the better of you.

Chriſalus. What? Do you think me an idiot?

Henrietta. God forbid!

Chriſalus. Am I a fool, pray?

Henrietta. I do not ſay ſo.

Chriſalus. Am I thought incapable of the firm ſentiments of a reaſonable man?

Henrietta. No, father.

Chriſalus. Have not I ſenſe enough at this age to be maſter of my houſe?

Henrietta. Certainly.

Chriſalus. Am I ſo weak as to allow myſelf to be led by the noſe by my wife?

Henrietta. Oh! no, father.

Chriſalus. How now! What do you mean then?

I think you are very merry in talking to me in this manner.

Henrietta. If I have offended you, I did not intend it.

Chrisalus. My will ought to be followed intirely in this house.

Henrietta. Very well, father.

Chrisalus. No person besides myself has a right to govern in this house.

Henrietta. You are certainly right.

Chrisalus. It is I that hold the place of chief of the family.

Henrietta. Agreed.

Chrisalus. It is I who ought to dispose of my daughter.

Henrietta. Certainly.

Chrisalus. Heaven gives me full authority over you.

Henrietta. No body contradicts it.

Chrisalus. And I will let you see that in taking a husband, it is your father you must obey, not your mother.

Henrietta. Alas! in that you flatter my softest desires; all that I wish is to obey you.

Chrisalus. We shall see if my wife prove rebellious to my desires———

Clitander. Here she brings the Notary with her.

Chrisalus. All of you must second me.

Martina. Let me alone; I will take care to encourage you, if there be any necessity for it.

SCENE III.

PHILAMINTA, BELISA, ARMANDA, TRIS-
SOTIN, THE NOTARY, CHRISALUS,
CLITANDER, HENRIET-
TA, MARTINA.

PHILAMINTA to the Notary.

CANNOT you change your barbarous ſtile, and draw up a contract in good language?

The Notary. I ſhould be a blockhead, madam, if I attempted to change the leaſt word in it, the ſtile is very good.

Beliſa. Ah! What barbariſm in the middle of France! But, however, Sir, for learning ſake, inſtead of pounds, ſhillings, and pence, let the portion be ex-preſſed in mines and talents; and date by the words ides and kalends.

The Notary. I? Why, were I to agree with your deſires, I ſhould have all my companions laughing at me.

Philaminta. In vain we complain of this barbariſm. Come, Sir, take the table and write. [Seeing Marti-na.] How, how! dares that impudent huſſy ſhew her face here? Pray, why do you bring her to my houſe again?

Chriſalus. We ſhall tell you why preſently at lei-ſure. We have another thing to reſolve at preſent.

The Notary. Let us proceed to the contract. Where is the intended bride?

Philaminta. She I marry is the younger daughter.

The Notary. Very well.

Chriſalus pointing to Henrietta.] Ay, Sir, this is ſhe; her name is Henrietta.

The Notary. Very well. And where is the bridegroom?

Philaminta pointing to Triſſotin.] This gentleman is the huſband I give her.

Chriſalus pointing to Clitander.] And this gentleman is the perſon I intend ſhe ſhall marry.

The Notary. Two huſbands! that is too many, according to the uſual cuſtom.

Philaminta to the Notary.] Why do you ſtop? Write down Mr. Triſſotin for my ſon-in-law.

Chriſalus. For my ſon-in-law, write down Mr. Clitander.

The Notary. Pray be at concord then; and upon mature judgment ſee and agree between yourſelves upon a bridegroom.

Philaminta. Pray, Sir, follow the choice I have fixed on.

Chriſalus. Do, Sir, do what I have reſolved on.

The Notary. Acquaint me firſt which of the two I muſt obey.

Philaminta to Chriſalus.] What! do you then diſpute my deſire?

Chriſalus. I cannot endure that my daughter ſhould be ſought after only for ſake of the wealth that is in my family.

Philaminta. Indeed your riches are very much thought of here; and it is a very worthy ſuſpicion for a wiſe man.

Chriſalus. In ſhort, I have made choice of Clitander for her huſband.

Philaminta. And here is the man, [pointing to Triſſotin.] I have choſen for her huſband; and my reſolution ſhall be followed, that is a determined point.

Chriſalus. Heyday! You pitch on him there in a very abſolute manner!

Martina. It is not proper for the wife to prescribe; and I am for giving the upper part in every thing to the men.

Chrisalus. Well said.

Martina. My discharge was often given me, that is true; but the hen ought not to crow before the cock.

Chrisalus. By no means.

Martina. And we see that people jeer at a man when his wife wears the breeches.

Chrisalus. Certainly.

Martina. If I were married, I must needs say I would have my husband to be master of the house; I should not love him if he proved a booby; and if I contested with him out of whim, or spoke too loud, I should think it right if he lowered my tone with a few stripes.

Chrisalus. She speaks rationally.

Martina. My master is in the right to design an agreeable husband for his daughter.

Chrisalus. Yes.

Martina. Why should he refuse her. Clitander, young and handsome as he is? And wherefore, pray, should he give her a scolard, who is always a criticizin? She must have a husband, not a school-master; and not desiring to understand Greek or Latin, she has no need of Mr. Triffotin.

Chrisalus. Very good.

Philaminta. We must allow her to prate at her ease.

Martina. Scolards are good for nothing but to preach in a pulpit; and I have said a hundred times, that I would never marry a man of learning. Learning is not at all what is necessary in a family; books agree ill with matrimony; and if ever I plight my troth, I will have a husband that has no other book but me; who, no offence to my mistress, knows neither A, nor B; and, in one word, is a doctor only for his wife.

Philaminta to Chrisalus.] Have you done? And have I long enough listened quietly to your worthy interpreter?

Chrisalus. What she says is true.

Philaminta. To shorten this dispute, I will absolutely have my desire executed. [pointing to Trissotin.] Henrietta and the gentleman shall be married directly; I have said it, and it shall be so; make me no answer. If you have given your word to Clitander, offer him her elder sister for a match.

Chrisalus. Here is an accommodation of the affair. See; [To Henrietta and Clitander.] do you give your consent?

Henrietta. What, father!

Clitander to Chrisalus.] How, Sir!

Belisa. She might easily have proposals made to her which would please her much better; but we establish a sort of love which must be as refined as the morning-star; the thinking substance may be admitted into it, but we banish from it the extended substance.

S C E N E IV.

ARISTUS, CHRISALUS, PHILAMINTA, BELISA, HENRIETTA, ARMANDA, TRISSOTIN, A NOTARY, CLITANDER, MARTINA.

ARISTUS.

I AM sorry to disturb these joyful rites by the grief I am obliged to bring hither. These two letters make me the bearer of two pieces of news, which have

given me very great concern for you; [to Philaminta.] one for you, came to me from my attorney;
[to Chrisalus.] the other, for you, came to me from
Lyons.

Philaminta. What misfortune can be sent us word
of, that ought to trouble us?

Ariftus. This letter contains one, as you may read.

PHILAMINTA.

" Madam, I have desired your brother to deliver
" you this letter, which will inform you of what I
" durst not come to tell you. Your great negligence
" in your affairs has been the cause that the clerk of
" your reporting-judge did not give me notice; and
" you have absolutely loft your fuit, which you might
" otherwife have gained."

Chrisalus to Philaminta.] What! have you loft
your fuit?

Philaminta to Chrisalus.] You are too much con-
-cerned! My heart is not at all shaken with this blow.
Shew a more noble foul, and brave, like me, the
ftrokes of fate.

" Your want of care cofts you forty thoufand crowns;
" and it is to pay that fum with the charges, that you
" are condemned by the order of court."

Condemned? Ah! That word is shocking, and
ought only to be applied to criminals.

Ariftus. He is to blame indeed, and you juftly exclaim againft him. He fhould have faid, that you are
defired by order of court to pay only forty thoufand
crowns, and the neceffary charges.

Philaminta. Let us fee the other.

CHRISALUS.

" Sir, the friendfhip which binds me to your bro-
" ther, makes me intereft myfelf in all that concerns
" you. I know that you have put your money into

" the hands of Argantes and Damon, and I muft
" inform you, that they both became bankrupts on
" the fame day."
O heavens! to lofe all my money at once in this
manner!

Philaminta to Chrifalus.] Ah! what a fhameful
tranfport! Fie. All this is trifling; to a truly wife
man, no change of fortune is fatal; and though he
lofe every thing, he ftill continues firm to himfelf.
Let us finifh our affairs, and quit your concern. His
wealth, [pointing to Triffotin.] may fuffice both for
us and himfelf.

Triffotin. No, madam, do not prefs this affair. I
fee the whole world is averfe to this match, and I have
no intention to put a force upon people.

Philaminta. This reflexion came fuddenly to you! It
follows very clofe, Sir, upon our misfortune.

Triffotin. I am at laft tired with fo much refiftance.
I would rather renounce all this confufion, and do not
defire a heart that will not furrender itfelf.

Philaminta. I fee in you, not for your honour,
what I have hitherto refufed to believe.

Triffotin. You may fee in me what you pleafe, and
I do not care how you take it: but I am not a man
who would fuffer the infamy of an injurious refufal,
which I muft have undergone here; I would have people fet a great value on me, and whoever will not, I
fhall have nothing to do with them.

SCENE THE LAST.

ARISTUS, CHRISALUS, PHILAMINTA, BE-
LISA, ARMANDA, HENRIETTA, CLI-
TANDER, A NOTARY, MARTINA.

PHILAMINTA.

I NOW plainly see his mercenary soul; and how little philosophy is in this action of his!

Clitander. I do not pretend to be a philosopher; yet, madam, I cleave to your destiny; and dare offer you with my person whatever wealth fortune has bless-ed me with.

Philaminta. You delight me, Sir, by this generous act; for which reason I will crown your amorous de-sires. Yes, I grant Henrietta to the eager ardour——

Henrietta. I have now altered my mind, mother; allow me to resist your intention.

Clitander. What! does Henrietta oppose my happiness? And when I find every one agree to my love——

Henrietta. Clitander, I am not unacquainted with the smallness of your fortune, and always wished to be your wife, when I knew my marrying you would settle your affairs as well as satisfy my tender desires; but since the fates are so cruel, I will not load you with our adversity; my love for you is too great to do so.

Clitander. Any destiny with you would be agreea-ble to me; and, without you, none would be sup-portable.

Henrietta. Love always talks in this manner in its transports, but let us avoid the disquiet of vexatious re-flexions. Nothing wears out so much the ardour of the knot that ties us, as the grievous want of necessa-

ry poffeffions; and people often accufe each other of
the direful forrow which proceeds from fuch engage-
ments.

Ariftus to Henrietta.] Is what we have juft now
learnt, the only motive which makes you refufe to
marry Clitander?

Henrietta. Otherwife you fhould fee me haften to
it with pleafure; and I only refufe to take him, becaufe I love him too well.

Ariftus. Allow yourfelf then to be bound by fuch
an amiable union. The news I brought you was
falfe; it was a ftratagem, a furprifing device which I
determined to try, in order to ferve your love, to undeceive my fifter, and let her fee what her philofopher
would prove upon trial.

Chrifalus. God be thanked!

Philaminta. The vexation which the bafe deferter
will feel will give me great pleafure. To fee this
match concluded in a fplendid manner, will be the
greateft punifhment to his fordid avarice.

Chrifalus to Clitander.] I knew very well that you
would have her.

Armanda to Philamina.] Will you facrifice me
then in this manner to their inclinations?

Philaminta. It will not be you that I facrifice to
them; you have the fupport of philofophy, and can
with fatisfaction fee their ardour crowned.

Belifa. Let him, however, be careful to retain me
in his heart. People often marry through a fudden
defpair, which they afterwards repent of all their days.

Chrifalus to the Notary.] You have not forgotten,
I fuppofe, the orders I gave you when you came, begin therefore, and draw up the contract agreeable
thereto.